MW01136982

A NATION SEVERED:
-WAR OF BROTHERS-

T.A. MANCHESTER

Published by Lulu Enterprises, Inc

First Edition: February 2012

ISBN 978-1-105-55082-9

For those who lived, and those who died.

❧PART ONE❧

Chapter I: Homecoming
 C3❧80

The sky was as black as iron. The moon above held a silver glimmer as it cascaded its mystic beauty over the crushing waves below. William Hinkley rested, lying on the grainy deck of the ship. He felt nothing; he felt lifeless. The cool misty spray from the blue depths below showered his face as graceful spouts of water flew what seemed like miles above the deck, and then came trickling down on to him. A low humming sound around him made the place seem surreal.

As William was lying in his benumbed state, two men in military uniforms ran over to him, their faces blurred, and their skin cold. As they spoke to William, their voices seemed inaudible; a low growl amongst the crashing of waves.

The surrounding environment became visible, yet the two men were still just a blur. The sails above were filled with gaping holes; the mainmast of the ship was shattered in half, toppled down over the port side of the vessel. As William began to take notice at the sights around him, the low hum became increasingly louder. He saw bodies red with blood, their faces frozen as if made of stone; they were nothing more than lifeless corpses that littered the

6

splintered decks. Cannons tipped over by an unknown source became deadly obstacles. What men survived ran about the decks shouting, yet again, their words rendered inaudible. One of the two sailors leaning over William pulled on his face to direct his attention. Upon the fo'c'sle deck stood a boy, his clothes riddled with holes, his wounds exposed. In his hands, he held a knife. William could see this boy's face. The low hum finally started to become known noise: the concussion of cannons rumbled like thunder, the high pitched screaming pain of dying men became unbearable, yet through all of this the boy stood unfazed, his face a blank canvas, his piercing blue eyes staring right at William. William could not breathe; his voice choked; he sat helplessly watching the boy as chunks of wood flew up from the ship, and shrapnel exploded just feet away from the tattered youth. The knife in the blue-eyed boy's hands rose up to his neck, the cold steel a gateway to death. The boy pressed it hard against his own throat and spoke one word, one word that was spoken with such a quiet tone; however, it sounded as if it were whispered in Will's ear, "William."

The brakes on the train drove the mechanical beast to a halt. With a thunderous sound, steam was expelled from the engine and clouded the small platform where the train docked. On board, William opened his eyes, his head still resting upon the glass window. The dream seemed so real to him. Ever since leaving the docks in Providence, his nightmares had become more and more vivid, only this one seemed to sting more than the rest, yet he could not think of why.

William blinked a few times trying to recollect his thoughts. He had dozed off at some point during the long ride back from Rhode Island. Looking around the car, he noticed that no one was in his presence. The men who had accompanied him leaving the docks were nothing more than mere memories. He felt a deep heaviness in his chest; the friends he made back on the *Liberty*, the ship on which he served just prior to the outbreak of war, were off on their own adventures in a world tearing at the seams. As William sat in thought, a gentleman dressed in a dark blue, denim worker's outfit from the engine room entered the car.

"Pardon me, Sir, but we have stopped."

William's gaze shifted onto the man. Upon the young sailor's face sat an expression of remorse for not being awake to see his friends leave, as well as an expression of grogginess from sleep-deprivation.

"Sir," repeated the man.

William breathed in quickly, breaking his own trance. "Yes, thank you, Sir. Let me gather my things."

"Would you like some help, Sir?" asked the worker.

"No thank you; I can manage," answered William.

The worker nodded and turned around, but not before replying, "Welcome home, Sir."

William shook his head in thanks and then stood almost hitting his head atop the low ceiling of the train car. Pulling his uniform jacket down to expel the wrinkles, William moved across the walkway running down the middle of the car and pulled two cases from the storage rack that hung over the rows of seats. He did not have much; one shoulder bag for his shoes, and a small locker that he kept his extra shirt and toiletries in. If he learned anything while in the Navy, he learned to pack light and make the best use out of everything you carried on you; one shirt was plenty for the sailor.

Before exiting the train, he glanced again around the car. He still envisioned his one-time crewmates sitting in the rows of seats before him. Captain Baring's words echoed in the back of his mind: *You are all heroes; you all have earned the right to call each other your family. You have overcome a huge diversity, and put aside your differences to save one another...you are all friends now...a string in a world of knives.*

Will wondered what that bond would be like again if he ever met Samuel, or Braxton, or any of the other sailors who went on to support the southern cause, after all, there was no United States Navy; it was the Union Navy, and the Confederate Navy...and they were enemies.

William shook his head, throwing the thoughts away. He pulled his starched naval cap straight down on his shaven head and walked toward the exit.

He slowly stepped off the train and onto the old wooden boardwalk of the railway platform as the steam billowed around him in the cool April wind. Up until then the thought had not set in, he was truly home.

The worker stood beside the entrance to the train and tipped his dirty hat toward William, "Welcome home again, Sir."

William smiled for what felt like the first time in months. Turning to his left, the young man walked out from under the awning that shaded the platform, and looked up squinting in the Virginian sun. A gust of wind flew through the exposed area and lifted the cap right off of Will's head. The breeze felt soothing on the man's skin, which was still slightly sun burnt from the hot African sun, where he and his fellow crew mates fought attempting to stop the illegal slave-trade.

"Ride, Sir?" questioned a nearby voice.

William looked forward to see a horse and carriage resting a stone's throw away from his position with a man perched atop.

The sailor chewed on the thought for a beat before deciding. "I think I'll walk!" he exclaimed with a cocky smile.

Pulling his bags tight around his body, the strong lad set off down the country road, feeling enthusiastic about the trek ahead of him, leaving the driver of the carriage sitting in confusion as to why someone would pass up a perfectly good ride.

A good hundred yards from the station, William was sprinting; his heart raced sending pulses of adrenaline through his veins. It had been so long since he had seen any of his family. They were the only ones he thought about while on duty.

Slowing to catch his breath, he tried to guess his brother's ages. *Was Logan twelve, and Jed nine? No, Logan was ten and Jed seven.* Scanning his brain, the answer finally hit him when he remembered celebrating Jed's birthday before he shipped out. *Jed was eleven, which meant Logan, was fourteen. Both boys had to be a full year older by now,* William guessed. More and more thoughts started to race through the man's mind as he picked up his pace and started to walk the trail again. *Would they be different than I remember? Would Cousin Nathan and Cousin Maxwell remember my face?*

With all the questions about his family racing through his head, the battle-hardened sailor grew nervous. He had not told anyone he was coming home, for he thought it better to surprise everyone so they did not throw him a coming-home party. All that attention on him made him anxious and ill at ease.

As William rounded the winding path downhill, the brush thickened. Not paying attention to his surroundings, Will ran headfirst into the branch of a walnut tree, the leaves and stems scraping his face, which effectively broke his train of thought.

"Ouch." he groaned, rubbing the imprint of a branch on his cheek.

William looked up at the tree, which towered over him with intimidating height. The tree seemed familiar to the man; its twisted shape was very unusual. Upon further examination, the jutting roots and two initials carved into the dark brown bark ignited a hailstorm of flashbacks from Will's childhood.

"Those are my initials…" the man took note. "Then who is M.S.?" William remembered being with a girl the day he carved those initials only he could not put his finger on who she was. Suddenly, it hit him. Mary Sutherland was her name. She was the daughter of Arthur Sutherland, the town apothecary, whom had strong relations to William's father. Mary was Arthur's eighth child out of ten, the only girl.

Will smiled remembering that day. He and Mary had announced their love for each other, and decided to make it publicly known; however, William feared Mr. Sutherland due to the fact that his only daughter was "still too young to be seeing boys," in Mr. Sutherland's exact words. So to play it safe, they picked the walnut tree to share their feelings. The tree was a local spot for kids their age to play, because it was the tallest tree in the area, and was just about the only exciting place to be in the town of Hampton.

*Mary Sutherland…*William recollected. He remembered her rosy cheeks and her dazzling green eyes. Her hair had to be made of silk, its texture too smooth to be of any natural human substance. All of her features complimented each other, and made the then eighteen-year-old Will extremely nervous to be in her

10

presence. She had to have changed by now, having been stuck living with all those brothers. William made a mental note to try to visit her before he went back to the service.

The man gleamed at the tree one last time, and then continued on his way. The house was not that far. It lie just down the hill, upon which William was standing, however, large hedgerows blocked the view of the small home.

All around him, trees were bright green and yellow, the dirt and grass on the ground was crisp and moist, and the Sun was shining just enough to illuminate the yellow daises that lined his path. In between the offset hedgerows, large rolling fields of alfalfa filled the windswept plains for miles to see. Will had fallen in love with that sight at a very young age, and it still held a place in his heart. Its mere beauty was something one can only truly appreciate if they were there, words cannot describe.

Lost in the marvel of the landscape, Will had not noticed that he had come out of the thickened brush that guarded the path, and was now looking at his house. Straight ahead of him, it rested on the top of a small bluff; its two-story foundation seemed the perfect backdrop to the scene Mother Nature had painted. Off to the right side of the house with red shutters stood a barn with white trim, this ironically was larger than the house. A lone windmill was the only structure standing to the left, hugging the edge of the alfalfa fields.

William looked around. He saw no one, but heard faint laughter from the field, a sound that echoed throughout the landscape. Slowly, he started the hundred-yard walk from the dirty path to the front steps of the home. Nerves kicked him in the stomach as he approached. He removed his cap briefly and wiped the sweat off of his brow. As the battle-hardened sailor moved closer to the home, the screen door was the only thing blocking his path inside. He could hear voices talking, the sound escaping filling the fresh air. Suddenly, William stopped; he looked at the three white wooden steps that led up to the porch of the small prairie house where a lone American flag waved graciously in the

11

breeze. He took one step, the toe of his boot clanking on the board. He took another with the same response, and then the third...he was finally on the porch. Looking left, Will approached the porch swing that was rocking in the late afternoon breeze. Carefully, he sat down on it and leaned back with a relaxing sigh. The man's nerves had conclusively subsided, and he scanned the heaven-reminiscent landscape; the laughter of children off in the distance completing the angelic atmosphere. From the barn a kite hung fluttering in the wind, its freedom held captive by the arm of a tree.

Closing his eyes, William took in the sounds of the land, feeling an overwhelming sentiment of relaxation and sanctity. He examined the kite with curiosity, and then looked back forward closing his eyes. He sensed something suddenly. Looking toward the door, William saw a man leaning on the frame, the screen door pushed open. Like a child caught in the act of mischief, William shot up swallowing hard.

"Father!" he said, his eyes wide and his mouth muttering nonsense as he searched for words.

Jedediah Hinkley smiled at his son, and nodded his head, motioning for William to direct his gaze out to the field.

"Children, time for supper!" the middle-aged man called out to non-seen figures.

William looked his father up and down, taking in his features; the aging man was the same as he had been when Will left; his hair graying, his eyes shielded by bifocals and his dress the same: a flannelled button down, with brown pants, and laced boots.

Obeying his father's command, William watched the field. The alfalfa swayed gracefully in the breeze, except for two lines, which cut through the field like razors. Two children exploded through the grain and onto the grass neither looking toward the house, yet both running as fast as possible, laughing all the way. Father Jed pointed toward the barn; two taller children exited from the doors, holding tools, one toting a small wagon. The two taller children squinted in the sun as they looked toward the house at the mysterious man standing beside Father Jed.

Nervously, William sat back down on the swing, rubbing his head.

"Easy, Son," Father Jed chuckled, noting William's anxiety.

The two small, younger children arrived at the porch first, while the two oldest trotted up shortly after. William coughed and stood, the group's attention now focused on him. The first child, a short brown haired boy with green eyes and a dirtied face, stopped in his tracks, his jaw dropped.

"William?!" he called with a tone filled with excitement and longing for his role model. The child ran and hugged William's waist.

"Little Jed! Or do you still go by Roo?" asked William, returning the hug to his littlest brother.

"Roo!" exclaimed the bewildered child, his round face glowing with excitement.

The other small child with similar features, whose face held a huge grin ran and joined in on the hug. Father Jed marveled at the sight.

"Cousin Maxwell, I have missed you as well!" William proclaimed.

Maxwell continued to smile and sat down on the porch swing as the two older boys ran up the steps to William.

"Logan!" William laughed as the dark-blond haired boy hugged him, his head even with Will's chest. Logan was about five feet tall, and resembled his older brother the most out of the children. He had a skinny frame; mainly due to the fact that he did not take in enough calories to compete with how much running he did to pass the time around the farm. He had fair skin, and lacked the usual sunburn that you would find on most farm hands that worked out in the heat of the Virginian summer. His face held an innocent, yet confident persona which made him particularly eye catching to the girls his age around Hampton, whose other choices in boys were the typical farm-type of the town: filthy, mud-soaked vermin who appeared to take better care of their livestock than their own personal hygiene.

As Logan backed away smiling, he looked at William, the boy's striking blue eyes forced the smile away from William's face. The sailor pictured the kid from his dream standing in the hellish grave that was the destroyed ship; the haunting blank expression of lifelessness that rested on the child's face chilled his bones.

"Will, are you okay? You look…well, like you have seen a ghost…" asked Logan to his brother.

William snapped back to reality. "I am fine, Logan, sorry, It just seems like forever since I last saw all of you." Turning to the last boy, William chuckled as Nathan, the jokester of the group, stood with his tongue sticking out, his face contorted into a twisted shape making him look like a deranged monkey.

"Cousin Nathan. You were about a foot shorter last I saw you! And more appealing to the eye…I guess being around these two has really turned you something awful!" teased William pointing to his two younger siblings.

With all the excitement on the porch causing a loud commotion, an older woman with hair tied up into a bun on the back of her head came running out from the house shouting.

"What in God's name is all…" she stopped when she saw the foreign figure standing erect on the porch. "It cannot be!" she cried as she wiped her hands on her apron repeating herself. "William?!" the woman lunged across the deck and embraced the man as tears fell from her face, leaving marks on the sailor's uniform.

"Mother, it is so good to see you!" exclaimed William.

"My dear William, I have counted the days since you left hoping that each one would be the day you returned to us, I have rehearsed what I would say to you when I saw you, and now, well now, here you are and I have nothing to proclaim except *William*!"

William's mother's heightened emotion and elated mood brought the rest of the family onto the porch of the small wooden deck.

"Well bless it anyhow…William Hinkley!" said a shorter man with a beard that stretched the length of his neck, the frenzied hairs tied at the middle with a piece of string.

"Uncle Moses, it is good to see you, how have you been?!" wondered William.

"Well, things could be better around here, Mother Nature has been pretty irritable lately, I haven't had the chance to even plant my summer crop yet, and it's April!"

14

"Forgive him, William, he is just trying to find an excuse for his chronic laziness." joked a fair woman stepping out from behind the grizzly man.

"Aunty Sue!" William shouted embracing the woman, whose frail arms and dainty wrists wrapped around the masculine man's neck.

As the family all gathered around each other, a cry was heard from inside the house.

"Oh the baby, forgive me, but I must go feed her." apologized Sue, returning into the house with red shutters.

"Baby?!" exclaimed William with a twist of confusion in his voice.

"Yes, Son, your Aunt Sue gave birth; no less than two months ago…her name is Abigail."

William grinned ear to ear. His love for children had become significantly greater since he was away. He had considered children of his own if he had time to settle down with a woman, yet his demanding job in the Navy was far too strenuous to find the time to be a father, at least, the kind of father who would be there to watch his kid grow day by day, the kind of father he remembered his being when he was young.

"Congratulations, Uncle Moses, you must be overjoyed!" William announced.

"Well, kids are truly a blessing, however, I'm losing my foothold in the family, we men outnumbered Sue, but now she'll have one to second her opinion in a few years." teased the burly man causing the group to laugh.

William looked to Logan and Jed with a look of feverish delight. "I've got some stuff to show you boys after supper! Same goes for you, Nathan and Max!"

"A gun?!" shouted Jed Jr. in an almost pleading tone.

"No, Roo! Not a gun, but it is just as neat, you'll see soon."

Jed Jr. let out a sigh of disappointment, followed by a yelp as Logan punched his arm in a joshing matter. Jed hopped off of the porch rail and retaliated with a lunge at Logan's waist. Before the air even escaped Logan's lips, Nathan was in on the ruckus.

"Now, now children let's break it up, run along inside and be seated, Amelia should have dinner set by now." Father Jed said with a forceful tone.

The gaggle of boys ran in the house like a stampede of wild buffalo, followed by little Maxwell toting a stuffed bear. Father Jed turned around and started to head inside the house, but not before William stopped him.

"It is good to see you, Father." Will's face showed signs something was bothering him as he half-smirked at his dad.

"You too, Son, we will talk after dinner. I'm afraid if we wait much longer, your brothers will eat each other." Father Jed said foolhardily.

"If they are anything like me, then it may be too late." cracked William slowly easing the expression of nerves on his face.

Once the family's joyous excitement wore off, and the children settled down, the group moved into the dining room of the house with red shutters. Amelia, the slave owned by Mr. Moses Hinkley, had prepared a wonderful meal of roast turkey and wine, accompanied by a side of green asparagus, green beans, and rich, creamy white-corn. The meal was by far one of the best that the woman had made; in fact, it was almost as if she knew that William would be attending dinner that night, for the table was more extravagant than usual.

Amelia herself had been with the Hinkley family since Jed Jr. was born. Against Jedediah Hinkley's wish, his brother went ahead and bought her from a group of slave trader's outside of Hampton. The fact that Jedediah had been overruled, considering that the house Moses and his family stayed in did not belong to them, did not sit well with the old fashioned farmer, who felt that slavery was immoral, despite living in the south. Nevertheless, Amelia had become a part of the family. Jed Jr. saw her as his secondary mother, and the older boys grew to respect her. She was heavyset and short, only standing about four and a half feet off of the ground, give or take a few inches. Her hair was trimmed short on her head and she always wore a baby blue bonnet that hugged the sides of her face. Her eyes shined a darkened green color in the light, however some beckoned that they were brown. Her round face gave her a very soft and welcoming appeal, one of the reasons that the littlest children felt so comfortable around her, and her drive and spirit were that of a bull, with a thoughtfulness and caring personality that rounded out her motherly ways. Amelia was the perfect woman to be around and almost everyone in the house knew that.

As the family sat gathered around the long oak table that lay in the small dining room, Amelia put the finishing touches on the meal. Upon the dark tabletop, a red velvet cloth was spread out, its furled edges draping off of the side. On top of that, sat the food; a gourmet of delicious delight. Candles, whose wax twisted in oblong shapes, were plugged into small golden towers that rested down the middle of the feast, positioned around the many plates of food.

"Is everything okay, Mr. Hinkley?" asked Amelia to the man of the house, who sat positioned at the farthest end of the table, opposite his brother, Moses.

"It is lovely, Amelia, you may go rest now."

"Thank you, Sir." said the woman as she bowed her head and walked out of the food-filled room.

Jedediah Hinkley sat looking at the faces of the starving children who bounced in their seats, eager to dive into the smorgasbord of delectable treats. To his left sat William and Nathan, the two eyeing him with pleading faces. William smirked at his father, guessing what he was playing at; however, Nathan was not so quick as to pick up on the silliness. He sat clenching his teeth, the muscles in his jaw contracting and releasing as he bit down hard on his invisible meal. To the right of the table sat Jed Jr. and Logan; both boys had wide eyes and hollow faces as they stared at their father wondering what the wait was for. At the opposite end of the table was Sue, Moses, Mary and little Maxwell, all fiddling with their plates, except Sue who was focused on the baby, Abigail, who sat content on her mother's lap. Father Jed cleared his throat...the few beside him looked. He waited and cleared again, this time the whole room looked at him, a barrier of silence blocked out every sound. His eyes flexed as he closely watched each child again; each one held the same expression this time around: hungry eyes, and dripping mouths uttering soft spoken words, pleading to eat. A grin slowly worked its way onto the old farmer's face, and he began to laugh. Confused and thrown off by the sudden laughing fit, the family looked at him as if he had gone mad.

"Aren't we forgetting something?" asked the father in a woeful tone.

The family all looked at each other in confusion as each tried to guess what was missing.

"Say thank you to Amelia!" Jedediah shouted, chuckling at the table's ignorance.

In an uproar, the family yelled their thanks, however, with each person shouting at a different time, the words were jumbled and hardly decipherable. Amelia apparently understood, because a response from the kitchen showed that she acknowledged the gratitude.

"Now can we eat?!" snapped little Maxwell, who was already picking through the pile of meat on the platter.

"Now you may eat." announced Jedediah.

In an instant, hands snatched up food from all directions filling plates with whatever they could hold. Little Abigail watched like a peasant at a king's feast, her eyes moving around the table noting every motion that the family made.

The table was quiet, excluding the sounds of silverware on plates, and the chewing of food. Finally, Moses broke the silence.

"So William, now that you have seen combat, you think we all can stomach a good ole war story?"

William drew a half-smirk, unappeased at the comment. Mary immediately jumped on the aging man.

"Moses, I do not think now is the time for such talk. The children need not hear such violence at their age."

"Oh Mary, relax, William knows how to keep discretion I am sure, right Boy?" Moses asked looking at the sailor with a know-it-all grin.

"Sorry, Uncle Moses, there are no stories to tell...we barely even saw a ship, much less engaged one." William lied.

William's father sensed his son's incorrect notion and winked in approval.

"Ah, 'tis a darn shame, I could have used a good story about what was going on out in the world. Your father runs a tight ship here...not a damn paper enters this house."

18

"Moses Hinkley!" snapped Sue, "Watch your language in front of the little ones!"

Jed Jr. chuckled at the word, and after hearing the forty-year-old man be chewed out like a child.

Moses bit his lip and shook his head seething with anger. Little Abigail stared at her father with large eyes watching his every move, just as Logan finished a bite of food and spoke aloud to the table.

"So does anyone want to go into town tomorrow? I'm sure William is anxious to see what has changed."

Father Jed shook his head in disapproval while he finished chewing, and then announced, "Not tomorrow, Son; I need all the help I can get out in that field, perhaps Wednesday."

Logan hung his head in disappointment; his lengthy, dark-blond bangs hanging down off of his forehead just barely shielded his eyes.

"Ah come on, Pa!" Jed spoke up with a giggle.

Logan immediately shot his head up, his eyes staring wide at Jed.

"Why do you want to go, Jed?" asked the boy's father.

"Well, not really for me, but for-" Jed was interrupted mid-sentence by a swift kick to the shin that made the whole wooden table jump up.

"Logan! What did you do that for?!" snapped Mary, glaring at her son for his odd behavior.

"Logan has a crush!" Jed yelled out before he could be shut up.

"Do not!" yelped Logan jumping on the sentence.

"Ah I see..." Father Jed said nodding his head, finally figuring out the true reason for the trip into town.

The whole table seemed to find the boy's crush a form of entertainment. Maxwell and Jed began chanting, "Logan likes a girl," while the adults began chatting about when William had announced his crush on Mary Sutherland. Yet, through all of this Logan did not speak, he sat gripping his pant leg with an angry fist. Nathan noticed his cousin's fury and flung a green bean at him across the table to get his attention. Logan looked up toward the direction of the shot. Nathan was grinning ear to ear as he motioned for Logan to do the same to Jed, only with a more devilish intent. Logan moved his hand over to his spoon and gripped it tight. He scooped up a pile of corn and positioned it in his hand so that he could aim it in the direction of his brother.

The adults still teased about the crush and talked of the past affairs of William, which made the attempt to defile Jed's moral almost unnoticeable. Logan bit his lips, his tongue extruding from his mouth as he concentrated. Just as he was about to let go of the spoon to send the corn flying, a swift smack came to the back of his head so hard so that it made him fly into the edge of the table with a loud thud.

"Don't you dare think about it, Logan Hiram Hinkley!" commanded a voice.

Behind Logan standing in the kitchen doorway stood Amelia with a mitt in her hand. "My food is for eating not throwing!" she scolded.

The room's attention was on the lover-boy now, who was rubbing the back of his head groaning in pain.

"...Serves you right!" Jed sneered.

Logan looked at Nathan in disgust for not getting in trouble for instigating the plan. Nathan held his hand over his mouth trying not to laugh. He looked toward the kitchen where Amelia stood; her eyes fixed on the dusty-haired boy pointing her short stubby finger in his direction. Nathan immediately dropped his hand onto his lap, drawing up a blank face.

"Logan, why are you so embarrassed at liking a girl," Father Jed asked, "It is normal for a kid your age."

"Because I knew that you would all gang up on me and crack jokes!" admitted the embarrassed teen.

"Oh Logan, we are family, it is what we do!" Jedediah spoke trying to break the boy's shy nature.

The lover-boy shrugged and tried to change the topic, but was shot down before he even was able to open his mouth.

"He kissed her!" Jed snapped.

All eyes shifted from Jed to Logan, as the sudden news seemed to shock the table. Logan's jaw was dropped in disbelief, his face revealed an inconceivable expression. No one at the table spoke, they all just looked at Logan, each with a dumbfounded look thanks to Jed's blunt nature, and at the fact that Logan had not spoken of his kiss with the girl of whom they did not even know the name of.

"It's true, I saw it!" Jed added with a smile that took up his whole face.

Jedediah started to speak, but Logan ignored, and through his gritting teeth he foretold Jed's fate, "Tomorrow, you are dead."

"Logan?" Jedediah asked.

"I'm sorry, Father, I did not hear, what did you ask?"

"Who is this girl?"

Logan swallowed hard before answering.

"She is in my class. Her name is Rebecca. Her Father works at the butcher shop in town…" he confessed.

"I see, so that is why you wanted to go into town. She lives there." Jedediah said, once again putting two and two together.

"Little boy has himself a lady-friend!" Moses yelled disturbing the relatively quiet conversation.

Logan looked up at William with sorrowful eyes hoping to find sympathy in his eldest brother for having had to endure the verbal abuse and emotional agony of the last five minutes. William winked at his little brother noting that it was nothing new. To Logan, it meant a lot. The fact that his role model of a brother had been in his shoes at one point was a calming thought.

"Well, enough badgering the boy let us drink; Amelia, the cognac." Moses called to the servant. "Children, why don't you go get changed for bed while the adults talk."

With a group sigh, the children stood up and hobbled off to their bedroom, while William and Moses sat pouring the alcoholic beverage into their glasses. Mary wandered off, following the children into the bedroom, and Sue went off into the den with baby Abigail.

"Drink, brother?!" asked Moses to Jedediah in a way that made him sound as if he had already been drinking.

"Not tonight, Moses, I'm going to go outside for some fresh air." Father Jed replied walking out of the dining room.

As the children obeyed their parents and went off to the bedroom to prepare for bed, Jedediah walked out onto the porch and sat down on the swing, the old wooden beams flexed with a creak as the old man leaned back with a sigh of relaxation. The sun gracefully descended over the rolling hills, which were covered in alfalfa bearing the late-afternoon dew. The final rays of light reflected off the plains of grass, giving the atmosphere an enticing, yet quaint aura. Not a bird took flight in the sky, nor a mouse scurry in the field, all was peaceful.

Jedediah breathed in slowly as he thought about the day's events. From his pocket he pulled a pipe. The man put it up to his lips and filled the cup with a pinch of tobacco. He struck a match against the arm of the swing, and with a hiss it immediately glowed at the end. With a few puffs, a steady stream of opaque smoke rose from the cup. Jedediah brushed his rough hand through his graying hair; his eyes gently scanned the panorama, taking in the luscious sight. Smoke from the pipe rose up from the ashes and swirled around his clean-shaven face; the man's glasses sat resting on his knee.

From the house, William walked outside over to the railing that lined the old white porch. The screen door slammed shut behind him with a clap. The young man looked out over the field; the fading sun's rays struck his face inviting shadows to dance across his features. The children, who had once filled the house with an exuberant and almost obnoxious noise, where finally silenced, just like the animals of the day were hushed, and replaced by the creatures of the night.

"What's on your mind, Son?" asked Jedediah in a quiet voice.

William glanced down to the ground, then back up at the sky before turning around to face his father.

"It is good to be home." he said, a hint of melancholy in his voice.

Jedediah eyed him with a curious gaze; his glasses found their way back on his face, where they rested slightly on the bridge of his nose.

"Would you like to sit down?" asked Jedediah.

William crossed over to the opposite side of the porch swing, and sat down gently, resting his elbows on his knees. "You know I really missed this place."

Jedediah did not reply, he only puffed on his pipe and watched his son.

"You are hurting aren't you?" the aging man finally asked.

William let out a gasp of air that resembled brief laughter; he moved his hand over his mouth, moving it back and forth as if he were wiping away dirt from his face.

"Father, I cannot begin to describe what I feel." William paused and looked at his hands, which shook steadily out of fright.

Jedediah rested, still watching his son gather his words.

"When I was there…on the ship, there was a moment when I thought that it was over, that my time had come. We had chased the traders for two hundred miles out to the open ocean where we sailed up beside them. They opened fire…the noise was so deafening that I lost my balance; as I fell onto the deck, I remember looking back up and I watched as my friend was ripped in half by the broadside. I remember looking at my hands, his blood soaked them and I tried to wash them clean, only every time I brought my hands out of the water that soaked the deck, the red liquid was there yet again. I tried to stand and get to my post, but I could not. My body did not listen, and I was left quivering like a child on the deck while my friends were blown to bloody pieces all around me."

William paused and looked up, his eyes wet. He bit his tongue and sniffled before starting again.

"I finally mustered the courage to get back up to my feet, and I worked my way slowly to my post, only when I got there, it was gone. A hole six feet wide was blown into the ship, and Percy Woodrow, he was the only person who wasn't afraid that day, was stuck under a broken timber of wood. At first, I was going to leave him there. To this day I cannot understand why I thought that, but I did, and I feel like I would not have regretted it, but I listened to my heart. I pulled him from the wreckage and brought him below deck, and that is where I truly saw what the consequences are like when Man hates one another. It was as if God had turned his head, only for a brief instant, and what had happened in that instant was of unspeakable terror. Our ship had only one surgeon on board, and surrounding his little workstation the bodies of broken men, fifty, sixty…maybe more, rested. Upon each face was a look of…a look of nothing. It was as if someone had captured their soul and left the shell, the life was taken from their eyes. To this day, that very look haunts me in my dreams…anyway it was down there that I almost lost it. I was about to walk back up on deck when another shot tore through the hull, and a splinter the size of a house cat was flung across my path. I told my body to duck and hide, but I could not move in time. I looked down and saw a pool of blood on the wooden deck, the source of it from my chest. The wooden stake had cut a ten-inch gash two centimeters deep in my body. It was at that moment that I could hear the voices. I could hear some woman crying out for me to follow her; there was a little girl who told me not to be scared."

William laughed at the last thought and looked to his father. "I don't know what that means, but I heard it. But then I heard you. I heard you say that you were proud of me, and that it was okay to go…and that angered me. It was too easy to die. I couldn't die…and what frightens me the most about that day, is that when I was fading, I didn't even think about Mother, or Logan, or anyone of them…what does that mean?"

William examined his father with pleading eyes, searching for an answer. Jedediah was looking at the ground in front of William. He blinked a few times, and breathed in deeply.

"William, what you experienced that day was something that no one can ever truly understand. What you saw was the very thing that most people go their whole lives without seeing, yet they feel the need to criticize and ostracize the ones who fought on the way they fought, and the way they should act even thereafter. You are a very brave man, and your family and I are proud to call you our son and brother; as for why you did not think of the rest of the family, I cannot say, however, if you are questioning your love for them, stop. I can see the way you treat them, and I can hear the way you talk to them, and I will stand before God and swear to him that your love for your family is unfathomable." Jedediah stared at his son with the eyes of a lion. He knew how his son felt, yet at the same time, he did not. Jedediah was never shot at, nor was he a soldier; however, he had lived long enough to see what war does to men and what it does to their character, and judgment of the world.

William licked his lips and looked back at his father; his face showed that he was still not satisfied with what he had spoken.

"How can I go back? How can I go back and deal with that again? To face death is a life-changing thing…those who have felt its insidious touch are never the same, yet this country is now demanding me to go back and taunt it yet again. That one battle on the shores of Africa was against strangers, those whose faces I had never seen, nor whose pasts I have never known…and now, I am being told that I must go stand against my brethren and raise the sword of so-called liberty, and put my friends under the blade…put them in the very place that I, myself, fear above all else. What kind of man does that make me? What kind of creature does that turn me into?"

William's blood was racing as he tried to force his feelings into words. The confusion in his mind and body made him feel as if he were no longer who he once was. Before he joined the Navy, he was an adventurous, anxious teenager desperately wanting to become a man, and now that he had knocked on hell's door, he was changed; he was no longer a boy, yet at the same time, he longed to redeem the innocence of his youth. "If you know what I should do, then please, by all means tell me!" he said in a desperate plea.

"William now is the moment that will truly define your character. Whether you chose to embrace the call, or to run from it, it is your choice. I will judge you no less than I ever have…but how will you judge yourself? That is what you will need to decide."

Jedediah stood up from the swing and walked back inside the house, leaving William to sit alone on the porch. The sun was no longer visible, and was replaced by the incandescent glow of the moon.

The children were finally changed into their pajamas except little Maxwell, who refused to put on his nightshirt. Mary, Maxwell's aunt, was wrestling the boy when William walked into the medium sized room. The room was a large rectangle, and the cage-like walls of the room were wooden with no color on them to separate the ceiling from the actual wall. Tucked away in each corner were the small cots, each just big enough to fit the bodies that occupied them. At the middle of the left wall was the door, which had two steps that led down into the sunken room; beside that door sat a long oak dresser with a small round mirror that hung just above it. The walls contained no pictures or brilliance of any kind, beside Maxwell's drawings of the family; the charcoaled figures sprawled all over the page, their body parts in complete disfiguration compared to their true nature.

When William stepped further into the room, the children jumped up with excitement.

"William!" they all cried.

Little Maxwell immediately ran to the man and hugged his legs, looking up at him with big round eyes, and a grin the size of a banana.

"Well, maybe he'll get dressed for you!" teased Mary in complete exhaustion after battling the little child.

Kneeling down, William looked the boy in his eyes and drew closer until their noses touched. Maxwell shivered in anticipation almost sensing what the sailor was about to do. William raised his hands slowly, and in a sudden jolt, gripped the boy and tickled him under the arms. Maxwell shrieked like a girl as William carried him over to the bed and tossed him down. All the other children laughed at the sight of the large man fighting with the small boy.

"Maxwell! I am going to tickle you until you wet yourself!" shouted William in a monstrous voice, making the room explode with laughter from the other kids.

"No!" screamed the nine year old in a high-pitched voice.

William stopped suddenly; crouching with his hands perched on the floor, his head just poking up above the bed. His stance resembled a cat about to pounce on its prey.

"Then do you know what you have to do?!" he asked quickly.

"What?!" pleaded Maxwell.

"Put your shirt on! It is the only way that you can defend yourself!"

Maxwell speedily threw the white t-shirt over his head, and hid under the blue covers that blanketed his bed. Wiping the sweat from his forehead, William breathed heavily and looked to Mary who stood shaking her head at the silliness of the situation.

"He is heavier than he looks!" laughed William.

"Well at least he is dressed! Goodnight children." Mary announced to the room before exiting.

"William, what have you brought for us?!" screamed Logan sitting up on his knees.

"Brought you? What do you mean?" asked the sailor, acting dumbfounded.

"The surprise, the gun!" shouted Jed Jr. who sat beside Nathan, opposite Logan.

"Uh, not ringing any bells…" William teased scratching his head.

"Will, tell us…or else!" threatened Jed, standing up from the bed.

William smirked at his little brother's aggressive act. Logan looked at Nathan and nodded his head; both boys smiled slyly and moved around the backside of William.

William enticed the boy, "Or else what, Roo?" Out of the corner of his eye he saw Nathan and Logan creep around the back, plotting to ambush him.

"Now!" yelled Nathan, jumping on to William followed by Logan, and Jed.

William tumbled down onto the bed and faked dead, his body motionless, his breath non-apparent.

Logan stood up and put his ear to Will's chest and listened carefully. "Oh no, Jed…we killed him!"

Nathan rose to his feet as well and held his hand over his mouth. "I am telling Uncle Jedediah!" he confessed.

Jed Jr. ran over to William and felt his neck for a pulse. In that instant, William jumped up and tackled the boy onto the floor with a loud crash. A knock on the door followed instantly, and all the children ran to their beds. William was the last to get up; he slowly moved over to Jed's bed and sat down. Nathan and Logan kicked off their covers and followed, flopping down beside Jed causing the little bed to groan at the weight of the group.

"Alright boys, I'll show you what I brought." William reached into his pocket and pulled out a bundle of papers.

Jed's green eyes anxiously examined the parchment that lay nestled in William's hand. William gently unfolded the papers and handed one to each child.

"They're notes I wrote you guys while I was away. I never sent them because I did not trust them in the hands of someone else…I wanted to give them to you personally."

The group all read the notes in silence. William rubbed his chest feeling the scar that served as a reminder of his brush with death.

"Did you really see a whale, William?!" marveled Jed reading a passage from the letter.

"Yes I did! It was a quiet day on the ship, and I was watching the horizon," William did his best to reenact the scene as he spoke, "When all of a sudden, the whale jumped out of the water completely, it's body as big as our ship, and it came splashing down with a loud clap! The waves it sent up rocked the ship so much, that I thought we would tip over!"

"No way!" shouted Jed with excitement and wonder showing all over his face.

"There's more, but I'll let you kids read those on your own. There are a few pictures in there too; I had my buddy draw them. I'm not so good with pictures." laughed the sailor.

"Thanks, Will!" spoke Logan.

"You're welcome…all of you. Now you best get some sleep, you don't want to be too tired for the morning. Pa says he's going to put us all to work now that I'm here to give a helping hand."

William stood up and walked to the door; the boys were all still gathered on the bed looking at the letters with amazement, hardly believing what each one contained. Will looked at them for a minute, and then walked out of the room shutting the door behind him with a quiet thud.

Jedediah was in his bedroom rocking in his chair that sat beside the window. In his hand he held a brown, leather book. The title etched in gold letters read *A Tale of Two Cities*. Mary was folding laundry beside the large bed that rested on the backside of the beige-colored wall. The only light in the room was the oil lamp that rested on the ornate nightstand beside the bed frame.

"So what did William have to say?" wondered Mary.

Jedediah kept on studying his book as he answered, "He does not know what to do."

"Does not know what to do as far as what?" Mary asked.

"...Whether he should go back to fight in the war or not. He is confused on the morality of it."

"...Morality in war?" Mary laughed with subtlety.

Jedediah placed a page-marker in his book and closed it gently, resting it on the seat of the rocker as he stood up with a groan. "I am happy to have him back." he said.

"He has changed a lot. He seems to appreciate the little things now…"

Jedediah moved over to the window and stared out it in thought; Mary still folded the clothes as she watched her husband.

"Do you remember when he threw a fit about us telling him to water the flowers on the window sill?" Jedediah asked.

"That is coming up on three years ago, now." Mary noted.

"Well, just today I told him that I need his help out in the fields tomorrow, and he agreed without a fuss. Imagine that!" Jedediah exclaimed with excitement.

"He has grown up, Jed. That is what the service does to these boys now. They go off children and they come back men. It truly is a miracle of a system." Mary spoke.

Jedediah nodded his head in agreement, and then moved over to his wife, coming up behind her, wrapping his arms around her waist.

"What do you think he should do?" questioned Mrs. Hinkley.

Jedediah closed his eyes and rested his chin on Mary's shoulder. He thought for a while, taking his time, breathing in and out softly as he held his wife of thirty years. The two were inseparable since meeting back when Jedediah first moved to

Virginia from Georgia. Jedediah and Mary did everything together, and through the tough times they had encountered over the years, their love for each other only grew, and truly stood the test of time.

"I don't feel my opinion matters much," Jedediah said while wrapping his hands around Mary's waist.

Mary took her husband's hand and caressed his rough, wrinkled skin. "He looks up to you. He admires you."

Jedediah took in a deep breath and spun his wife around to face him. "The decision is his to make. He is a smart man now."

"Did you give him *any* advice?" Mary asked starring deep into her husband's eyes.

"I told him that we will always love him no matter his choice."

Mary walked over to the bed and tossed the folded clothes into the hamper as Jedediah strolled over to the window.

"The children admire him as well. The way they looked at him tonight…he is their hero."

Jedediah nodded in agreement.

Mary undid her bonnet and let her thin hair fall to her shoulders. She gently slipped into bed and eyed her husband who glowed in the light of the lamp. "Jedediah, I must ask something of you."

Jedediah did not move; his gaze remained cast on the fields outside the window.

"William knows not of the arguing between you and Moses. I must ask that you make peace with you brother, at least until William leaves, should he decide that as his choice."

"I will try, dear."

"That is all I ask. He is under a lot of stress; the fighting will only make it worse, and effect his decision."

Jedediah crossed from the window to the lamp and turned the knob, effectively cutting the source of fuel from the fire. The room became black, colorless.

"You have my word, dear." Jedediah finished.

The aging man unbuttoned his shirt and climbed in to bed, covering himself with the warm sheets. He leaned to his wife and pressed his smooth lips to her cheek. With no more words, the two of them turned over and closed their eyes, not to open them until the light of a new day.

"He is finally home…" Logan said through a yawning mouth. Turning to his side, Logan laid in his cot, listening to the world outside his bedroom window. Crickets chirped softly in the night, expelling songs that filled the vacant hills and mountains that surrounded the alfalfa fields that he knew as home.

"Do you think he was scared?" Logan asked to a dark room.

After a moment's pause, Jed spoke up, "William?"

"Yeah, when he was fighting?"

"Probably…would you be?"

Logan turned over on his back and looked up at the ceiling where small shadows danced across the surface brought forth by the dying candlelight. In the back of his mind he tried to convince himself that if he ever were faced with a situation like that of William's, that he would be calm and steady, and the bravery that flowed through his brother would ultimately take a hold of him.

"No." he answered.

The sounds of Jed turning over in his bed filled Logan's ears as he started to realize that the true fact of the matter was he would have no idea how he would act in battle. "I hope I never have to be brave…"

"What?" questioned little Jed after a long, drawn out yawn.

"I hope I never have to fight like William. I'm scared I will fail." Logan's inner feelings swirled through his head as he tried to conjure up all the possible scenarios that would call on his ability to be strong in a moment of true danger.

"Yeah whatever, Logan; Goodnight," Jed replied turning over once more.

"Goodnight, Roo."

"Will you two hush up already?!" said Nathan's groggy voice.

Turning over on to his side away from the world, Logan closed his eyes, slowly slipping off into a gentle sleep.

As the morning mist started to dissipate from the early air, and the fingers of the sun's rays tickled the gentle orange sky, Jedediah awoke to a sleeping house. Rubbing his cleanly shaven face, he carefully descended the stairs from his bedroom loft, buttoning this flannel work shirt. He rolled his cotton sleeves in a precise manner, being sure to get each cuff at equal length.

Upon reaching the landing, Jedediah walked over to the kitchen and removed one small mug from the white cupboard and filled it with a brew from the previous night; a mix of water and ground coffee beans. The mixture proved to be ample in raising one's level of alertness; however the taste of such an inconsistent solution was less than satisfactory. Nevertheless, Jedediah seemed not to mind, for he repeated the task every morning of his adult life. Sipping away at the concoction, he looked out the window at the horizon, watching as the early birds fluttered above the alfalfa fields hunting for worms, and other insects. There was a deep thought rumbling through the confines of his brain, yet his face remained significantly plain.

As if on cue, the thump from the morning post hitting the weeping porch drew Jedediah's attention away from the field. The man was quick to act, moving from the kitchen to the front room, and finally out of the house. Bending over with a deep groan, the aging man gripped the bundled papers and examined the title. All over the front page was news on the growing war, followed by lists of names that belonged to soldiers that had joined the rebel cause. With a sigh of disgruntled defiance, Jedediah tossed the paper onto the porch swing and took another sip of his brew, the man's thoughts finally becoming clearer.

"Good morning, Father." a groggy-voice called.

Jedediah looked behind him to see his son, Jed, standing in the doorway still in his nightgown; the porch storm door stood open behind him.

"Well, good morning, Jed. I was going to let you sleep in this morning. With William here, the work should not take as long today."

The tired boy walked over beside his father and rested his hands on the splintered wooden rail of the white porch; his upper body just barely tall enough to let him peer over the rail at the rising sun. "I heard a noise out here. It woke me up." he announced whilst yawning.

"Oh, that was nothing, just the paper." Jedediah explained.

"Can I read it?!" questioned the boy now fully alert.

Shaking his head with uncertainty, Jedediah responded, "I do not think that is a good idea, Son, I…"

"Please, Dad!" Jed shouted, cutting him off.

Jedediah looked at his child who put on his best sympathy act.

"Not yet, Son, maybe in a year or two…" the man ruled working his way back inside.

"But, Father, by then the war could be over; all the news will be boring then!"

"God willing…" Jedediah mumbled under his breath, walking back inside leaving Jed Jr. on the porch.

The green-eyed boy sighed with frustration and self-pity as he flopped down on the porch swing, his bare feet just skimming the old floorboards. Twisting in confusion at what he was sitting upon, Jed pulled the bundle of papers out from under him. His face lit up in excitement. He had feared his father would have taken the paper with him; however, his father's lack to do so had resulted in his win. The boy tucked the papers under his shirt and pranced inside, only pausing to question his disobedient act once, yet in the boy's mind, he was not breaking any rules seeing as how his father had said nothing about taking the paper, only reading it.

Once inside, Jed Jr. ran to his room, doing his best to avoid his father at all costs. Entering the room and slamming the door shut, he forced the other sleeping children to moan and shift in their beds.

"You guys!" Jed whispered in an anxious tone, his body leaning back on the shut door.

The room was unresponsive…

"You guys, get up!" Jed shouted louder and louder until he received a pillow in the face from the direction of Logan's bed.

"Shush, Jed, we're sleepin'!" moaned Logan with annoyance.

"But…"

"He said Shush, Jed!" Nathan chimed in.

Irritated, Jed Jr. walked over to Logan's bedside and knelt down beside it until his eyes were even with the boy's face. He studied his sleeping brother with a keen eye, looking for a way to wake him up and not receive the almost certain fist that would fly his way.

Logan's face was scrunched up as he tried to cover his eyes from the Sun's light penetrating the blinds on the window; his hands cupped together by his head like a spider waiting to pounce on its attacker if provoked. Jed reached his hand out until it was only a mere centimeter from Logan's face. He curled his fingers into a circular shape and waited. Just as Logan started to turn over, Jed released his grip, letting his forefinger slam right into Logan's cheek. In a wild flash, followed by a mass pile of blankets flying in the air, Logan leapt out of bed on top of Jed, burying him in the pillows as they descended to the ground.

"You twerp, you know better than to bother me when I'm sleeping!" shouted the riled teen.

"I have to show you something!" Jed replied gasping for breath under his older brother's weight; his words muffled by the mountain of pillows and blankets atop him.

By now, Nathan and Maxwell were up. Laughing with a devilish delight, Nathan ran over to help torment Jed, leaving Maxwell behind to watch with sleepy eyes at the chaos unfolding.

"Logan, get off!" screamed Jed, panicking at the presence of a second body crushing him.

"No! You're gonna' learn to shut up when we say!"

Kicking with all of his might, Jed searched for any possible escape route. Both his cousin and brother were too strong to beat off by force, so he resorted to the last possible solution; a solution that would most certainly work, a solution that was his only hope of escaping before his lungs collapsed…Mom.

"Mom!" Jed shrieked.

As if someone had fired a gun into the air, both Nathan and Logan sat up and looked at each other with huge eyes. A look as if they had just witnessed a murder.

"Mo-" Jed tried to call out again, but was silenced by Logan's hand.

"Okay, okay! Don't call her, we give…" Logan pleaded.

Satisfied with his victory, Jed rolled out from under the pile of sheets and bodies, and walked over to the bureau that sat under the mirror.

"I was trying to show you this…" Jed pulled out the bundle of papers from his gown. "I hid them from Pa…"

All of the boys huddled together in front of the mirror, each one of them trying to get a piece of the forbidden prize.

"Maxwell, fetch me the knife from under my bed." Nathan ordered his brother.

Little Maxwell hustled over to the dark oaken bed frame and reached under it with a grunt as he stretched his joints to their limits trying to snag the handle of the hunting knife. The child grabbed the calcified bone grip, and ran it over to his brother.

"I thought Aunt Sue told you to get rid of that thing…" Jed noted looking at the long blade dangling from Maxwell's hand.

"Well what she don't know, don't hurt her. And besides, you aren't exactly obeying either." Nathan fired back causing Jed to frown with guilt.

Nathan took the knife from Max and cut the string that held the bundle of newspaper together. Like starving thieves in a bread shop, the children attacked the stack of parchment, with the exception of Jed.

"Wait you guys," he said grabbing up the papers from each kids' hand.

"What, Roo?" Logan snapped with frustration at his brother's shift in mood.

"Maybe we shouldn't read this…"

"Why not, we already have it opened?!" announced Nathan grabbing the stack from Jed.

"Because, what if there is a reason that my father doesn't want us to read this?" asked Jed in curiosity, whilst retrieving the stolen papers again.

"Pa just doesn't want us to have nightmares or something like that…" Logan explained.

"What do you mean?" asked Jed.

"Never mind it, Roo; I heard him say a while ago that sometimes they publish things that children shouldn't read. But you are twelve and I'm fifteen…we're practically adults."

Jed shrugged in agreement even though a part of him still regretted disobeying. Logan, while smart for his age, was as stubborn as a board. He had not really encompassed the whole idea of what war was. To him, and the rest of the children in the home, it was a glorified conflict; death seemed a thing of fiction to them, while the stark reality of it was just the opposite.

Unbeknownst to the adults, the children started to read the bold, black headlines of the press. In silence, they lounged around in the center of their room, still in their nightgowns; their hair tufted up like feathers. Logan sat across from Maxwell, his feet rested in the center of the circle; little Maxwell mimicked his oldest cousin watching every move he made. Peering over the paper slowly, Logan giggled at his cousin's ostentatious behavior; the little child's toes tickled the bottom of Logan's feet as he rocked side-to-side humming an unknown tune. Upon his face sat a look of wonderment as he marveled at the older boy's features, and insouciant behavior.

"Hey, Maxy…want to hand me that other sheet?" Logan asked, motioning to the pile of untouched documents.

In a fit of determination, Maxwell jumped up from the circle, and stumbled into the stack of parchment, sending it flying across the room.

"Grab it, Max!" shouted Nathan to his brother as a sheet slid closer and closer to the door.

As if karma had stepped in, the paper jutted up into the air, and out the crack under the white door, and into the dining room.

Every face in the room turned white. Jed looked to Logan, Logan looked to Nathan, and Nathan looked at the figure standing in the open doorway: Father Jed.

William snapped awake in a sweat, his body shaking as he sat up and turned on the oil lamp that resided next to his bed. Every time he closed his eyes to shake off the visions of the blue-eyed boy, the piercing eyes became more vivid. *What does it mean?* He asked himself as he ran a hand over his wet face.

The room around him was pitch black, besides the light that shown from the lamp which cascaded a gentle glimmer into the kitchen where the sounds of Amelia cooking breakfast on the heated iron-range were growing increasingly audible.

Rising from the bed and throwing on a loose fitting shirt, William opened his door and walked down the small corridor, following the smells of crackling bacon. Amelia was rushing around the kitchen singing to herself as she tried to tackle six activities at once.

"Good morning, Amelia." William said while yawning.

Caught off guard by the man, Amelia jumped and turned to face the sailor.

"My heavens, good morning Master William; how did you sleep?" she asked in a giddied tone.

"I'm afraid not very good…not good at all actually."

Amelia pitied the man's answer and handed him a stick of bacon. "Here eat this; hopefully it will get your mood up."

William chewed on the piece of thick bacon and took a seat at the table; leaning his head back he sighed as he stretched his legs. The morning sun was shining brightly through the thick glass windows that were positioned directly in front of the table, and slight morning breezes whooshed in under the lifted pane. William thought as he examined passing birds out the window, that if everything besides the set back of his dream continued to improve, then the day had the makings to be wonderful.

"No!" a loud scream came from a distant room in the house, which caused Will to pause.

"Amelia, what was that? Where is Father?" he asked aloud.

"No, Pa I swear it, we just found them, we wasn't reading anything!" cried Logan pleading the children's case.

"You *were not* reading anything; *wasn't,* is not the correct term." Father Jed corrected.

"Yeah that! You have to believe us!" the boy finished.

Father Jed stood erect in the doorway glaring at each boy with eyes that seemed to pierce their souls. Each child sat nervously looking up at Jedediah with apathy.

"I have a tough time believing you boys, considering I left the papers on the porch swing…"

All eyes in the room shifted to Jed, who lowered his head in self-pity. He knew that he had condemned every one of them. At that moment, William poked his head through the door. Little Jed popped up at the sight of his brother. Immediately, he started scheming.

"What is going on in here?" William wondered.

"Your brothers and cousins *happened* upon a copy of this morning's paper." Jedediah emphasized the accusatory word.

Standing up and walking over to William, Jed began to work his magic. "What Father claims is that we took them, but I found them in the room when I came walking back in…"

"I see," noted William being led by the hand by Jed over to the bed, away from their father.

Leaning in close to the sailor, Jed spoke quietly, so quietly that not even Nathan who sat less than two feet away could make out the words.

"Look, help me get out of this one and I'll give you a chunk of my allowance."

William rubbed his chin in thought, "How much?"

"Ten percent…"

"…Ten percent of what?" Will asked.

"It's five cents, okay?" Jed spoke anxiously.

"…Deal." William said shaking hands with little Jed.

Spinning around, William tucked his hands behind his back and strolled forward toward his father, acting like he was some high-classed attorney. At the sight, the boys giggled like toddlers looking up at the goofy man.

"My dear, sweet father…what Jed seems to be saying is that he could not have possibly taken the paper, for he was never on the porch…"

"Yes, I was…" Jed coughed quietly.

"I mean he was! However, that does not mean he took the paper!"

Father Jed cocked a half smile, crossing his arms.

"…And seeing as how you were no longer present on the porch when young Jed left to return to his room, you cannot possibly prove, behind a shadow of a doubt, that he took the papers!"

Jedediah rubbed his face and stepped farther into the room, pausing before he made his counterpoint. "If I was not present on the porch, and nor were you, then how can you possibly know he did not take the paper?" Jedediah paused waiting for the reply.

Little Jed's jaw dropped; his father had just shut down William's defense.

"Well…uh…" William recollected his thoughts. "Well, Father, I do not think court works that way."

The aging man laughed at his son's obvious defeat. "Do not let me catch you with the paper again." he said rubbing Jed's furry head; he then walked out of the room.

"Dang, William, way to go you almost blew it!" Jed hollered punching his brother's arm.

"Roo, you are the one who hired me!" William pointed out.

Laughing mischievously, Nathan spoke up, "Hey guys, he never said to give the paper back!"

William tapped his jokester cousin on the back of the head. "Hand me the papers you guys, Pa is right, there's no sense in getting all worked up about this war."

The room gave a unanimous groan as they passed Will the newspapers.

"I'm taking my money back!" Jed yelled.

William looked at the dresser beside him and swiped his hand across it collecting loose change. Counting it briefly, he shook his hand and winked at Jed, "Good luck, little brother!"

Logan laughed at Jed's loss and tackled him to the floor. "He showed you, Jed!"

"Buck off, Logan. He would'a done the same to you!" Jed noted.

"Yeah, but the difference is, I'm broke so he would have stolen your money anyway!"

"But it wouldn't be your money to give!" Jed protested.

"That's the beauty of it!" Logan kissed his fingers like a chef after creating a masterpiece.

Jed sat watching his dork of a brother in confusion, as he ran out into the kitchen with Nathan following.

Jed motioned for Maxwell to stand up. "Maxy, I sure hope Nathan's moved out by the time you are my age, brothers can be a handful…"

The quiet child nodded in agreement, even though he really did not understand what Jed meant. The two boys ran out of the room, throwing the door closed behind them; it shut with a loud thud.

Moses and Sue were present at the breakfast table when the children entered the kitchen. They were feasting on the creation Amelia had been cooking all morning. Little Abigail sat in a high chair beside Sue, whining every time her mother withdrew her hand from the child's grip.

"Good morning, Amelia!" Logan announced flying into the room grabbing the back of an empty chair and spinning to a stop.

"Good morning, Mr. Logan." Amelia said, glancing toward Moses with a look of cowardice.

"How are you today?" Logan asked.

Amelia opened her mouth to speak, but paused when she caught Moses' eyes glaring at her.

"Logan, let Amelia be." Moses announced.

Caught in the grasp of a sudden hype, Logan said nothing more to the servant, nor did he question Moses' command. Instead, he looked for William's shadow down the hall, hoping to catch the man before he headed out to the fields. "Uncle Moses, where is William?" he questioned.

"You just missed him; he walked outside with your father."

Logan swung at the air with irritancy.

Moses set his fork down and pointed a finger toward the child. "You my friend, best get moving and head out to the fields yourself. There's a storm brewing and those crops have to be planted!"

"Oh, Moses, hush!" Sue said with one hand occupied by Abigail's slobbery grasp. "You are just too lazy to get up and do the work yourself…"

"Sue, I would do the work, but I'm helping with Abigail!"

"You most certainly are not!" the woman fired back.

Logan watched the couple bicker and formed a mental note on how to potentially escape chores his parents, or anyone for that matter, ordered him to do: *take credit for helping others, even if you are blatantly doing the opposite.* While it was not the best idea, he figured it was worth a shot to try.

"Okay, well I am going to head back to the room, I will see you guys later…" Logan said trying to leave the scene before his mother arrived.

"Where is it you said you are off to, Son?"

The boy froze. His mother's voice stung his ears like a needle to a balloon.

"I'm, uh…" desperately, the boy searched for an escape. He knew that if he told her the truth, she would direct him to the field to help William and his father.

"I'm going to get Jed to… help…help you!" Inside he prepared to use the tactic his uncle had successfully utilized.

"Help me?" Mary asked in confusion.

"Yes, Mother. I was going to help you by watching the house, while you and Sue go into town. That was the plan right?"

Mary looked to Sue who shook her head in disagreement. "We had no such plans."

Logan knew that his plan was failing quickly. With all eyes in the room on him, he knew he had to act fast. "Okay, well I'm so busy right now; I helped Father in the field yesterday, and it has gotten me behind on my other chores." Feeling confident, the blue-eyed boy turned his back to walk toward the sanctity of his room.

One-step…no response from his mother.

Two steps…

Three steps… "Logan."

The child turned as his hopes for escaping were narrowing by the second, "Yes, my darling Mother?"

"Nice try, Son, but no one worked in the field yesterday." Mary said through a half-cocked smile.

Logan knew his plan was shot. "Can I do the field tomorrow?"

Straightening her bonnet, Mary looked outside the kitchen window at the sky above. "No, it is going to rain. These crops will need as much water as possible, so you best get them in today."

"Come on," pleaded the depressed teen.

"Run along now. Maybe William will teach you kids baseball after you finish…weather permitting that is."

Baseball, Logan thought. He knew the game, yet he had never played. Father Jed had bought him a ball for his birthday when he was fourteen; however, it sat at the bottom of the clothes hamper ever since…never touched.

"Alright…" Logan said sulking as he walked outside onto the rickety front porch.

Thick gray clouds had already rolled in above the sweeping plains when Logan had set foot through the door and out onto the deck of the house. William was already in the field beside his father with hoe in hand, appearing diminutive when compared to the rising mountains on the horizon behind him. Sulking with self-pity, the teen marched his way through the green grass out toward the two men, where the grass transformed into tall blades of brown and tan wheat. The dry grain brushed across the boy's legs as he maneuvered his way through the maze, allowing his hands to skim across the top of the needle-like plants; his fingers tugged at the frayed tips, which sent tingling sensations through his palms.

The rows of alfalfa dissipated as Logan neared his brother and father, and rich, black soil filled the void. Long rows of small green plants poked their heads out of the dirt as if trying to touch Logan's mud-caked shoes as he passed through the aisles.

"Ah, just in time, Logan." Father Jed announced handing the boy a shovel and a bag of seeds.

Frowning with bitterness, the teen shook his hair out of his eyes to examine the crops around him. "They haven't grown much…if at all…"

William drew a hardened look toward his father who wiped a dirty hand across his brow leaving a trail with the outline of three fingers just below his hairline.

"It's going to be another tough year, Bud." William said in place of his father.

"So then what is the point of handing me more seeds?" asked the blue-eyed boy in frustration.

"We have to go back through and plant another row of seeds. Half of these crops will die within the next week." Jedediah announced raising his voice.

"So let me get this straight…" Logan began.

William pointed a finger at his younger brother, and bit his tongue trying to hold in a sudden streak of anger. Inside he felt a malevolent emotion that spawned from pity for his father and his family's current state.

Jedediah walked away from his sons and out further into field where he threw his rake toward the mountains. "Just one year is all I ask. One year to be able to put food on the table for my family!"

Logan buried his words as he watched his father spill his emotions like he never had before. He did not quite understand what his father meant, for they had plenty of food. Suddenly, it struck him. The continuous trips into town by his mother over the past few months seemed to explain their recent shortage of money and over abundance of food, which was quickly diminishing.

Jedediah calmed his breathing and turned his attention back to his boys. "You kids can go on. I'll handle this."

"No, Dad we-"

"William, go. Neither of you have to help me today. I'm sure there is something else you kids would rather be doing with your day."

A low groan of thunder rumbled throughout the valley as William and Logan watched their father pace the ground, pulling up the dead arms of deceased crops as cold rain started to trickle down atop their heads.

"Go!" shouted Father Jed.

Logan pulled on the back of his brother's shirt and the two made their way back to the house leaving their father in the field alone.

Will ran a hand through his brother's blond hair and shook it back and forth tossing around his golden locks. "Things will be alright, Logy; he's just stressed. Give it two weeks or so, and I bet that ground will be throwing food at us."

Logan fixed his hair and kicked a stone out of his path. "I've never seen him lose it like that. He normally is calm around us."

"People need to release that built up emotion from time to time, he'll be alright."

Logan let William's words soothe his mind and he began to toss around the idea of playing baseball; a desire that strangely called to him. "Want to play catch?"

Taken aback, the sailor laughed for a moment. "What did you say?"

"Baseball…do you want to play?"

"Uh, yeah, sure…I thought sports weren't your thing?" Will said.

"I never said that. I'm too old for tag with Jed and Max, but baseball seems fun."

"Grab your brother and Nathan."

Logan scurried off into the house anxious to learn the game.

"And grab something to use as a bat!"

William chuckled at the sight of his brother's sudden appetite to play the game that William himself had only learned to play months ago when he was docked for re-supply in New York.

The young sailor was taught by a member of the prestigious New York Knickerbockers, a connection that was introduced by the Captain of the *Liberty* himself.

Moment's later, Logan burst through the screen door of the house with red shutters carrying a long wooden stick, and his baseball. Atop his mop of hair rested a blue cap with a long bill that cast a gentle shadow over his face.

Following Logan was Jed, who ran out of the house in frenzy.

"I want to bat first!" hollered Jed, who raced passed Logan to his brother who had started to mark out the bases of the diamond.

"Easy Jed, everyone will have a chance. So I don't suppose you two know any of the rules?" asked William expecting the answer.

Anxious grins found their way onto the boy's faces as they shook their heads, denying any knowledge of the game.

"I figured. Well first thing is, Jed why don't you go step behind that plate over there." ordered William pointing to a rock that was set to act as home plate. "Be sure to stand about ten feet back so the ball doesn't hurt your hands when you catch it."

The young boy ran to the rock and stood awkwardly behind it waiting for further orders.

"Now, you are called the *behind*. Your job is to catch the ball if Logan doesn't hit it."

"Logan gets to bat first?!" shouted Jed impatiently.

"Yes, it was his idea to play, therefore he bats first." explained William.

Out of view, Logan's tongue pierced his lips as he mocked Jed's grief.

"Now Jed, crouch down real low and let you knees line up over your toes."

Jed did as told and moved into position.

"Good! Relax a bit though. You should be perfectly balanced with your hands out ready to catch the ball." William pushed on the boy's chest causing him to rock back a hair. "There, perfect balance!"

Jed grinned feverishly as he awaited the throw from William right over home plate.

Inside the house, Mary had been watching through the window at her children playing together, a sight that warmed her heart.

"The children seem to be getting along great!" she exclaimed to the room.

Seated at the kitchen table was Sue, with baby Abigail absent for what seemed to be the first time in history. Also present in the room was Amelia, who was sweeping vigorously trying to remove the crumbs of leftover food that had wandered off the table and onto the floor.

Mary worked her way over to the table where she sat down across from Sue, and folded her hands neatly on her lap. The steady pitter-patter of rain on the roof drowned out the silence that was threatening to take hold of the room. Out of the corner of her eye, Mary watched Amelia work tirelessly; the woman panted as she crossed the house to put away the broom.

In her absence, Mary spoke, "That poor woman."

Sue lifted her eyes to catch Mary's. "Whatever do you mean?"

"Amelia. She works and works without a break or any sort of reward."

Confused, Sue tilted her head as she tried to find Mary's reasoning. "It is what she was brought here to do, Mary."

Mary grunted with frustration. "Well, I feel sympathy for her. She must receive a break sometime in her life." Mary rose and went to hunt for the slave.

Sue began to realize Mary's intentions, and jumped up immediately. "Mary, do not take another step!" lowering her voice, she continued, "If Moses finds out…"

"Moses will not know of this, Sue. Please…"

Sue paused second guessing herself, but finally withdrew her grasp on Mary's arm.

Mrs. Hinckley nodded in thanks, and proceeded down the hallway following in Amelia's footsteps.

As she reached the end of the corridor, she stepped carefully on the wooden beams below. With each step, the wooden floor seemed to flex and moan with pain. Stopping her motion, Mary listened.

From one of the bedrooms, she could hear tender weeping, and hushed words. Mary checked behind her for the illusive Moses before entering the room.

"Amelia?"

As the peach colored door to William's room was pushed open, Mary saw Amelia sitting upon the edge of the bed, with little Maxwell and Nathan present by her side.

Amelia's eyes were wet as she held her shoulder, overwrought with sorrow.

Carefully, Mary entered the room with a stone cold face. Once inside, hundreds of thoughts raced through her mind as to the reason for Amelia's woebegone state. Looking toward the children, she could sense in their hearts that something had occurred; something that sent shock waves through what they considered morally right.

Amelia did not look up from her position on the bed; her eyes remained fixed on a small spot on the floor in front of her.

Mary opened her mouth to speak; yet nothing came out.

"I will be alright, Mrs. Hinkley, you may go." Amelia said through a shaken voice in response to Mary's breath of air.

Striking up the nerve to talk, Mary stood up straight and swallowed hard. Her eyes glimmered in the candlelight that took the place of the sun, whose absence was due to the growing storm on the horizon. "Who did this?" she muttered.

Amelia sat unresponsive, yet the children's gazes answered her question as they shot startled looks toward the door.

Cautiously, Mother Hinkley brought her attention around to the open doorway where the grizzly silhouette of Moses was present resting on the frame.

"You have done this?" demanded the woman.

Moses did not speak, and he remained out of the light of the flame.

Mary remained focused on man. "Children, go join your cousins in the yard."

In quick time, both Max and Nathan walked toward the door with an awkward pace where they cringed while passing their father.

"What has Amelia done to deserve this, Moses?" Mary asked after waiting for the sound of the screen door to slam.

The quiet man stepped menacingly into the candle light, "Nothing in particular."

The words rolled off his tongue in a slithering manner, a manner in which one would quickly feel threatened.

"Amelia, you may leave." Mary announced.

The damaged servant shifted her stare onto Moses who did not acknowledge her presence. Apprehensively, Amelia exited the room, her blue bonnet left behind on the bed.

Moses crept ever closer to Mary until their faces were but inches apart. The woman's nostrils picked up the strong scent of whiskey and tobacco as rancid breath escaped the scraggly man's mouth like fire from a dragon's lungs.

"You think you are in control little woman, but let me tell you this, if you ever think that the slave will become a member of this family, then you best realize that your world will shake and fall like mountains…"

Mary backed away as Moses' whiskers tickled her cheek. "And if you think that hitting a woman in front of children, and then threatening another will make you strong in the eyes of others, you have another thing coming." Strong-willed, she lifted her dress so that her feet would not catch the loose fabric, and left the room leaving Moses to reflect on her words.

As the emotional incident involving Amelia passed from the minds' of the boys, Maxwell and Nathan wandered out into the yard to watch their cousins attempt to play a game of baseball. With hands in his pockets, Nathan encircled the group, eyeing Logan who was still at bat; each step he took forced the ground to gargle as puddles of rain slowly tried to hide beneath the thick grass.

"No, Logan, bend your knees more." William shouted from across the makeshift diamond as Logan's swing passed high over the ball.

"I'm trying, Will. It is harder than it looks!" groaned the boy growing increasingly frustrated.

Moving closer toward home plate Nathan spoke up, "I'll give it a shot."

Logan paused for a moment as he tried to decipher if he was truly ready to hand over the wooden stick.

"Good luck." he said sarcastically as Nathan gripped the end of the bat.

Slowing his breathing, the dusty-haired boy took up his position just off to the side of the rock serving as home plate. He twisted the bat in his hands, squeezing the object to gain further control. As he bent his knees, and looked off toward William, squinting through the little sunlight that started to break through the blackened horizon. "Throw it."

William wound up and tossed the ball overhand toward the determined teen. With one fluid motion Nathan dropped the bat level with the ball, and cracked it over William's head and out into the long, brown grain that was the field.

Every jaw around the boy dropped as he smirked with hubris before taking off around the bases.

"How did you learn to hit like that?!" asked Jed whose jaw remained open while he picked up pieces of the shattered stick.

"I guess I have a knack for sports!" shouted Nathan leaping into the air in celebration as he continued to round second base.

"Logan, what kind of bat did you grab?!" William asked in disbelief of the event that just occurred.

Out of breath, Nathan jogged back toward the group who gathered around the stick; a smile still present on his face from ear to ear.

"Nathan, that is ridi-coo-lase…" Maxwell muttered pointing at the bat.

"You mean ridiculous, Maxy." Logan corrected.

"Hey, don't blame the player, blame the bat-boy!" Nathan joshed, punching Logan's arm.

"It is fine guys; the ball is lost anyway…" William consoled.

"So that's it?" asked Jed in disappointment.

Nodding his head, William answered, "For now, we'll have to get new equipment…being a ball and actual bat."

"Oh well, it was fun while it lasted." Nathan said content with his performance.

"Yeah, easy for you to say, you got to bat!" cried Jed as the group headed back for the house.

Not long after the boys entered the home did Father Jed walk through the door. Covered with dirt, the man walked past the kitchen where the children all sipped on water out of tall, porcelain mugs. Without a word, he moved down the corridor toward his room.

"Think he is mad?" asked Logan anticipating the slam of the wooden door against its frame.

To his surprise, the door clicked shut almost without noise.

"He told us to go do something else, he has no reason to be upset." said William.

Mary entered the room watching the children and William with a keen eye. "Have you done something to upset your father?"

"No, but Nathan lost the ball!" Jed said dropping his voice to a whisper halfway through the sentence, for fear of Jedediah's hearing.

Removing a plate of cookies from the cupboard, Mary tilted her head with stupefaction. "He lost the ball...how did he manage that?"

"He hit it," the group announced in unity as the proud, yet quiet teen stood in the corner of the small galley.

After a moment's pause, Mary looked to the boy with a look of admiration. "Nathan, I did not know you were good at sports?"

Reaching through the group, Nate took a burnt cookie from the plate. "I didn't either. I guess I've found a hobby."

Father Jed's footsteps echoed in the hallway as Nathan's voice subsided. Grabbing a cookie each, the kids shoved them into their mouths to act occupied just in case the aging man was truly upset.

Menacingly, Jedediah turned his attention to the group as he stopped in front of the kitchen. After a moment of deep concentration, the man's face broke as a smile worked its way upon his cheeks, which were cleared of dirt. "Good hit." he laughed tossing what remained of the ball to the dusty-haired boy.

Catching the tattered cloth that once made up a ball, Nathan's brown eyes swelled with wonderment and fascination as his fingers caressed the torn seams. "I did this?" he asked in amazement.

"That you did…good hit." repeated Jedediah as he walked over to his wife and kissed her cheek before exiting the room toward the porch.

"I did this," said Nathan through a triumphant smile.

When the children awoke the next day, the smiling face of Amelia greeted them. It was a rare occasion when Amelia got them up in the morning, for it was normally one of the other adults, so to the children that meant only one thing…bath day.

"No!" screamed little Maxwell running around the bedroom like a crazed animal. The rest of the children hid in the corner of the room while Max distracted the servant's attention. Breathing heavily as if under attack by an Indian raiding party, Logan, Jed, and Nathan sat low to the ground behind the beige curtains that hung down the bleak wall. Clutching pillows like rifles, they devised their plan.

"Alright, Jed, when I say, I want you to sprint like hell to the door and run out into the kitchen, from there, Nathan and I will meet you in front of William's door…he's our only hope to get out of this mess."

"Got it!" nodded the green-eyed boy accepting the order.

Logan looked to Nathan who wiped the sweat from his face.

"Nate, I want you to combat crawl your way over to her right flank and hold for the order to attack; when I give it, you throw your pillow and we dart like bats outta' hell to rendezvous with Jed at Will's room. Clear?"

"I hear ya!"

Logan looked at each face in the circle; on each one was a look of hardened determination to take down the opposition: Amelia. The thought of what the other grown-ups would do if they escaped her never crossed their minds, for they had never escaped a cleansing. However, they had become a well-trained force to be reckoned with; each time, their tactics had grown as effective as the last, and their military-like precision had increased to the point that they now figured that they were ready to take to the battlefields of the Great War.

"Now!" shouted Logan standing up and tossing his pillow at the robust woman, hitting her in the back, right shoulder. Jed darted to the door hunched over as if dodging a hail of bullets. Nathan dove to the ground and slid his way behind Maxwell's bed where he awaited Logan's order to fire. Maxwell shrieked like a girl as he was picked up into the air by Amelia, who turned around and looked at Logan standing awestruck, frozen in time.

"-Logan," Nathan yelled growing weary of the plan's downfall.

"Uh…" was the only sound to escape Logan's mouth.

Amelia started her menacing walk over to Logan; every step seemed to shake the room's wooden floorboards.

"Logan, what's the signal?!" screamed Nathan in a last ditch attempt to save the operation.

"I don't know!" the blue-eyed boy cried.

"You don't know? What kind of plan did you have in mind?!"

"Run!"

And with that order, Nathan chucked his pillow at Amelia's blue bonnet, hitting her square in the head. In a mad dash, one that would surely win the boy's a badge of courage…if in war…the remaining duo darted for the door. Fumbling the handle, Logan started to yell as the fear of Amelia's hand scratching down his back became increasingly real. Nathan's sweating hands rolled over the knob trying to get a grip, however each attempt ended with another lost second.

"Nathan!" shouted the anxious, fear-stricken Logan.

"I'm trying for God sakes!"

Logan knocked Nathan out of the way and grasped the handle with all his might, throwing his body against the door.

"Master Logan, ya'll best obey now before I get all ugly on you!" Amelia groaned lunging for the boys.

Finally, in the last split second possible before Amelia's wrinkled hand yanked the back of his cotton shirt, Logan hit the door again sending it flying open, exposing a blinding light that caused the boys to fall to their knees.

"Quick, to William's room," Logan murmured through gasps for air.

As the cousins stood up and sprinted across the kitchen toward the dark hallway that led to William's room, a thin figure stepped out in front of them, Jed a prisoner in its grasp.

"Not today, boys…" Mary Hinkley announced crossing her arms.

"Cold!" cried Jed as the icy water splashed down his bare back.

Dressed in their undergarments, Nathan, Logan, and Jed all stood in a line as if waiting for soup at a local kitchen. At the command of Amelia, one at a time they would step forward to be dowsed with the chilled water from the woman's bucket. Littlest Maxwell sat in a copper tub out in the lawn, watching his siblings shiver in the freezing water, while he enjoyed the heated comfort of the tub.

"Way to go, Jed…" seethed Logan, his wet, dripping hair covered his eyes as drops of sparkling water fell off of his nose and lips, and onto the grassy ground.

"Me? It was your plan!" Jed proclaimed.

Logan shook his head disregarding the fact, and stepped forward to receive another splash of the frigid drink. He shook ferociously throwing his arms around his core, rubbing his

53

shoulders trying to produce heat. "Hand me the soap." he demanded.

Jed held out the small black bar of foaming cleanser to his brother, who snatched it with anger.

Nathan walked over to his cousin, while the servant doused Jed once more.

"Ya'll should'a listened to me and you could'a enjoyed some heated water…" Amelia scolded over and over.

Beads of the water marbled in the hot sun on Nathan's chest, causing him to shine like a diamond under intense light. Unfortunately for him, no matter how hot the sun was, it did not take away from the chilly touch of Amelia's dreaded liquid.

"Why do we have to bathe? Derek from class doesn't, nor Peter…" Nathan complained.

"Beats me, all I know is, we should be sitting in that bath with Maxwell, not standing out here to freeze."

"Well, if your plan didn't suck, we would be…"

"Easy!" Logan drew back in offense.

"Well it's true. You stood there with ants in your pants while I was waiting to attack…" Nathan explained.

"Look, we can sit here and point fingers, or we can get even…"

Shivering, Nathan looked at Logan with curious eyes. Smiling in a malevolent manner, Logan dug his toes into the ground and stirred up a filthy blend of worms and mud. The boy bent over and stuck his hand into the wet ground and picked up a handful of the brown, musky mixture.

"Watch this," he ordered.

Amelia pointed a finger at Logan and Nathan. "You two behave, I'll be back; I have to fetch more water."

"Yes, Ma'am," the scheming cousins agreed with angelic attitudes.

Amelia walked back toward the house, and the gaggle of children watched her disappear into the open doorway. At the same time, Logan and Nathan turned their attention to Jed.

"What?" he questioned, his head tilted to the side like a confused dog.

Logan brought his mud-caked hand forward from behind his back and raised it with malicious intent.

"No, Logan, don't do it!" Jed pleaded backing away from his brother in fear.

"Why, Roo, it's only mud…." Logan said in a tone that was deceitfully innocent.

Jed paused for one more second watching his deranged brother before taking off toward the field.

"Get back here, runt!" shouted Nathan joining in on the maniacal masquerade.

As the bare-skinned kids reached the edge of the grass that lined the field, they surrounded Jed on both sides. In a way, they looked like savages with their exposed flesh, and dripping, mud-soaked bodies. Logan poked his fingers into the muck that he cupped in his hand and ran two lines under his eyes to add to the savage appearance.

Panting, the doomed Jed fell to his knees trying to catch his breath. "Please, Logan, stop!" he shouted on the brink of tears.

Without a second thought, Logan chucked the mud at Jed and hit him right in the chest. The impact of the mud ball caused a splatter effect that flew up onto the victim's face. Nathan drew up an expression of shock; he had not thought that Logan would actually throw the mud. Jed slowly brought his hand up to his body and scraped the dirt off, flinging it to the ground. In a matter of seconds, he began to breathe heavier; his fists closed together clutching an imaginary weapon. Logan started to step backwards, Nathan doing the same.

"Easy Jed, it was only a joke," announced Nathan trying to smooth out the situation.

Shaking his head, Jed replied, "No way, Nathan, you two crossed the line this time."

With that threat, the two older boys were off to the races squealing like frightened pigs back to the house with red shutters. Jed was tight on their trail, only a few paces behind. As Jed rounded the bathtub with little Maxwell still occupying it, he bent down and snatched up the bar of soap. In a frantic attempt to get even, the vengeance-stricken child launched the soap through the air. Logan turned back and watched as the bar flew wide left, skipped off of a small rock, and bounced under the porch. Instantly, Jed threw his hands over his mouth. Losing the soap was a crime that would not be taken lightly by the adults, for the foaming cleanser was a rarity, an expensive one at that.

"Jed…what did you do?" Logan moaned finally serious.

"Logan, hide me, get me out of here!" pleaded Jed, his hands clasped together as he begged on his knees.

At that moment, Amelia walked back out into the yard singing a tune that was light on the ears, however, to the children, the song meant that she had not seen what had happened, for if she did, the song would quickly turn into a tirade of threats followed by swinging hands.

"Children, time to finish…" Amelia started, but suddenly stopped when she looked at the children. "Good heavens! Ya'll are dirtier that mules in an outhouse!"

"Sorry Amelia, we fell…" Nathan tried to convince the confused servant.

"Well we don't have time to be bathing ya'll again. Towel off and run along inside, your parents want to be leaving for town by noon."

Jed smirked at his brother and cousin in joy for having evaded the wrath of Amelia.

"…Soap." Maxwell muttered. The word struck Jed's eardrum like a bat on metal.

"Where is the soap, Master Maxwell?" Amelia asked in a voice that one usually reserves for infants.

Logan and Nathan turned around with dropped jaws.

Jed lowered his head accepting his fate. "Amelia, I-"

"He forgot to tell you…he, uh, he forgot to thank you for taking the time to clean us!" Logan covered for the youth.

Amelia laughed at the comment. In a flash, the children ran toward the house before the servant discovered the missing soap.

In the sanctity of their room, the boys toweled off, snickering at their close brush with trouble. Logan hopped over to the bureau that held their clothes. Pushing Jed's shirts out of the way, the driven teen searched for his best outfit.

"Hey Logan, toss me my green shirt, the buttoned one." Jed asked politely.

Logan disregarded Jed's voice as he dug even deeper in the drawer.

"…Or not…" Jed sulked in irritation.

"Never mind him, Jed, he's love struck!" Nathan mocked.

Those words drew Logan's attention like the smell of candy to a toddler. "Am not!" he shouted.

"Are too, Logan, ever since Uncle Jedediah mentioned the possibility of going into town, you have been in a daze." Nathan explained.

"So sue me!" the love-struck teen said finally giving up the denial act.

Nathan nudged Jed on the shoulder and pranced over to the mirror above the bureau. Picking up one of Logan's long sleeve shirts, he held it up to his chest spinning around in the mirror admiring the way it looked. "My name is Logan, and I am in love!"

"Stop that!" Logan demanded.

Jed giggled at Nathan's act.

"…Might as well change my name to Romeo!" Nathan continued.

"Cut it out, Nate!"

Jed was cracking up, rolling over with laughter; his encouragement pushed Nathan to continue his mockery. Folding the shirt over his head like a bonnet, Nathan struck his best girl impression.

"I am Rebecca…kiss me, Logan Hinkley!" Nathan lost himself keeling over in laughter while trying to run away from Logan's flying fists.

"Take it easy, Logan!" Nathan ordered as the kid tackled him into the bed.

"Seriously guys, I'm nervous…" Logan confessed.

"Why? She is just a girl…" spoke Jed.

"You don't get it, Jed, when I talk to her I get all choked up; it's weird."

Jed shrugged in confusion. He could not understand why a girl would be tough to talk to. He talked to them all the time at school; he just treated them like one of the guys.

"Maybe William will help you talk to her?" Nathan wondered.

"Possibly…either way, I need some privacy to get ready, so beat it." Logan bossed the two boys.

Begrudgingly, Nathan and Jed grabbed their clothes and walked out of the room while Logan continued to search for the perfect outfit to impress his love.

A few hours later, the family rolled into town in their wooden wagon. The usual canopy that covered their cart was no longer present, as the weather proved to be quite stupendous. While the family entered Hampton, the children marveled at the sights and smells that flooded their senses.

A small brick wall served as a boundary marker for where the town's limits started and ended. Immediately following the wall, the buildings shut up into the sky like towering Gods. From the shop windows, banners and signs hung down swaying in the wind, advertising all sorts of items.

Bustling about beside the carriage were people of all shapes and sizes. Men with combed hair and straw hats walked beside men with suits and shiny shoes. Women both big and small mingled with each other, talking about the latest fashions and gossip.

In front of the carriage was a long line of traffic. Horses and carts clogged the cobblestone streets. That was the one problem in Hampton; no one obeyed the right of way. Laws in Hampton Square were seemingly considered optional, seeing as how there was a small police force of two men, both being known drunks. Still, the town was considerably peaceful given the circumstances of the law.

Maxwell took in the scenery with large eyes. He had only been to Hampton once in his nine years of life, and that was when he was three. The bright sights and colorful people amazed his childish senses. On the surface, Hampton was perfect; a place completely separated from the whispers of war...so it seemed.

William sat in the front of the carriage with his father and mother; Moses and Sue behind him, and in the back, the children. Slithering his way to the front, Logan tugged on Will's sleeve.

"Hey Will, think I can talk to you for a second when we stop?"

"Sure, little brother, when we stop."

Excited at the fact that he was actually going to be able to talk to his dream-girl, yet nervous for the same reason, Logan's palms began to sweat. His mind started to race as he tried to figure out how he would approach the girl.

"It looks like we'll be stuck here for a while, kids," Jedediah announced with an irritated sigh.

"Awe, come on!" shouted Jed, already growing tired of the minor wait.

"I'm sorry, but I cannot control the traffic!" Jedediah explained growing impatient himself.

Sue turned around in her seat and leaned back toward the children. "Little Jed, do you remember the time that I had to play with you in the yard because you were so upset that you could not go work in the fields with Jedediah, Will, and Logan?"

Jed tried ignoring his aunt, but found it hard when Logan chimed in.

"I remember that! He cried for hours because he wasn't old enough to hold a shovel!"

"That's right, and your mother was too ill with influenza to help watch you, Jed, so I promised her I would keep you busy if she would keep an eye on Maxwell while he slept; he was just a baby then." Sue added in.

Jed became ever more allured by the story, and soon let the past memories flood his mind. "Why would I cry about working? I'd do anything to skip out on it now!"

Sue laughed, "Because you wanted to be like your big brothers."

Jed looked at Logan who sneered jokingly at the boy.

"I must have been insane…" Jed laughed.

"Hey, Aunty Sue, were you the one who cuddled me to sleep whenever we would get a thunderstorm?" Logan asked curiously as the whole carriage seemed to listen in on the conversation.

"That I did, Logan. You were about Maxwell's age back then. Whenever the dark clouds would fill the sky, you would come running for my arms pouring sweat, and shaking with fright."

Logan smiled as he dreamt of his younger days.

"What a baby!" fired Jed with animosity.

"You did the same with me, Jed." Mary said from the front of the wagon.

"I did?" the boy asked puzzled.

"Yes, you did. You were worse though! Whenever the rain would hit, you would fall fast asleep, eventually we would tell you that a storm was coming just to get you to go to bed." The adults chuckled at the comment, which forced Jed to blush with embarrassment.

"Hey, give me a break, I was little!" the green-eyed boy pleaded.

"Hey, Mother, was it me or Maxwell who you said used to run around naked after our day at the beach?" asked Nathan laughing at the matter.

"You did what?!" Logan asked taken back by the odd question.

"Both of you boys did." Sue answered. Looking to Logan and Jed, Sue explained, "When your cousins were younger, Moses and I used to take them to the beach. We would go vacation right on the water in a small house that was surrounded by sagging willow trees. It was truly beautiful. Wasn't it, Moses?"

Moses nodded in agreement. "But that was a long time ago…"

"Anyway," Sue continued, "we would arrive back home after a day in the sun, and the boys' clothes would be filled with sand, so the two of them would strip and run around the house before we were finally able to catch them and force them to wash off."

"That's weird!" Logan said whilst laughing at his cousins.

"It's not like we did it recently, I was seven and Maxwell was only about two." Nathan explained in his defense.

"Well, what do you know, traffic is moving!" Jedediah yelled aloud as the horse pulling the carriage began to pick up speed.

The thought of Rebecca began to swirl around Logan's head again, as did the hundreds of butterflies taking flight in his stomach. Nervously, the boy adjusted the buttons on his collar and fixed his hair, waiting for the moment when he would be face-to-face with the beautiful girl.

Meanwhile, Jed and Nathan continued to reminisce on their childhood as Maxwell watched curiously at baby Abigail who sat tugging on her mother's blouse hoping to be fed.

"Alright, go ahead and disembark people, I'll tie up the horse." Father Jed announced, jumping down from the rickety wagon.

"Hey, Will…" Logan muttered through tight lips as he motioned for the sailor to follow him.

Jedediah tied a half-hitch knot around the wooden stake that served as a tie-up for the horse. "Everybody ready?" he asked counting the family to be sure all were present.

"That we are!" cheered the children, wrought with excitement.

"Give us a moment, Father." William said cocking his head toward the nervous Logan.

Father Jed smirked in acknowledgement as he directed the family toward a small bakery further inside the town.

"All right, Bud, let's go," said William pulling Logan with him toward a vacant alley. William towered over the boy, even when he leaned in close to him to whisper, as to not cause a scene for the sake of Logan's pride.

Double-checking to be sure no one was within earshot; Logan licked his lips as his face filled with the painful look of anxiety. "Okay, so how do I even approach her?"

"…Like you always have." William confessed.

"That's not what I mean. How do I come off? Should I act tough and strong-willed, or shy and mysterious?"

William chuckled at his brother's dilemma. "Just be yourself, Logan. If you try to act like someone else, it'll only make her think you aren't confident, and she'll lose interest."

Logan nodded in understanding as he leaned in closer toward William, away from the damp reclusive nature of the brick walls at his back. "Right, so have confidence!"

"Yup, confidence is the key."

"Confidence is the key!" Logan repeated as he tried to build himself up.

"Yup, and remember, treat her as you normally would, talk about things that interest her, complement her hair, ask her how life is…things like that."

"Whoa, slow down!" Logan shouted. "I won't remember all that!"

"Just be yourself, and be honest! You have already kissed her, and if she didn't hit you, then that means she likes you!"

"Shush!" said Logan putting his finger over his lips signaling for William to be quiet as a man passed by. "I don't want people to hear! And besides, what happened before wasn't really a kiss, kiss; it was more of an accidental kiss."

"Be brave and confident. And do it quick, because here she comes!" William walked out of the alleyway leaving Logan in shock as the blonde girl made her way from the row of shops across the street toward the dimly lit alley.

"Logan Hinkley?" the girl asked.

"Uh, hi…Rebecca!" called the blue-eyed boy as he tried to remain calm.

"What are you doing in the alley?" laughed the girl as she pulled the boy out onto the street.

"I, uh, dropped my hat…" Logan said quickly. After he said those words, a sour look ran across his face as he immediately realized how dull his excuse was.

"You aren't wearing a hat…" Rebecca noted.

"Yeah…never mind. So how are you?!" the boy said trying to revert the topic.

Smiling shyly, the blonde girl began to walk down the cobbled road toward her father's shop. "I'm doing fine. How are you?"

Logan looked to William who rested beside the carriage a few yards away. "Follow her!" he whispered to his dumbfounded brother.

The boy quickly caught back up to the girl. "I'm doing well."

Rebecca nodded awkwardly as she looked around waiting for the boy to make his next move.

"So..." he uttered.

"So?"

"So...how are you?" Logan asked again grimacing, realizing he was blowing the conversation.

"You already asked me that!" Rebecca laughed.

"Yeah, I was just kidding!" said the boy turning toward William with a look of terror. "Help me!" he mouthed.

"So, I have a question." Rebecca stated.

Logan immediately snapped his head back to face her.

"Do you think that you would miss me if I ever left?"

"What do you mean?!" Logan asked worriedly. Suddenly, his nerves began to subside.

"I'm sorry; it wasn't my place to ask that..." Rebecca said shying away.

"No, go on." Logan urged as he scanned the fair girl with emotion.

"Nothing, it is just that my father is threatening to move north."

"Why would he do that?" asked Logan.

"People here..." Rebecca paused and pulled Logan into the doorway of the nearby shop. "People here talk. They talk about how my father supports the North, and they don't like it. It could get dangerous around here soon...for me at least." The girl dropped her round hazel eyes to the ground as she tried to straighten her thoughts.

"I would miss you no matter where you went." confessed the love-stricken teen.

Rebecca lifted her gaze to where her green eyes met the intensity of Logan's crystal blue stare.

"You are just saying that..."

"No, I mean it, Rebecca! To be honest, I was in that alley trying to think of what I would say to you when I saw you. You make me feel..."

Rebecca perked up as a hopeful look passed over her face. She pulled her hands close to her body as she awaited the next words from Logan's mouth.

"I like you." Logan announced as he remembered what William had told him about being honest.

A golden smile worked its way across Rebecca's hollow face. "I like…"

"You like what, Rebecca?" asked a deep, groggy voice.

"Father!" she said jumping with fright as the large, muscular man walked out of the shop's front door.

Logan jumped back in alarm. "Good afternoon, Sir!"

"Who are you?!" asked the man through a thick beard that covered the entirety of his middle-aged face.

"I'm…"

"Logan, come along!" called Father Jed from across the street.

Logan seized the moment, and said his goodbyes, "Nice to meet you, Sir, but I have to run!"

Rebecca's father sneered at the boy, and then returned to the shop. Logan stopped halfway in the street and glanced back at the girl of his dreams. The gleaming smile returned to her and she blew a kiss toward the fleeing teen, who returned it with a proper bow, then returned to his place among the ranks of his siblings.

"I hope I'll see her again soon." Logan murmured to himself. "How did I do, Will?"

"Just fine, little brother." said the man rubbing his hand over the boy's hair, causing tufts of it to stand up.

"So kids, where to now?" asked Mary as the group worked their way further into town.

Moses approached Mary and motioned to a small shop on the corner of the two intersecting streets of Wabash Lane, and Helms Borrow Avenue.

"I'm going to take a step inside; I need to refill my pipe." said Moses while he coughed.

64

"Jedediah, why don't you follow Moses?" Mary asked, almost demanding.

Jedediah shrugged off the comment, but could not excuse the harsh look that followed. "Yes, dear." he said pulling open the door to the small convenient store.

Nathan pushed his way past Max and Jed and up to Logan's side. Sneakily, he pulled the boy out into the open street to where the two had a clean view of the opposite street corner.

"You see it?" Nathan asked pointing a finger in the direction of a small newsstand on the corner block.

"Yeah, I see it, what about it?" Logan wondered peering through the moving carts and buggies with a keen eye.

"Now is our chance to read the post! Our fathers are inside and will never see us!" Nathan began to squirm with excitement as he continued to scheme.

Logan bit his lip and pulled away, back toward the sidewalk. "I don't know Nate, if we get caught again, we're in for it, and I mean bad...possibly even the paddle."

"Will you just chance it one more time?! What is there to lose?"

"Um, I won't have a sore butt..."

"Logan, you are killing me!" Nathan ran in front of his cousin to block his escape. "Look, if we get caught, I'll take the blame."

Logan chewed on his tongue considering the situation. "All of it?"

"All of it. Cross my heart and hope to die." Nathan swirled his finger around his heart and kissed his pinky.

"Deal, let's hurry before my mother sees us."

The two boys hustled off across the busy street, running through the center of town. Once in the clear, the two skipped up from the cobbled street and onto the smooth sidewalk. Nathan pulled a cap out of his pocket and pulled it down tight on his head.

"What is that for?" Logan asked.

"Just in case anyone should recognize us," the dusty-haired boy explained.

Ten feet away from the boys there sat the small wooden newsstand. Behind it, the doorway of *McHarvey's Book Emporium* served as social center for the citizens crowding the cramped walkway. Directly in front of the tiny stand stood a small boy, no older than Maxwell shouting, "War spreads to Hampton, read here folks!"

"Follow my lead..." Nathan said poking Logan's shoulder, "Pardon me, Kid."

The small boy looked up to see Nathan towering over him. Logan looked around nervously, afraid of being caught by his mother.

"May we trouble you for a paper?" Nathan asked in a kind voice.

"Five cents, Bubo." the child replied.

Nathan turned to Logan with irritancy. "Five cents?!" he whispered.

"Just give it to him." urged Logan.

"Here..." Nathan held out his palm and gave the boy the money and in return received a fat stack of newspaper articles.

Logan tugged on Nathan's arm. He was already tearing apart the string holding together the thick bundle. "Let's get out of here."

The two darted into the doorway of the bookstore and looked around for a place to be seated.

"Mother, where is Logan?" Jed asked moments after the boys had left the group.

"They were just with us. Perhaps they went to grab a snack?" Mary replied without worry.

Knowing that the two would not run off without telling their mothers of their whereabouts, Jed started to suspect that they were up to something. The boy looked to his mother, whom was busy window-shopping while awaiting the return of Moses and Jedediah. "Mom, I am going to go find a place to use the washroom. Okay?"

"Of course, dear, hurry along." the fair woman replied.

Jed scurried off away from the adults and crossed the busy streets of Hampton. All around him people walked waist to waist forcing him to squeeze through any gaps possible. Finally, the child reached the newsstand where the small boy was still busy shouting the headlines. Curious, Jed halted in his tracks and began to read the bulletin posted on the wooden framework of the stand, for a moment he forgot his mission of finding his older siblings.

As the child's green eyes scanned the thick, black print painted on the wooden sign before him, his mind began to soar as news from the frontlines filled his brain. The information he desperately craved was now at his feet.

"Hey kid, how much for a paper?" Jed asked the boy aloud.

The kid pointed to a sign behind him that listed the price.

"I'll make you a deal." Jed said after realizing he was completely broke.

"No deals mate. Pay it or move on…"

Filled with irritancy, Jed moved on toward the doors of the bookstore where Logan and Nathan sat in peace.

"Oh no it's Jed!" Logan shouted as he looked up from the print to see his brother trotting up toward the store entrance, completely unaware of the two older boy's whereabouts.

"So?" Nathan commented with a non-caring attitude.

"So he might rat us out, or worse, he won't shut up if he sees the papers and our parents will kill us."

Logan stood up from his seat in the leather armchair that was just inside the doorway to the lounge, adjacent the main entrance of the building.

"If we can get back outside without him seeing us, we should be fine I'd think." Logan assumed.

Nathan shook his head in disagreement. "Follow me to the back of the store. We can hide there and wait him out. I paid five cents for these papers, and I'm sure not about to lose 'em."

Logan followed close behind Nathan who slithered like a snake between the chairs filled with sharply dressed men sucking on porcelain pipes. The two stopped short of the bookcases and

67

prepared to cross the open divide that separated the lounge from the actual shopping center. Nathan peered up from his crouched position and examined the surrounding area, hoping that Jed had not seen them leave. To their liking, the boy was still stuck at the entrance navigating through a mob of leaving customers.

"Run now!" Logan said as he pushed his cousin forward.

The two boys darted across the open walkway and took up refuge amongst the towering bookcases.

Across the street from the old bookstore, Moses was searching for tobacco to fill his brittle pipe; Jedediah was in his company, to the dismay of both characters. Examining the shelves of the infinitesimal shop, Moses hummed an old tune to himself.

Jedediah kept his distance, watching his brother with strained eyes.

"I can sense you are about to make some abusive remark…"

Jedediah kept his tongue.

"So let me save you the trouble. Yes, I am buying tobacco; all I need to know is, flavored, or non-flavored?" Moses paused looking to his brother. A cocky grin worked its way across his face, blossoming into a full-blown chuckle.

"I find your sense of humor disturbing, Moses." Jedediah said whilst shaking his head.

The two began to move toward the counter to pay for the tattered tin of tobacco. Jedediah took the lead, pushing past his shorter sibling who walked painfully slow; his hands stuffed in his pockets.

"Are you in a rush, big fella?" Moses asked hoping to spark some sort of argument.

"You walk much to slow." consoled Father Jed.

"Jedediah, what is eating at you? It seems to me you just won't admit to yourself that you are having a grand ole time shopping with me!" said Moses brimming with sarcasm.

"I find it painfully vexing to be in your presence."

Moses drew up a snarling expression, realizing that the fight was on. "You aren't so pleasant yourself you know."

"Is that so?" Jedediah asked turning to face his brother.

"That it is. Do you know what it is like being around a prodigious hypocrite?" Moses asked going on the attack.

"I'd imagine it being the same as being around a depreciative little racist, whose looks are a gateway to the dull, malignant insides that swirl through his veins."

Moses stopped in his tracks and glared intensely at the man before him.

Jedediah glared right back and drew himself closer to his shorter brother. "Mother had always told me that this day would come. She said that once she was gone she knew we would fight like this. And do you know why? Not because we have different views on life, but because you were always jealous and stubborn. I have allowed you to live in my home, eat my food, and give your kids a chance to grow up with others their own age."

"I did not have the luxury they have, Jedediah! You think that I am not grateful for what you have done? I spent five years of my childhood alone on the farm waiting for you to return to us. You left us to chase a dream, and in doing so, you left us behind."

Jedediah examined his brother with eyes struck in awe. "Moses, no one left you. You were just too blind to see that."

"What is that supposed to mean?" asked the man raising his voice at Jedediah, who left the store, the bell above the door chiming as he exited.

Logan and Nathan still sat unseen in the darkened corner of *McHarvey's Book Emporium*. The colossal bookcases gave off an eerie sense of entrapment, forcing Logan to squirm sheepishly as he grew impatient. Nathan examined the doorway, still keeping an eye on the ever-searching Jed. Time passed, and familiar thought began to transpire in the confines of Logan's brain.

"Hey, Nate…" Logan whispered in a drizzling tone, staring at the tower of novels in front of him.

"What is it?" responded Nathan on high alert.

"Can I ask you something?"

"Make it quick."

Logan's eyes grew wide as he spoke from his heart. "What is really going to happen to all of us if this war continues?"

"I don't know, cousin; I'm not too worried about that right now." Nathan said.

"Rebecca might be leaving…"

Nathan removed his eyes from Jed, who still navigated the lounge area across the store. "You are still thinking about her?"

"It never stops." Logan admitted.

"I wouldn't worry too much about it."

"No, Nathan, listen to me. I really, really like her; if she leaves, it will hurt…a lot. She said she was leaving because her father favors the North…what will happen if one of us ever has to leave?"

"Why would we ever have to do that?"

"Look at our fathers. They can never agree and they argue more and more by the day." Logan paused as his gaze fell back upon the row of books before him. "If she leaves, it will hurt me…if you or Maxwell leave…it will kill me."

Nathan looked his cousin up and down as he replayed the words in his head over and over. "It will kill me too, Logan."

Moses finally exited the convenient store and found his place with the rest of the group. Jedediah avoided all eye contact once the man joined the ranks beside the women, who walked and peered into the thick glass windows of the shops simultaneously.

"Did you buy something, dear?" Sue asked her husband. Abigail cuddled close to her mother.

"Nothing special," Moses replied.

Sue and Mary looked at each other, then to their husbands.

"Jedediah, we seem to be missing children." Mary spoke out, trying to change the tense nature.

"Father-" William said directing Jedediah's attention to two boys standing just out front of a bookstore.

"Logan and Nathan," Sue finished.

"Boys," Jedediah called out over the bustling traffic.

The two kids hurried across the street, dodging carriages and people along the way. Panting for breath, they laughed to themselves. Everyone eyed them curiously.

"What is so funny, Nathan?" Moses asked; his tone was riddled with irritancy.

"Nothin, Father," Nathan giggled.

"Logan, where is Jed?" Father Jedediah asked.

Logan and Nathan busted out in hysterics. They directed their attention to the bookstore where Jed stood out front looking at the newsstand.

Mary tapped Logan on the head.

"What was that for?!" he cried.

"You know better than to ditch him. This is a city, Logan!"

Sulking, Logan slinked his way over to Jed and helped corral him across the street, and over to the family who still waited outside the convenient store."

"Pa, Ma, they left me!"

"We know, Jed." William replied in a monotone fashion.

"Jerks," Jed cried out.

Logan pushed the boy back causing him to fall into the street. Jed rolled over and rubbed his elbow that had smashed into the cobbled road. He began to weep.

"Logan Hinkley!" hissed Mary grabbing her son by the arm.

"He started it, Ma!" Logan attested.

Mary tossed Logan up against the wall and smacked him on the rear.

"Don't embarrass the boy here; it will only make things worse." Moses chimed in.

Jedediah stepped forward. "Do not tell her how to punish our child, Moses."

Moses did not listen, "It is like dealing with a slave. The only way they learn is when you seclude them from the group and give them a good lashing. No one can see them cry. They will conform."

Nathan and Maxwell watched wide-eyed as their father rambled on.

"Moses, not in front of the kids," Sue yelped in abhorrence.

"Shut it, Susan."

Mary released her grip on Logan and turned toward her brother-in-law. "Moses…" she shook her head in disbelief.

Moses stepped forward from the back of the group and lifted Jed off of the ground. "Stand up! If this were war, you would be dead! Wipe your tears and stand like a man!"

"Let him go!" Jedediah thundered.

Jed watched in shock as Moses and Jedediah fought over him.

"If you refuse to raise your boy like a man, then I will, Jedediah!"

"Moses, this is not war, this is not your son. Unhand my child before you burn a bridge."

"This *is* a war. This is a Civil War. Look 'round brother! There are banners all around. Propaganda posters litter the streets; men in uniform walk the same sidewalks as us! You are blind to it all!"

Jedediah pushed Jed out of the way as he encroached upon Moses. "I am not blind. I choose to ignore it. We have children who are innocent. Should their eyes see us acting *like this,* should they see us gossip about war and slavery they will grow weak, they will taste the bitterness of hate. One day they will savor that taste, but not now…not this young."

Moses gripped his brother's suspenders. "Sooner or later, you and I will reach our climax…and everything you know will change."

The two separated. All eyes looked on, trying to interpret the event.

Mary overcame the effects of the numbing argument and let out a shrill voice. "Let us run along to the carriage, children."

When the family arrived back at their home, the kids tramped through the yard, and immediately went off to bed. Once in their room with the door shut, they maneuvered to their respected beds, but not before Logan assisted Nathan in tucking the sleeping Maxwell in his cot, covering him until the blankets rested just below his chin.

"He falls asleep fast." Logan announced as he undressed and clambered into bed.

"It was the wagon ride back." Nathan explained.

Jed laid in silence with his hands supporting his head.

After moments of painful silence, Nathan spoke up. "Can someone close the curtains on the window? The sun is blinding me."

Logan tugged the fabric over the window, shielding the sun from the room.

"Did you hear what they said?" Jed asked.

Nathan and Logan did not answer; they glared off into space.

Fiddling with his covers, Jed asked, "Why do they call it Civil War if there ain't nothin' civil about it?"

"That's not what it means, Jed." Logan answered. "It means we are fightin' ourselves."

"Our country?" asked the green-eyed boy.

"Yeah…" Nathan said.

"Do you think Uncle Moses and Pa argue like that a lot?"

"I don't know, Roo…if they do, they hide it." Logan grimaced.

Jed tucked himself down deep in the covers. "William leaves tomorrow morning."

Logan nodded solemnly.

"Think he'll stay if we beg him?"

"I don't know, Jed! Go to sleep."

"He was just asking a question, Logan," said Nathan.

"Go to sleep." Logan pulled the blankets over his head and hid from the others in the room.

Jed rolled over and rubbed the sore bruise on his elbow, leaving Nathan to stare at the darkening room on his own.

In the darkened hall of the house with red shutters, William awakened several hours before the rest of the family. He sat in a wicker rocker in the corner of his dull bedroom looking out the opened window at the dark sky and the sweeping fields as if waiting for a breeze to sweep in and carry him to the outside world. His face was hardened as if in deep thought, yet his mind was at ease. On his cot rested his shoulder bag for his shoes, and the small locker that he kept his extra shirt neatly folded in. A gentle knock upon the closed hardwood door forced his shimmering eyes to shift away from his fixation upon the blooming cardinal and burgundy shades of morning light of the rising sun.

"I am awake." William said calmly and quietly.

The door was pushed open slightly and the blue eyes of Logan stuck out in sharp contrast to the darkened hall as they peered into the room.

"You should be asleep still." William scolded but motioned for his brother to enter anyway.

Logan tiptoed into the pocket-sized room and shut the door, quietly, with a thud. "I just wanted to talk for a bit before you left," the boy admitted; a tone of grievance in his voice.

William glanced at his golden pocket watch, "I don't leave for another three hours."

Logan yawned with exhaustion; he seemed to have not slept at all during the night. "I do not want to waste a minute."

The two sat in silence for a moment, with only the breeze hitting the wind chimes outside filling the silent void. Logan moved over to the cot and sat down upon it, picking at his fingers. "Hey, William, are you scared?"

Will did not answer immediately, "What about?"

"Leaving; are you afraid about fighting?" Logan asked.

William swirled the images of the battle on the *Liberty* around in his head. The scar on his chest stung as the memories became real. In a flash, the blue-eyed boy with the knife in his nightmares filled the black in his mind, forcing him to lean forward and turn his full attention to Logan. It was then that William saw that both the eyes of the haunting child in his dreams, and that of Logan's were the same. An eerie sensation crept over him. *Is this*

74

a sign, he wondered. "Logan, when you are fighting, you do not have time to be afraid or to fear. You only think to survive; survival becomes your mind's only possession. It is when you stop and sit that you begin to realize that any second could very well be your last…and that is when you begin to fear." William licked his lips trying to gather his thoughts. "So I guess no; I am not scared to fight….I am scared to stop."

Logan watched his older brother with curiosity. "But what you have seen…how do you forget those images?"

"I do not. Nor do I think I will ever." William locked eyes with Logan and he could tell that the boy was admiring him for some reason he could not pinpoint. "Logan, I am no hero. I am not one to envy. I was a coward during my time on the ship; the one battle I was in, I almost left my friend to die…I almost died. Do me a favor and do not aspire to be like me or look up to me."

Logan batted his eyes as if taken by surprise. "Will, I-"

"I wish I never fought…I am different from other men." William interrupted. "Those who I fought, and those with whom I served, seemed to welcome death. I suppose if you can get your mind over dying, and rid yourself of the animalistic zone, conquer your adrenaline, you can think. And if you can think, you can plan; plan how to kill. That is something I could not and cannot do!"

Logan watched Will as he quickly tried to regain his composure.

"Forgive me. That was not right of me to yell." soothed the sailor.

William's brother shivered as a chilling gust of wind blew in through the window.

"Want me to shut that?" William asked motioning with his head toward the open pane.

"No, I'm alright," mumbled Logan, rubbing his arms.

William watched the blue-eyed kid; slowly, a smile began to work upward from the corners of the sailor's mouth.

"What?" Logan asked in wonderment.

William chuckled, "Nothing, just thinking."

Logan waited for his brother to continue, "About?"

"I was just thinking about when you were born, and the first night we all held you." William leaned back in his rocking chair as he let the memory swim through his mind; Logan sat up on the bed and crossed his legs together.

"Mother had started to recover from the pain and Father wanted something to cover you up in so she could hold you, but there was nothing. Days before she went into labor, Momma had knitted a stocking for me with my initials on it, and me being the problem solving child I was, grabbed that to use…."

Logan listened as his face drew up a venerating glow.

"…You were so small and frail, but they both let me wrap you in the stocking and hold you first. You had not opened your eyes yet until that moment, and when you did, they were as blue as they are now; crystal-like." William spaced off for a moment longer and rubbed his chin as the smile faded from his face, "Your shivering a moment ago reminded me of that."

"Don't stop." Logan said shattering the inner abstraction of William's mind.

"What else do you want to hear?" Will asked.

"Just tell me more about anything; I have never heard these stories." admitted Logan.

William smiled once more as he located another memory. "When you were three I used to push you around in the wagon."

"…The one in the barn now?" Logan asked excitedly.

"That's the one. I used to tie your hands together and pull you around the yard claiming that you were my prisoner. Mother did not approve of that one." William laughed aloud.

"You tied me up?!" Logan shouted, pretending to be upset.

"Yeah, but you always escaped anyway. You started to fight back, too. There was one time specifically when I was chasing you in the fields and you had enough of me harassing you so you picked up a small dirt clod and hurled it at me."

"I missed?" Logan asked hoping to be proven wrong.

"Nope; you hit me right in the jaw. You knocked out my loose tooth!" William said pointing toward his mouth.

Both boys giggled, reminiscing on the younger years.

"I am gonna miss you." William said.

Logan peered upwards at William, fighting the urge to ask his brother to change his mind about leaving.

"Yeah…" Logan mumbled; he stood up to leave the room. "The photographer will be here soon. I am going to get dressed."

William did not respond, instead, he returned to watch the sun rise in the morning sky.

A knock upon the front door of the home tolled the dreaded hour, William's last. Mary and Sue walked out onto the porch leaving the screen door open for William and the children to file out, followed by Moses and Jedediah, with Logan being the last to exit.

"Mr. Barker, pleasure!" Jedediah said, clasping hands with the photographer.

"Howdy, Mr. Hinkley, right here on the porch I presume?" Mr. Barker asked planning the shot.

"That will do just fine, Ted." Jedediah confirmed.

The family scuttled together awkwardly, trying to get all faces in the photo.

"Jed, you and Logan move down to the left," Mary ordered trying to adjust the children.

William moved in beside his father and placed an arm on his shoulder. "Thank you for everything, Father." he spoke in hushed tone.

"Thank you for coming back." replied Father Jed patting his boy on the back.

"Okay, all faces on me!" Ted Barker shouted as he prepped the camera.

William, Jedediah, Sue, Moses, and Mary stood tall in the back with Jed, Logan, Nathan, and Maxwell huddled together in the front row; baby Abigail laid in the grass at the group's feet.

"Three, two, one…" Barker counted. The snap from the camera captured the image, and then relaxed with a low hiss. "Just give me a moment, and I can get this developed.

Mr. Barker walked off fiddling with his large camera. William nodded to his father, and turned to his mother and embraced her in his strong arms.

"You be careful out there, William." she spoke holding back tears.

"Always will be, Mother." William withdrew.

Sue wrapped her dainty wrists around the sailor's neck, "Will, you be sure to visit soon."

"I shall return as soon as possible, I promise," said William returning the hug, and shaking Moses' large hand simultaneously. He turned to face the group of children as Sue backed away toward her husband. "Nathan, you be a good kid for your parents. I will send you notes from the frontlines."

Nathan nodded in agreement and half-hugged the tall man.

"Maxy, take care you hear? Next time I see you, you will probably be big enough to hold your own against me when we wrestle to get you dressed!" teased William running his hand through the child's dusty hair. "Logan and Roo…" he sighed turning to face his younger brothers.

"William, please stay longer." little Jed whined.

"Stay longer? How much longer?" he asked.

"Forever…" Logan said.

William looked back and forth between the two boys before pulling them in tight to his chest and rubbing their backs. "You two behave for Mom and Pop. They will need you to hold down the fort."

Jed withdrew from the hug leaving tear streaks upon the sailor's uniform. Logan continued to hold onto his older brother. "If you will not stay, let me go with you."

"I am sorry, Logan, but I cannot…" he hunched down until he was even with the boy's blue eyes. "Keep things around here together. Be brave, and be strong. I will write."

Logan pulled away and rejoined the family. William pulled a small photograph from his pocket and handed it to the boy. "Keep this. It is from my graduation from training."

Logan took the small tintype in his clammy hands and examined it. William sat tall against a bleak wall that let his uniform stand out vibrantly in the frame. "Thank you." replied the sorrow-stricken boy.

"Here you be!" Mr. Barker spoke up with enthusiasm, handing the photo to Sue.

"How much do we owe you, Ted?" Jedediah asked digging into his pocket for payment.

"Free of charge, Jedediah," he said pushing back the man's hand, "Good luck, William, and Godspeed."

William nodded in acceptance. He looked one last time around at his family, letting his eyes say the final goodbye.

"Shall we share a cab?" Ted Barker asked the sailor.

"That'd be great, thank you."

The two turned and walked off toward the crest of the hill, leaving the family alone on the porch of the house with red shutters, leaving footsteps in the dusty trail.

Chapter II: Tensions rise
ରେ

It had been exactly one week since William had left to
return to service, and already, his name seemed like a stranger's.
Tensions between Moses and Jedediah had been brewing, and their
arguments made the days when William was home seem distant
and that of a dream. In the back of every mind was the question
that no one could answer: what would become of the family if
things continued to worsen?

The school bell rang three times on the calm, late summer
day that brought children from all over the surrounding land to the
tiny, dated schoolhouse. The confines of Logan's mind had been
occupied by the alluring thoughts of Rebecca since the day he left
her company in the town square. Those very thoughts and
memories became a portal, bringing the boy back to the feeling of
intense nerves that kicked inside him whenever he saw the girl, or
even thought about her.

Finding his seat amongst the rows of students, Logan
watched the graceful Rebecca as she entered the room. Just the
way she walked awakened an urge to run and hide, inside him; he
stood awestruck by her beauty that seemed unmatched by any
other girl in the room. Swallowing hard, Logan's piercing blue
eyes fixated on the satin dress that flowed down the curves of the
young lady.

"Class, please be seated so we may begin today's lesson."
hollered the voice of the teacher, Mrs. Craven.

Logan's ears did not receive the message; he was in a momentary state of shock as he devised a plan to approach the lovely Ms. Rebecca.

"Young man?" called Mrs. Craven.

All eyes in the room shifted toward the center where the awkward boy stood erect, staring off into space toward the direction of the girl.

"Young man what is your name?"

Reality finally hit Logan like a train. Feeling a sudden swell of embarrassment, he breathed in deeply and sank down into the bench underneath him; he ran his sweaty palms down the sides of his legs as he tried to cool down.

"You did not answer me..." Mrs. Craven continued.

Sighing with frustration over the painful shock of the class's attention, Logan spoke up, "Logan Hinkley, Ma'am."

Breaking through the growing giggles in the room, Mrs. Craven raised her voice, "Ah, yes; please do pay attention. There will be time in the future to court the lovely Ms. Rebecca, but for now, we learn."

Moving on, Mrs. Craven started the lesson, yet her ultimatum was ineffective, for Logan's lust and love for the girl would continue to hold him prisoner; her addictive qualities, the rope that tied his mind.

Curious about her admirer, Rebecca looked back to see the boy staring and drooling like a dog. A small smile crept onto her face as she raised a graceful hand and waved.

Logan's senses erupted as he realized that the girl made contact with him. Trying desperately to play off the situation, he nodded his head and pretended to tip his hat.

The remaining hours would be a test to the boy's will and patience, as he counted the hours till the last bell chimed and he could approach the fair girl that he thought so fond of, once more.

Mrs. Craven's voice was angelic as she dismissed the class, trying to out-sing the reverberations of the bell. Finally, the moment had arrived.

"Are we racin' Max and Nathan home?!" Jed asked as he muscled his way through the mob of kids to get to his anxious brother.

"No, I've got to-" Logan paused as he glanced toward Rebecca, who stood beside the door motionless as if waiting for the boy to accompany her. "Do something." He finished.

"Are you kidding me?! You promised this morning," whined Jed.

"And we lose every time. Now beat it." said Logan dismissing Jed's presence.

Jed watched as Logan fought through the exiting children to get to Rebecca, a girl who once seemed untouchable. "What am I supposed to tell Father?"

Logan's momentary tunnel vision ceased as he took his eyes off of the girl's smile. "Tell him I got side tracked."

Jed shook his head in vexation and joined the final wave of students exiting the wooden building.

Logan wiped his palms on his smooth pants as the clamminess that he so often felt around Rebecca began to surface once again.

Rebecca took the boy's hand and pulled him out of the schoolhouse. "Hi, Logan." she said as she took him over to a large rock just outside of the schoolyard fence.

"Hey-" Logan mouthed awkwardly.

"So I saw you staring at me earlier." giggled the fair girl.

"It was that obvious, huh?"

"Mrs. Craven helped to point it out."

"I guess she did a little, didn't she?" Logan said laughing off his embarrassment.

Both sat down beside the rock, letting the grass tickle to underside of their legs.

Rebecca tugged on a small red ribbon sewed to the bottom hem of her dress. "So, there is something that I wanted to do back when we were in that alley in town, but I never had the chance to."

Logan studied the features upon her face as he waited for her to confess the actions that had yet to be completed.

"Well, I suppose I better just get it over with." Rebecca leaned in toward the blue-eyed boy's lips and stopped just shy of them. He could feel the warmth from her breath leave her mouth, and gently move over the tops of his lips that hung open as if trying to make the decision to lean in and complete the situational embrace, or to let it die quicker than it had arisen. Logan's eyes settled upon Rebecca's as he searched for any sign of hesitation or uncertainty through her closed lids, yet found none. His piercing blue gaze disappeared as the darkness and security of his fantasies surfaced in to one tiny motion; one small tilt of his head forward until he felt the foreign skin he had longed for, and desired so. As the moment passed, and their lips parted, Rebecca said nothing. Logan could still feel her breath upon his face; his eyes remained closed, replaying the last image of the girl before the kiss.

As the shock of his senses numbed his racing mind, and a heated sensation pulsed through his veins, Logan leaned forward once more, tasting the sweetness of the fruit he once thought forbidden.

When the boy opened his eyes once more, the sky was darkening and the sun was already tucked away behind the mountains in the distance.

Rebecca sat quietly, searching the boy's face for something Logan could not pinpoint. As he was about to stand to leave, she settled her head upon his chest and listened to his racing heart, "Do not leave." she whispered innocently.

Logan closed his eyes and leaned his head back until the cold stone caught him like a pillow, "Never."

Rebecca's breathing slowed, until finally she seemed to be lifeless. Logan scanned her flowing hair that was brushed so perfect and fine; not a piece was out of place. He gently ran a hand down the length of her neck, tucking little strands of the blond, thread-like locks in his fingers. Feeling the warmth and comfort of her skin, he sunk down into a restful state, allowing his mind to wander off into the distance of the sleeping landscape.

"You know this will end soon?" Rebecca's voice caused Logan to jump.

"I don't want it to." he sighed.

"Nor do I; we could run off you know? Travel as far west as the trains will take us, and find a place to live. I hear it is quieter country out there…no one to bother you. You can literally disappear."

"We could find land, and I could farm it." Logan added.

Rebecca tucked her hands up close to her cheek, marveling at the image unfolding in her head. "I could cook and do the chores."

"I'm a good hunter, too. William showed me how to once."

"Eventually we could have kids of our own…" Rebecca implied with a hesitant tone.

Logan's eyes still searched the empty horizon. "And we can raise them away from war and violence. There won't be a North or South, just a home."

Silence took hold of both kids.

"It is a nice thought." Rebecca stated, shattering the dreams and images of a peaceful life.

"Rebecca?" Logan spoke.

"Yeah?" she replied.

"Do you love me?"

Rebecca shifted her weight off of Logan's chest and sat up, letting her eyes meet his shifting gaze.

"I just want--no, I need to hear you say it if you do." Logan looked into her soul. "I may never get a chance to hear it in my life once you are gone."

Rebecca leaned in and wrapped her arms around his neck, embracing him with every ounce of strength she could gather. "I love you, Logan."

Days after his moment with Rebecca by the rock, Logan sat in his room alone with the door closed. Outside, birds sang songs that would lift anyone's spirit, except Logan ignored them. Instead, he focused on a photograph of William in his naval uniform that he had been given before Will left. The sulking boy desperately missed his brother; yet even more so, he missed the way things were when he was around. Father Jed had not once pitched the idea of going into town again, nor had he made any notion to play with his children. Logan felt invisible.

Rolling over, the boy set the picture down on the turquoise sheet that covered his bed. Gently, he rested his head on his pillow and closed his eyes. A single tear escaped from his long lashes and dripped onto the pillow, leaving a tiny, damp circle where it had fallen. A sudden knock at the door startled him. Sniffling, the boy called out, "Who's there?"

"Nathan…" came the reply.

Logan quickly rubbed his eyes and hid the photograph under the pillow. "Come in," he announced.

Nathan entered the room and glanced at his cousin, who sat upright and looked out the window. The dusty-haired boy could tell that something was the matter by the way Logan avoided eye contact.

"…I just need to grab my shoes." Nathan explained.

Logan nodded his head as he swallowed. He tried not to show weakness or give away his feelings to his cousin, for if he did, he felt that Nathan would think less of him.

Nathan carefully sat down on the bed directly across from Logan, causing the mattress to moan and creak. The dusty-haired boy unbuckled the clasp on his leather shoe and slipped it on his foot. Both teens glanced at each other periodically, yet neither spoke a word.

Once finished, Nathan stood up and headed for the door, but stopped shy of it.

"Hey, I'm sorry if my father said anything to you…he's been irritated lately." he said looking at Logan, his body half turned to face him.

Logan's lips were coiled tight. Slowly raising his eyes to look at Nathan, he shook his head, signaling no.

Nathan nodded in acknowledgement and walked out of the room awkwardly.

The blue-eyed boy thought for a moment, and then rolled back over onto the bed, tucking his legs up to his chest.

Out in the yard, Nathan joined Jed and his brother, Maxwell, in the grass playing with a toy wagon.

"Where's Logan?" asked Jed.

"He's inside, he doesn't feel like playing." Nathan said understanding the way Logan must have been feeling.

"Gosh, he has been acting weird since Will left, I think he might be mental." announced Jed not fully grasping the meaning of the word mental.

"He just feels alone right now, Jed. The way our pa's have been acting has him worried."

Jed tossed a handful of dirt into the wagon and pushed it toward Maxwell who pounded the payload into a flat surface.

"What's there to be worried about? Father and Uncle Moses are just upset at this war, that's all." Jed said pulling the wagon back toward his direction.

Nathan picked at a few pieces of grass, and crossed his legs Indian-style. "No, it's more than that, Jed; they don't get along very well, and this war is just an added stressor."

"Big whoop..." Jed said bluntly, not even paying attention to what Nathan was saying.

Growing tired of the childish games Nathan rose to his feet and squinted through the sun back toward the deck. Upon its warped beams sat Jedediah on the porch swing on one side, and Moses in a rocking chair on the other. Biting his lip in thought, Nathan walked over toward the barn on the far side of the house to where he was out of view. Once in the clear, he sprinted over to the children's room window that was positioned just above eye level on the backside of the house with red shutters.

"Logan!" shouted Nathan in a contained whisper. After pausing for a few seconds, Nathan repeated the call and tapped the window.

Slowly, the glass was lifted up into the air, and two blue eyes peered out.

"Logan!" Nathan jeered.

"Nathan? What are you-" the blue-eyed boy started to speak, but was interrupted.

"Logan, grab the rifles from you pa's room and let's go hunting!"

Logan lifted the window open more and stuck his entire head out. "Are you crazy?! Father will kill me if he found out!"

Nathan shook his head in disagreement. "He ain't gonna find out! I know a spot back by farmer Dave's woods where the shots will be muffled by the trees."

Logan started to sigh in defiance, "I don't know, Nate, what if one of us gets hurt?"

"Look, you want to be stuck inside pouting all day, or go have some fun?" Nathan could tell he was getting to his cousin; putting on his charm, he went in for the kill, "What would William do?"

Logan pondered for a moment and backed away from the window. A moment later he returned with two rifles, and small leather bag containing the necessary ammunition and percussion caps.

"If we get caught, I'm killing you!" Logan said whilst clambering down the side of the wall from the window.

"You have another match, brother?" Moses asked Jedediah coldly.

"One left…" the man said tossing his brother the small package. "You should really cut down on your smoking," he added.

"Oh save it, Jedediah, you ain't Mother." Moses said laughing at the thought of his brother in a dress.

Jedediah watched Jed and Maxwell play out in the yard as he gently rocked back and forth on the swing. "Where are our other boys?" he questioned.

Moses shrugged, not knowing, "Probably out terrorizing some girls."

Father Jed ignored the comment and stood up to get himself some more tea.

"Where are you off to?" demanded Moses.

"Refill…"

"Nonsense, sit yourself down, that is why I have a slave, brother."

87

Jedediah's face reddened as he tried to contain his thoughts, however, they slipped. "You know Moses, one day you will regret taking advantage of other people. One day, everything you do now will come back to haunt you."

Giggling at his brother's sudden prophetic remark, Moses fired back, "When that day comes, you and me will no longer be kin."

Jedediah walked into the house letting the screen door slam with a loud clap. Moments later, Sue walked out onto the deck holding Abigail.

"Have a seat, my wife." Moses invited, motioning to the swing.

"What is wrong with Jedediah?" she asked innocently.

"You mean sour-puss? He is criticizing me on our *maid*." Moses laughed hideously at his joke.

Sue frowned at her husband's vile humor. "You know, I was thinking...how's about we all go down to the ravine for the afternoon. It might do you some good to fish with your brother. You both used to love it."

Moses removed the pipe from his dry lips and spit onto the porch. "Used to, Sue...he is becoming just like our father, always judging me on what is morally right and wrong." Moses paused to look his wife in the eye. "Well you know something? Morals are the problem with this country. Everyone in power loves to sit around and decide what is right and wrong, and then they make laws on what we do. Sue, men like me built this country with hundreds of slaves, thousands of them. George Washington had slaves, Thomas Jefferson had slaves, but now it is wrong to own them...where is the morality in that?"

Sue hung her head looking at the nails that held the boards of the porch together. "Not even for one hour?" she asked hopeful.

Moses put the pipe back in his mouth. "Not unless he backs off."

Sue stood up and handed Abigail to her father and walked into the house.

"Mary, he is vile, he is vermin, and he drives me mad!" Jedediah shouted from the confines of the kitchen.

"Jedediah, give him some space. Think of how he is feeling! He fought for this country and put his life on the line, and he has yet to receive compensation for his injuries…"

Jedediah grunted at his wife's comment. "Injuries, Mary the man was hit in the shoulder with a falling rock, if anything the injury is to his head not his body!"

"Look, all I am saying is that things would be a whole lot better around here if you two could find some way to get along! Your sons are depressed; you haven't even talked to them on a personal level since William left!" Mary said making the children's feelings apparent.

Jedediah ran a sweaty hand over his mouth and leaned back against the iron range. "The man has his views, fine, but when he openly mocks me in front of my children, then he has crossed the line!" Jed Sr. stiffened; his voice grew louder.

"He has done no such thing!"

"Oh, do not play dumb, Mary! He already speaks badly about Amelia in front of her; it is only a matter of time until he takes that next step!"

Mary shook her head in frustration and walked out of the kitchen toward the door just as Sue came walking in. Both women stopped and glanced at each other before Mary exited the house.

"Moses says-"

"I do not care right now, Sue!" Jedediah shouted.

Sue held her hands together nervously at her waist and corrected her posture, "Maybe that is the problem…neither of you care." The emboldened woman turned toward the narrow, dimly lit hallway and walked down it.

Jedediah thought about the words Sue had just said to him when the door to his brother's bedroom clicked shut.

Nathan and Logan had covered a large portion of ground by the time the sun had started to set. Around them, the beasts of night had started to make their presence known as all other beings drifted into the shadows to wait for the next dawn.

Logan walked behind Nathan, his arms wrapped around the rifle clumsily, holding it like a child. He looked at the scenery with large eyes, somewhat worried about the increasing darkness, and the ever-growing thickness of the woods and brush. Buzzing about, mosquitoes nipped at whatever open areas of skin they could, leaving the boy to balance the rifle and swat the pests at the same time. Up ahead, Nathan leapt through the thistles and twigs with ease, cutting down what foliage he could with his walking stick.

As the two approached a small ravine, Nathan sought cover behind a rock. It took Logan a moment to reach the other boy's position, but when he did, he immediately knew what game Nathan was playing at.

"I have the ammo!" shouted Logan, running forward and diving behind the rock.

"Load it! I see three Redcoats up ahead, they are crossing the river!" Nathan exhumed.

Logan pulled the ramrod out of the musket and pretended to load it. He turned over on his stomach and rested the rifle on a small rock before him. "I've got 'em in my sights, Nate!" he acknowledged.

"Wait for it…fire!"

Both boys made a sound mimicking the roar of firing guns. Nathan stood up and ran over the top of the large rock, his fist raised in the air shouting, "Charge them!"

Logan gathered his effects and stood up to follow, only to stop dead in his tracks, while Nathan continued to battle the invisible enemy. "Logan, bring up the reinforcements!"

When Logan did not reply, Nathan turned around in question. He saw the grimaced look of fear on Logan's face; his eyes pointed directly atop the rise in scenery. The confused boy shifted his stance slowly to examine the apparition that was standing behind him. His hands became clammy; his heart sped faster. In his mind, one question tugged at his insides, *what is it?!*

Upon the hilltop that was covered with shed leaves, snarled a beast. Its fangs dripped with white saliva, its fur on edge. The Beast's eyes were red with the thirst of blood; from its throat came a noise which drowned out the flowing stream, a noise that bellowed from the bowels of hell itself, causing even the brave to perspire.

"Nathan…what is that?!" Logan's voice cracked in panic.

Nathan put his weight on his heels and carefully stepped backwards toward his cousin as a wave of horror flushed over him. "I think it is Mr. Mosley's dog…"

"-The one who went rabid," Logan whined.

A lump formed in Nathan's throat. No matter which way he moved, the Beast's gaze stuck on him like glue.

"Nate, get out of there; come to me!" Logan said motioning with his hand for Nathan to cross the creek.

"It's watching me!" cried the boy in fright. Nathan looked to the ground to find a foothold to make his move, but was stopped by the Beast's gruesome howl. "Logan, do something!"

Desperately, Logan searched the ground at his feet for something to use as a distraction to break the dog's fixation on Nathan. Bending down, he ran his hand through the red and orange leaves; the cool dirt of the earth found its way underneath his fingernails. Finally, a smooth stone tumbled its way into the adolescent's hand. He gripped it tightly and rose to his full height, the rifle in one hand, and the rock in the other.

"Do you have something?!" Nathan asked through clenched teeth.

"Yes." Logan replied.

"On three…" whispered Nathan, carefully shifting his weight onto his back foot.

Suddenly, the Beast lurched forward savagely, its muscular body bounded down the hill at an incredible pace.

"Run!" screamed Nathan lunging backwards toward the brook.

In a moment of sheer chaos, a crack echoed throughout the wood. Nathan fell to his knees in shock. A stinging pain made itself apparent as he moved his hand down his leg to where he felt the warm, syrupy drip of blood. Panic stricken, Nathan looked to Logan who held the smoking rifle in his hands.

"Oh, God…" he whimpered.

"What was that?!" questioned Jed standing up from the grassy field.

From the house, Father Jed came running outside, his pipe strangled between his lips.

"Did you hear that?" Jed asked his father, "It sounded like-"

"Gunfire-" the man said finishing Jed's sentence.

Mary and Moses stood up from their chairs on the porch and walked out into the yard, looking out over the horizon toward the direction of the shot. Jedediah glanced around the area and counted each family member; Maxwell and Jed were present, as were Abigail, Mary, and Moses, and Sue who made herself present on the scene.

"Where are Logan and Nathan?!"

No one answered the question…only looks of confusion filled the vacated silence.

"Jed, where did they go?!" snapped the aging man.

"I don't know! Nathan ran that way!" he confessed pointing to the backside of the house where a lone window was open; its drapes billowed in the breeze.

"…The woods!" Jedediah ran for the tree line, followed by Moses.

Feet away from Nathan laid the body of the Beast; its breath became more and more delayed, until finally…it ceased. The injured boy looked down at his bleeding leg and discovered a small scrape caused by a sharp rock beside the riverbed where he had fallen. Following a wave of relief, Nathan stood and turned to face the victim of the lone shot.

"I killed it…" Logan gasped with eyes of sorrow.

Both boys stood for another moment of silence, until Nathan spoke up.

"You did what you had to do…"

"But this was somebody's pet, Nate…"

"He was missing for weeks Logan, no one missed him." Nathan soothed.

"Still, it is not right…do I tell Mr. Mosley?"

Breathing heavily, Nathan turned away from the body of the animal and took the rifle from Logan. "Let's go home."

"Logan!" called a distant voice.

Turning around, the boys looked to see Jedediah running down the slopes of the tree-laden hill.

"Are you boys alright?!" asked the man catching his breath. Immediately, he noticed the sullen looks on the faces of the children and directed his gaze toward the body of the dog. "Who did this?" he questioned, his eyes shifted to Nathan holding the musket.

Logan stepped forward pulling the gun from his cousin's dirtied hands. "I did, Father."

"I see…" Jedediah groaned.

"I can explain, but not now…I just want to know…are you angry?"

Jedediah took a steady breath and shifted the spectacles on his face. Rubbing his chin, he spoke in an easy tone, "No, Son, I am not angry."

A brief look of contentment appeared on the boy's face, and then disappeared quicker than it had spawned. "Do I tell Mr. Mosley?" he asked ill-fatedly. "I do not know what to do."

Jedediah pulled his son closer to him, and let a hand fall on the boy's shoulder. Removing his glasses, he ran a hardened hand through his graying scalp. "Logan, sometimes deciding what to do in life can be a tough choice; with anything, there are two options. Think of them as roads and rivers. One path can be bumpy, the other smooth and free flowing. However, no matter which you choose, both have their twists and turns, and despite the calm nature of the river, keep in mind that with every body of water there are high tides…do not always take the easy way out, Son, for you may find that you cannot swim."

Jedediah let the thought sink in. Inside, Logan was fighting an emotional battle. It was not so much the fact of telling Mr. Mosley that his pet had been killed that bothered him, it was the feeling of loneliness that troubled him; he would no longer be dependent on his father to take the blame for him, he would have to take responsibility alone.

Moses had finally reached the group at the base of the steep incline by the time Logan had made his decision. The retired military-veteran was breathing heavily, and large damp patches formed under his arms and around his collar as he sucked in the warm, humid air.

"Remind me never to follow you again, Jedediah."

"I thought you were in shape, Moses?"

"I am…a round shape." the sweaty man proclaimed.

Nathan and Logan giggled innocently at the comment, which took their minds off of the somber situation for a brief moment. The two boys did not say it, but they were happy that for that minute, a small, tiny lapse of time, in which their parents were not at each other's throats, but instead, were joking with each other like they had before William had left.

"Well Logan, you must do what you have to do. We will be at home waiting for you." Jedediah rubbed his son's head and receded back up the hill, followed by Moses, who was mumbling profanities under his breath.

Logan looked to Nathan who watched humorously at the two grown men hobbling up the beaten path.

"Well, pal I'll go with if you want me too…" Nathan announced.

Logan shook his head in defiance. "No, this is something I have to do on my own."

Nathan nodded in understanding and took the rifle from Logan before heading up the hill, following his father's footsteps.

Once Nathan's silhouette had disappeared beyond the crest, Logan glanced around at the empty woods that surrounded him; beyond the vacancy of the stream, laid the lifeless body of the dog. He approached the animal and sat down beside it, finding a way to stomach his nerves. Carefully, he reached his hand out toward the mutt, but drew back instantly out of fear. After a moment of serenity, he cautiously held his hand out over the creature and let the tips of his fingers fall onto the soft, golden fur. Suddenly, the dog did not seem so frightening; in a way, its deviled nature was replaced with its inner beauty; the bit of sun that was still afloat in the sky, shined down through the thick green and orange canopy above, and fell onto the boy and the dog, illuminating the both of them.

"I'm sorry," he whispered to the silent animal.

The boy's hand began to make slow, drawn out passes down the yellow fur, each time, a clump of it sticking to his palms. "I know you did not mean to try and hurt us…it wasn't your fault you were the way you were; I guess life isn't fair, huh?"

Moments passed and nothing in the forest moved. It seemed as if Logan was the only creature alive in the darkening setting. Rising to his feet, the boy brushed the loose hair onto his pants, and drew in a warm breath of air. "Here goes nothing…" he spoke to himself as he followed the babbling stream toward the direction of Mr. Mosley's residence.

Days lingered on, and no one spoken of the dog. Punishment was exempt for the two older boys, which was perfectly fine in their regards. Logan and Nathan were awake and changed for school, however Jed still slept in his bed, coddled up with his mound of pillows.

"Look at him." Nathan said through a thick grin.

Logan took his attention away from his tie. "Jed? He is so weird."

"Wanna mess with him?" Nathan asked.

Logan nodded with a slim smirk.

Nathan rose from the edge of his sheets and tiptoed to Max's bed. He grabbed all the pillows. He then made his way to Jed, and carefully began mounding all the feathered fluff atop the sleeping boy.

"Nathan, he looks ridiculous!" Logan giggled, trying hard to suppress his laughter.

The sound of footsteps in the hall forced Nathan to retreat to the safety of his cot.

The door opened slowly and Maxwell meandered in wearily. His eyes were heavy with sleep, and his step had an awkward bounce to it.

"-Hey, Maxy," Logan said in a susurrant tone.

The small child ignored the greeting and hobbled to his bed. He slipped into his sheets, but found the vacant spot near his head. He sat up and glared at Jed with a face riddled with question and irritancy.

Nathan and Logan began to crack with laughter at Max's face. The child threw himself down in the bed and pulled the quilted blankets over his head.

"You see his face?" Nathan whispered.

A door slamming out in the main living area of the home forced both boys to listen.

The voice of Father Jed thundered from the corners of the home, "Moses, get that paper out of my house!"

Moses' response was quick to ensue, "Freedom of the press, Jedediah!"

"Not in this house. They can print whatever they wish in those pages, but there is no freedom in reading that war propaganda under my roof."

The boys in the room ran to the door and pressed their ears to the wooden board.

Moses roared again, "Amelia, take these papers to my study."

"Moses, do not force my hand! If the children find these they will become obsessed and I do not wish them to read this garbage!" Jedediah said.

"You push me to the brink brother; there will come a time. You cannot shut us out forever."

Silence followed.

Logan looked to Nathan. "That's the fourth time this week they have argued."

Nathan swallowed hard, but returned to his bed where he flopped down, causing the frame to creak.

"I'm gonna get Jed up. We're gonna head out earlier today I think."

Nathan looked up at Logan. "Going to school early? What a good little student!"

Logan disregarded the wink that followed and hurried to rouse his brother.

Logan and Jed Jr. had reached the schoolhouse early to relax with their thoughts before the mass pile of children from around town flooded the small log building. It would be their only real chance to be away from the harsh conditions at home. As they both approached the small building, Logan threw his knapsack down on the ground and walked over to a twisted stump that sat just outside of the schoolyard fence. Jed followed him, but kept his distance. He could tell that his brother was in a depression. Since William's departure, Logan had felt more alone than ever. The relationship between him and his father had started to grow continuously strained as the threat of a war in their backyard was becoming increasingly real, and was made even worse by the fact that Uncle Moses was adding stress onto the family's already lamentable situation by slinging his lucid standpoints of slavery onto the children.

While Logan sat in silent thought, Jed fiddled with his bow tie. Both of the boys were dressed in their best clothing with their hair neat, and shoes shined. At first glance, you would think that their lives were perfect, yet the image was superficial. With the tension at home rising, both boys, and even their cousins could tell that if something did not give, their lives would change drastically.

"Logan, is my tie straight?" questioned the boy.

"Quit messing with it, Jed."

"But, I…"

"Stop!" screamed Logan in a fit of rage, his eyes red and nostrils flared.

Jed stared at his brother in shock at the sudden outburst over a simple matter.

"…I just wanted to know…" Jed seethed in a hushed whisper through quivering lips.

Logan bit his tongue and gritted his teeth, as he looked back down to the patch of dirt he had been examining subconsciously; his head was in his hands, and his scrawny elbows rested on his knees.

Jed wiped his nose as he tried to cover up his tears. Logan had never lashed out at him like that, even when they would fight, the retaliation from Logan was somewhat controlled.

"Apologize!" demanded the hurt child.

Logan did not move…

"-Apologize!" shouted Jed even louder.

"Why, so you can feel better?! Why should I? All you have ever done is antagonize and cry, and expect me to forgive you the next second…well that all ends, now!"

Jed started to openly weep.

"You look like a baby." finished Logan.

"What is your problem, just because Father treats you differently lately?"

"You wouldn't know…" Logan mumbled.

"Is that it?!" Jed continued.

"You wouldn't know!"

"Yes, I would!" Jed snapped back quickly.

"How," Logan asked.

"You are doing it to me…what happened to my old brother, the one who was my friend?"

Logan sniffled trying to hold back tears of frustration. He knew Jed was right. He knew that he was doing the same thing that his father was doing to him, even if it was not intentional; he had been pushing Jed aside.

"Jed, I…"

"Don't explain." the green-eyed boy put coldly.

Logan stood up slowly, his head dropped; his chin fell to his chest. He stumbled over to the white picket fence and slid down it until he hit the ground. Pulling his knees up to his body, he hugged his shins and hid his face.

Jed stood looking at the flag wavering above the schoolhouse door; its thirteen stripes and little white stars seemed so diminutive compared to the trouble and heartbreak that was brought onto his family by a war that sought to preserve the symbol the flag stood for. *How can something that has nothing to do with us, be so hurtful and tormenting,* he wondered.

Slowly, the boy worked his way over to his weeping brother. Sitting down beside him, Jed put his arm around him and squeezed his shoulder.

"Roo, does Father know what he is doing?" Logan asked through bouts of tears.

"I'm sure he does not mean to make you hurt, Logan…"

"No, not that…I mean with all of us…does he know how to fix us? Since Will left, all we do is fight and argue…it's tearing us all apart, Jed!" Logan's face was red and streaked from tears; his blue eyes seemed like they were a pool of water left to flood through a small hole punctured by a needle of uncertainty.

Jed felt a sudden rush of uneasiness; seeing his older brother cry over something that he had never truly thought important woke him up. Did his father know what he was doing? Did he know how to fix all the problems that the family was fighting over? All of those questions filled his head in a mass rush. The man he thought invincible was quickly becoming a man to question.

"I hope he knows, Logan…" Jed murmured trailing off into thought.

The schoolhouse bell chimed instantaneously startling both boys. One by one, the children from town started to flock into the log building, some sprinting up to the door with looks of giddiness, others teasing the smaller, weaker children. Upon all of these children' faces were looks other than grief and fear; as for Logan and Jed, they carried both unfortunate looks that made them seem as alienated as ever.

All the kids were inside by the time Logan and Jed stood up. Logan fixed his hair and cleared his throat; his hand wiped away the salty tears from his face. Jed patted down his clothes and tightened his book bag around himself.

"Ready?" Logan asked his brother.

Jed nodded, and turned to walk the brick path that winded through the grass up to the door of the school. Nathan and Maxwell ran up behind the two panting like dogs trying to catch their breath.

"We late?" gasped Nathan.

"No, right on time…" Logan said breathing in, trying to push aside his feelings.

Together, all four kids walked into the log structure, the striped flag fluttering above them in the breeze.

Once inside, the children buzzed like bees all hyped up on a morning high. The Hinkley boys found their seats in the room and sat quietly, waiting for their teacher, Mrs. Craven, to arrive. Logan avoided looking to the left side of the room; out of the corner of his eye he could see the empty space surrounding the area that once belonged to Rebecca. No longer would his ears ring with her angelic voice; no longer would his eyes receive her delicate smile, and no longer would his body feel the warmth she exhumed from her heart when she hugged his slender frame. Rebecca Foster was gone; she had moved a world away…a world north of Virginia.

The schoolhouse was too small for all the children that attended school every Tuesday of the week. The individual desks were reserved for the oldest kids that were higher in grade at the back of the room, while the rest of the children were seated on long wooden benches with nothing more than a small chalkboard to use as a writing platform. All along the walls of the building were pictures of past presidents and papers of past students, framed to preserve their memories. One such paper belonged to a young William Hinkley. The paper served as a reminder to Logan that he was living in his brother's shadow, something that he did not particularly mind, but at the same time, he felt as though he would always be stuck in the dark, unable to shine his own light.

Sulking in their depressed state, Jed and Logan stared ahead at the large chalkboard that filled the front of the small room. With the slamming of the old door, Mrs. Craven entered, her red hair frizzled around her dainty face.

"Good morning, class!" she announced.

"Good morning, Mrs. Craven!" all the kids cheered aloud.

"Johnny Carson, do not forget that your parents owe three cents to the school."

"I won't forget to tell them, Mrs. Craven." replied a small third grader.

"Now class, let us all begin today's lesson with a reading from the Holy Bible."

The class reached under their seats and withdrew copies of the old tattered books.

"Flip through until you reach Genesis Chapter 4…" Mrs. Craven ordered.

Logan was slow to listen, and in doing so he drew the eye of the teacher.

"Logan isn't it?" she asked.

"Yes, Mrs. Craven."

"Why don't you read for us first?"

Logan cleared his throat and stood up, his eyes scanned the page before beginning, "…And Adam knew Eve his wife; she conceived, and bare-"

"…Not there Logan, farther down…" Mrs. Craven interrupted the boy.

Logan cleared his throat again and skimmed down on the page, "…And the Lord said unto Cain, Why art thou wroth? And why is thy countenance fallen?"

Logan looked up at his teacher, "Shall I continue?" he asked.

Mrs. Craven replied with a silent nodding of the head.

"…If thou doest well, shalt thou not be accepted? And if thou doest not well, sin lieth at the door. And unto thee shall be his desire, and thou shalt rule over him…And Cain talked with Abel his brother: and it came to pass, when they were in the field, that Cain rose up against Abel his brother…" Logan paused and looked at Jed across the room, "…and slew him."

Mrs. Craven's voice faded from Logan's ears as she started to ask the class what the passage meant, but Logan continued to stand, looking at Jed in thought. No matter what the true meaning of the passage was, Logan knew that unlike Abel to Cain, Jed was the only one in his life at the moment who would stand with him in the toughest of times, even when he was not truly appreciated by his father, he could find the love he needed in his brother.

Chapter III: A family Severed
 CƷ𝕭Ɔ

The Hinkley children were sound asleep on the gloomy morning that plagued the once sweet, majestic, and quaint landscape. Rain fell slowly onto the rolling fields that created an airy mist, drenching the alfalfa that so desperately craved water; the glowing sun that once shown bright in the sky was masked by an array of gray clouds; clouds that promised no silver lining.

In the children's room, all laid in their beds with covers pulled high to their faces. It was there that they dreamt of brave knights slaying dragons, and princesses with flowing, blond hair kissing the heroes on their cheeks to pay homage for their gallant actions. It was there that they hid from the dangers of the outside world that threatened to topple everything that they held dear; everything that they knew. In that room, innocence was abundant, and no one could guess how quickly that very innocence would fall and crumble, like a castle of sand.

Jed's eyes opened staring at the ceiling with a vacant expression. Something had caused him to snap awake. Lying in wait, the boy listened. In the distance he could hear mumbled voices; he could not make out what they were saying, he could only tell that their words were hostile by the sharp accents upon heated syllables.

Kicking off his covers, Jed hopped out of his bed and stumbled to the window, shaking off sleep along the way. On the porch he saw Uncle Moses shouting at Father Jed, who was carrying bags from the rain-soaked porch to a large carriage parked at the end of the dirt road at the edge of the property. In a panic, Jed ran from the window over to his brother's bedside, sliding the last few feet.

"Logan, wake up!"

Logan did not move; his eyes shifted back and forth behind closed lids.

Jed bounced up and down anxiously as if trying to keep from wetting himself. "Logan!" he said in a forced whisper.

Logan turned over in his bed making a face of discomfort, throwing a pillow over his exposed ear. "You know, you make it terribly hard to get some sleep around here, Jed…" he groaned.

"Logan, I swear it's important!"

Logan turned over and looked at Jed; his eyes squinted as he tried to focus on the child's disgruntled face. After a long pause he finally spoke. "You're fibbing."

"Am not," Jed protested, "It really is important!"

"You have thirty seconds." Logan said giving in.

"It's Pa and Uncle; they're at it again, except Pa has bags packed!"

Logan ran a hand over his face brushing away the grogginess, and jumped out of the cot to glance out the window. Jed followed close behind, stepping on his brother's heels.

Jedediah and Moses were still arguing intensely as the rain continued to fall.

"…Every damn thing I say, you disregard as malarkey!" Moses hollered.

"That is because every comment or remark that leaves your tobacco stained mouth is negative, and I will not tolerate it, especially when my children are present!" Jedediah fired back.

Moses stepped off of the porch and walked out onto the muddy lawn.

"Moses, you have always been the opposite of me, and now more than ever it has become too much to handle. You gamble, you cheat, and you speak of people like they are animals…" Jedediah paused as he walked toward his brother shaking with anger, "Your worst trait however, is the fact that you think that everything you say is right, and you feel no remorse for what you do. That is why I am taking the children, including Nathan and Maxwell."

"I will be damned if you take them! Brother, you criticize me for my actions, yet you are so obsessed with me that you let yourself go. Have you ever considered that you favor the wrong side? Have you ever thought that maybe our government is as oppressive now as it was when we were under the British flag? You are so blinded by your beliefs that you fail to see my side."

"Your side," Jedediah raised his voice, "Your side is reserved for traitors and fiends; your side wants to send children off to war to fight your revolution!"

"Children fight in wars Jedediah; it is a sad fact of life. War is not reserved for men; it affects all, even the unborn. It is not always optional; sometimes you must stand and fight, negotiation is not always a luxury!"

Jedediah ran his hand through his coarse hair and paced over to the porch; he stopped suddenly and pointed a thick finger at Moses. "What you just said is exactly what is wrong with this country...war has progressed so far that is has become a human emotion, such as hate. It is an act of instinct drilled into the mind through repetition; an act that is practiced by grown men, whose thought processes have become obscured by blood thirst, so much so, that they are willing to kill rather than converse...now do not get me wrong, there are times when war is justifiable, but when it threatens children who know nothing of its creed, then it is no longer war, it is sheer defiance to be civil. Now brother, I ask you, what kind of man are you, the kind who preaches war and passes it along like a hand-me-down or the kind who seeks alternatives to fighting?"

Moses Hinkley glared at Jedediah with eyes full of disgust. Both men were soaked from the weather's appalling conditions. The bearded man spat onto the ground, and then looked up at the falling rain. "You speak to me as if I know nothing of war's demeanor. Fifteen-years ago I fought in the bloodied sands of Mexico City to defend this country, this country that has so gratefully spit in my face. In all my time, I have seen many a thing...I have seen the atrocities of the corrupt...I have seen the vile acts of hate, the dissolution of a twisted mind...I have seen the ruthless slaughter of millions, the wicked dealings of murder in the name of God, race, and country...but in all of my time, nothing strikes me more than the heartless beatings of a soul left to rot in the wake of an oppression. An oppression that has taken on new colors: no longer red and gold, but red, white, and blue. I have killed, I have raped, and I have pillaged...I am nothing short of a villain myself. For if one asks me to describe my being to a man such as you, I shall answer this: I am thy bringer of death; I am a destroyer; hell holds no shackles on me, for I am evil."

Jedediah looked at Moses and shook his head in sheer abhorrence, "Then you are lost."

Moses stood perfectly still; his pose gave off the image that he was calm even though he was desperately trying to control his teeming rage. Jedediah picked up two more leather bags from the white porch and loaded them onto the carriage. Young Jed ran out of the house and stopped in his tracks when he saw his uncle standing motionless while his father continued to pack. The distraught adolescent was in his nightgown, its silk edges fluttered in the wind that had picked up rather violently, throwing his dark hair off to the side of his head.

"Father, what is happening?!" he yelled in fear, the words muffled by the gale.

Neither man answered the boy. They both retained their hard, unrelenting, grimaced attitudes, ignoring each other and Jed. Little Jed looked at the expression on his father's face; it was as coarse as a stone. Neither care, nor love was present in the cracks, only the look of exasperation. Slowly, Jed came to realize that everything he had once feared was coming true: his family was ripping apart in front of his eyes. He had been fooled by his mother's calming words, which soothed him to sleep at night; those words that echoed through his mind suddenly began to sting; he knew that they were so far from the truth.

"Somebody, answer me!" he begged.

Jedediah looked at his son; an infant in his eyes. "Get your brother and get in the carriage, son."

The words were a knife in his heart; the boy swallowed hard and tumbled backwards until he felt the cold, damp reclusive nature of the house's outside wall.

Jed opened his mouth to speak, however he was immediately silenced by Jedediah's sharp tongue saying, "You will obey me!"

Tears filled the child's mouth that hung open; he desperately wanted to scream for a way out, yet no matter how hard he tried to protest, the words were transformed into mournful sobs.

"Listen to me, Jedediah!" screamed the boy's father; he had never called his son by his full name, ever.

"What is happening out here?!" wailed Mary running out onto the rain soaked porch with Logan at her side.

Jed slowly cocked his head to look at his troubled mother. Mary's lower lip turned inward as she shook her head; reaching out, she grabbed her smallest son.

"Mother, stop him!" Jed balled into his mother's gown. Heartbroken, both embraced each other knowing that everything they once held dear was gone.

Logan was silent. He stood lifeless; watching as his father paced from the porch to the wagon, each time, some belonging of theirs was in his anger-driven hands.

"Father...Pa...please do not make us leave..." the older boy murmured.

Jedediah stopped and wiped heaven's tears from his brow. "Why Logan, so you can be forced to live with this man?!" he asked motioning to Moses.

Moses worked his way back to the porch and stopped just a few feet shy of the stairs. At that moment Nathan, Maxwell, and Sue came out of the house, Sue clutched baby Abigail to her chest.

"Jedediah, what is going on?!" Sue shouted in question.

The aging man disregarded the remark and continued packing the wagon.

"He claims to be taking the children..." Moses hollered.

Sue's face twisted in confusion, "What kids?!"

"All of them, every damn one of them!" Moses spat out in fury.

Every eye on the porch looked to Father Jed. Nathan stepped forward from the crowd of weeping faces. "Uncle Jedediah, why?" was all he spoke.

Jedediah breathed in deeply and walked over to Nathan. Scanning his brain for the right words, the hardened man scratched his face. "Nathan, Mary and I want to take you kids with us. The actions of your father are..." he stopped to correct his wording. "...It is not safe to live here anymore. We want you three kids to come with us."

"With us, with us where," Logan asked through falling tears at the realization that his father was not going to give in to the

107

demands of the rest of the family.

"Pennsylvania…it is far enough North that we can hopefully evade any conflict of the war. I tried to keep the reality of everything from you, kids, but I have failed. I did not want you to be scared…"

Nathan's gaze fell onto the ground; the whole situation had a cold, heartless feel.

"I guess this is goodbye then, huh?" sobbed the lanky boy.

Logan drew away from his cousin, his face contorted as a violent flood of built up calamity came cascading down his cheeks at once; the salty taste of tears were overwhelming to his senses. "Nathan, don't say that…" he cried.

Mary and Sue were forced to watch as the two forlorn children, who had spent the entirety of their younger years together, had to bear the task of saying goodbye. No one knew how long the separation would be; yet no one cared. The simple fact of having to say so long to blood was unbearable, even to the youngest of the boys.

Moses finally walked up the steps of the porch and into the house. Seconds later, he returned with a long, sleek object clutched in his riddled hands.

"Moses put the gun back inside!" Sue bellowed.

"If my brother wishes to become a Yankee, then let him, but I will not stand by and watch him take my children from me!"

The family stepped away from the crazed man, except for Jedediah who approached him with outstretched arms.

"Stay back, Jedediah! Do not make me shoot you!"

"Moses, put the gun down before someone gets hurt!" Jedediah said anxiously while trying to be as calm as possible.

"Mommy…" Jed Jr. ran to his mother and hugged her waist.

Nathan turned to face Logan who still did not want to believe the facts that everything would be different from then on. "Logan, take care of Jed, don't let him end up like our fathers…"

"Nate, stop it! This can't be it!" Logan glanced at his father who was busy trying to wrestle the gun from Moses. "You promised that nothing like this would happen!"

Nathan grabbed his cousin's arm and looked him in his wet, blue eyes. "It's over Logan, things have changed…"

Tossing the damp hair from his eyes, Logan opened his arms to give his cousin one final embrace. In that instant, a shot rang out. The deafening noise made thunder seem like a robin's chirp as it echoed throughout the surrounding valley. Out in the field, birds took flight, fluttering away from the pursuing sound waves. Logan looked down at Nathan's chest; the white fabric suddenly grew dark as a burgundy liquid began to ooze from the hole in the cloth. Everyone knew instantly that it was not the kind of blood you get from a roughed up knee or broken scab. Unable to breathe, the blue-eyed boy slowly brought his glare up to Nathan's face. Toppling over, Nathan fell onto Logan causing both boys to collapse on the rain-soaked deck. The blood from Nathan's wound began to flow like a steady stream, encircling the youthful bodies and dripping off the edge of the porch, settling into a pool in the grass.

Moses looked down at the musket that he and Jedediah both gripped in their hands. The muzzle was aimed right at Nathan's body; on the trigger, rested Moses' finger. Dropping the rifle, the bearded man fell to the boards; he began to rock back and forth, moaning in disbelief as his eyes started to pour salty water.

"Amelia!" screamed Jedediah rushing over to the jarred youth. Carefully, Father Jed rolled Nathan over on to his back, letting Logan slowly slip out from under his cousin. Logan's nightgown was stained with his cousin's fluid; drops of the red liquid were present on his face as well as arms. The child's blue eyes were held open in shock at the horror of the incident.

Nathan's jaw chattered as his body convulsed with pain. He was unable to mutter even the slightest syllable.

"Amelia, bring out a bucket of water and bandages now!" Jedediah shouted.

The family stood motionless, watching in horror as Nathan lay dying on the old porch soaked in his blood. Moses mumbled meaningless jargon as he continued to rock like a baby on his rear. Logan was no less than two feet from Nathan, and he watched as the fading boy gasped for air; the dying youth's hand gripped tight around Logan's forearm.

Amelia ran to Jedediah with the bucket and bandages. The two of them desperately tried to mend the wound, yet no matter how hard they tried, their efforts were futile. Slowly, the boy's body stopped twitching, and Father Jed sat up on the backs of his feet. His masculine hands were bright red, a stark contrast to the gray atmosphere.

Mary looked at her husband with hopeful eyes; however Jedediah responded with a solemn twisting of the head. "He is gone."

Sue let out a screeching cry as she fell to her knees. Mary took baby Abigail as the woman clawed at her son's lifeless body. Jed covered his eyes as he avoided looking at Nathan. Disheartened, Jedediah stood up and ran his forearm under his eye, removing a single tear; he walked over to Logan and lifted him up like he had done when he was just a little boy. Nathan's lifeless hand still gripped his cousin's sleeve. Unwilling to let go, Logan attached his hand to Nathan's.

"Let him go, Son."

Tucking his face into his father's shoulder, Logan shook his head in defiance. As the boy's tears stained the elderly man's flannel shirt, he cried out, "No!" repeating himself over and over, yet even though the words were spoken in a raised tone, they reached the ears as if covered by a mask.

"Son, he is gone now, let him go…" Jedediah tried his best to hold in his emotions, however seeing his second child so distraught brought him to the brink. Unable to walk any farther, the aging man collapsed on the steps of the porch and wept with his son as he ran his large hand through the boy's soft blond hair.

"God, forgive us…" he spoke through twisted lips as he sobbed uncontrollably, mimicking his boy.

The entire family remained scattered upon the deck, while Nathan's inanimate body laid sprawled out in an awkward fashion. There was nothing peaceful about his death; the actions of hate and anger had driven him to his untimely demise. Nathan Hinkley would forever remain a victim of the separation; a casualty of the broken link that the two brothers, Jedediah and Moses, had yet to mend.

Finding his strength, Jedediah stood up with Logan still clinging around his upper body like a child. In his hand, the blue-eyed boy held the tattered baseball that Nathan was once so fond of. Mary guided Jed toward the wagon where the family climbed on; only she was brave enough to look back, a sorrow built up in her eyes. Sue rested her head on Nathan's body hoping for a sign of life, however, no matter how much she hoped she knew he had passed on. Baby Abigail sat beside her mother playing with her dress, the poor child unable to comprehend what had just occurred.

Maxwell watched as a part of his family faded off into the distance, leaving behind two thin lines in the mud as the carriage crested the trail away from the home. The fluttering flag that hung from the house shook ferociously in the wind until finally it tore off of its pole, and circled in the air once before falling to the bloodstained grass.

Moses rose to his feet grunting as he tried to control the feelings of rage and grief that swelled inside of him. Walking over to the side of the porch, he grabbed two shovels and handed one to his nine-year-old son.

"It is time you become a man. Help me bury your brother." he muttered coldly.

Maxwell stared at his father with large, round eyes. The boy's innocence was as apparent as ever as he followed his grizzly father out into the yard. Without hesitation, Moses began to dig a hole, thrusting his shovel into the ground and churning up a large pile of dirt, and then tossing it over his shoulder. Maxwell looked back at his brother who lied frozen on the porch, then reverted his eyes to the ground, where he started to dig.

≫PART TWO≪

Chapter IV: We go marching
෬෩

The luscious Virginian grass that once bore the scares of a butchered youth and the footsteps of tampered love, swayed in the still, silent breeze. Two years had passed since the fateful day that tore a thick seam in the once sacred bond of family; no longer was the pain of a tearing heart, felt by either side…for in its place rose a wall of incertitude that things would return to the way they once were before the quivering injustice of a dying time, a time that would forever stain the innocence of the Hinkley children.

Nathan had become a name unspoken, a name whose syllables slithered off the tongue like a curse. Everything that the boy could have become in life was buried in the dirt along with his bones…despite the hopes of the family nothing could ever be like they once were.

It had been a long two years. The war had ravished the country in a bloody wake leaving behind it a form of unfathomable terror. Names like General Lee, and "Stonewall" Jackson had become synonymous with words like traitor and fiend to those who occupied the Northern states. Logan and Jed Jr., who had once thought themselves Southerners, found themselves denying their own pasts, forgetting that part of their kin still lied in an earthen tomb in Virginia. Both boys had grown in height and heart, yet their minds could not grow out of the memories they held. Father Jed and Mary had become tired of the separation from their true home, yet each denied feeling remorse for what had happened to their relationship with Moses and the rest of the family; the weight of the separation however, was apparent as their moods were so glum that many a day was spent staring off into a realm of their own creations far away from the reality of a life in hell.

Sue Hinkley had passed away shortly after the death of Nathan; her pain and grievance over a lost son, and the splitting of what was most dear to her left her heartbroken and weak…ultimately she chose her path and took the ill-fated steps into a world unknown.

At their new home in Pennsylvania, Jedediah and Mary desperately tried to heal their sons' grievances, yet their attempts were sub-par, for they could not even heal their own. The effect from the split had drawn the children apart from their parents like it had the family as a whole.

Logan and Jed Jr. were sitting alone in their room listening to the deathly quiet sounds of a house in mourning. Not a word was spoken between them for most of the day, and they had refused all of the meals their mother had made for them. This was the routine for the better part of the two years since the death of Nathan Hinkley.

"Logan," Jed called out one afternoon.

The boy's voice had begun to change, following his steps into adulthood. Logan was gripping a new baseball in his hands; his fingers maneuvered across the tops of the red seams.

"Do you want to play?" Jed continued, while watching his brother who retained his glum posture on his bed.

"Play what?" asked the blue-eyed boy.

Jed thought for a moment not knowing what to say. "…Baseball?"

Immediately after speaking, Jed realized his mistake. Logan sprang up and chucked the baseball at the wall, puncturing the thin wood that sealed off the room.

"I'm sorry!" Jed tried to console.

"What does it matter, Jed?" Logan asked with hands lifting toward the sky. The boy spun around and walked to the window that showered cracks of light into the depressed room. From his pocket he pulled the tattered remains of the baseball Nathan had shattered over two years ago.

Jed said nothing more. He watched with wide eyes and closed lips as his brother panted with emotion.

"What does it matter? Everyone is always sorry. No one ever means to make me upset or they apologize because they said the wrong thing. Well when does it end?"

Logan turned back toward his silent brother and sat down on his bed across from the green-eyed teen. "It has been two years since…you know…and it still feels like it all happened yesterday. I wake up every morning and I feel like he still sleeps across the room from me, only he is just out in the kitchen or on the porch, and that is why I can't see him. But that's not it…and that will never be it."

Shaking his head, and breathing through tight lips, Logan huffed heavily and crossed over to Jed who still retained his feeble stance on the edge of the bed.

"Jed, when will the pain I feel leave me? I feel like I am always putting up a wall, always pushing away what I'm feeling. His blood was on me for God sakes! How can I run from that; how can that make me stronger?"

Jed watched his older brother expel his deepest thoughts without second-guessing any of what he was saying. It was a surprise to the younger child, who had spent most of his childhood looking up to his brother for advice; the tables were turned.

"Logan, most people believe that it is holding on that makes one stronger, but sometimes it is letting go that truly heals us."

Logan cocked his head and looked at Jed with eyes of suffering, yet for a brief moment, there was a glimmer of relief and gratitude that broke its way through the watery pain.

"Who told you that?" the blue-eyed boy asked.

"Nathan…"

Logan sniffled, and nodded.

"…When my fish died…" Jed added.

The remark caught Logan off guard and as hard as he tried to suppress his laughter, he giggled, and wiped away the salty tears which had begun to form in the corners of his eyes.

Jed smiled with pride at having helped his hero overcome such a complex emotion that his whole family felt. "I'm sorry."

Logan walked over to the wall where the baseball had fallen and picked it up admiring its simple stitching. "Roo, let's forget about Nathan, at least for today. Want to play catch?" he asked.

Hesitating, Jed opened his mouth to ask for clarification, but stopped himself and simply replied, "Yes."

The two brothers threw on their sewn baseball caps and bolted from their room. Logan doubled back briefly and tossed the remains of Nathan's ball around in his hand. He crossed over to his dresser and carefully set the skin down inside the drawer and closed it gently. Breathing deeply, he looked around the room once, and then took off through the house, and out into the green yard that surrounded the quiet Pennsylvanian home.

Miles away in Virginia, Maxwell's life seemed to be halted in time. He had experienced two deaths within a matter of months and was forever surrounded by a state of loathing, as the memories of Nathan and his mother had become abasement shadows in a world caught in the clutches of desolation. Surrounded by the remnants of his family, Maxwell had begun to embrace this new world, yet not a day passed when he did not consider how differently things would have been had his father and uncle resolved their issues a long, long time ago.

"Goodnight, Son," Moses whispered to the boy as he blew out the last candle in the den.

Maxwell did not reply. He simply watched his father disappear from the moonlight shining through the panes in the window into the darkened corridor leading out into the quiet home. The child listened to hear the faint shutting of a door in the corners of the home before he rolled over to face the dark ceiling.

"Goodnight, Mom." his cracking voice whimpered through tight lips.

Sporadically the child's eyes scanned the dark space as if waiting to hear a response. When none came, he pulled his checkered blanket to his chin and closed his innocent eyes. No matter how hard he tried, he could not sit still. Deep inside, a feeling was becoming increasingly superficial as he returned to his initial position on the den's sofa, where his eyes opened to meet the closed door of his past room directly down the hall.

Languidly, Maxwell slipped his bare legs out from under his cotton covers, and stepped foot onto the cold floorboards of the den. Shivering feverishly, the child hugged his nightgown close to his body and crept his way down the darkened hall to the doorway of his old room.

Upon reaching the white door, he held a shaking hand out and grasped the brass knob. The boy pushed gently until the door opened up slightly, releasing a swift breeze that blew the hair on his forehead to the side. Apprehensively, he looked around the room before entering; everything inside the lonely bedroom had remained the same since the day he last saw his cousins, and brother. Pushing on the door again, Maxwell walked inside, stopping just after descending the steps into the sunken room.

The boy glanced around with huge eyes. Each bed was untouched and left the way it had been that fateful morning two years ago. The sheets on Nathan's cot were left bunched up at the end as if he had just kicked them off in a hurry to start a new day; sadly they were removed for an entirely different reason.

Maxwell's eyes moved upward along the wall where sheets of paper rested nailed into the paint; their faces were embellished with images he had scribbled of his family; above each figure was the name. Shying away, Maxwell looked to the ground and turned his back on the scene. He stumbled over to the oak bureau that still held his brother's clothing. Working up his nerves, the child looked in the mirror hanging over the dresser. All around him, the room was bleak and filled with shadows. He himself appeared dull and lifeless. Desperately, the boy tried to fight the urge to weep as memories and voices of his family began to haunt his mind. Peering at his self through decaying eyes, Maxwell began to notice how similar he and his brother looked; the dusty hair, which hung down to his forehead and the tops of his ears had started to flip out on the ends, creating a wavy appearance. Under his eyes, which were a watery fusion of green and light brown, were small freckles that seemed to spread to the bridge of his nose.

Stricken with heartfelt torment, the child flung his fist at the mirror, breaking the reflection in two, and fell to his knees with his face in his hands.

The door was suddenly flung open and Amelia ran into the room as if on cue. "Child what is going on in here?!" she cried out in the dark upon seeing the weeping boy curled up in a ball on the floor beside his brother's bed.

Speedily, the woman sat down beside him, and pulled the boy toward her lap.

"Amelia, why did he have to die?" wailed Maxwell through shimmering bouts of tears.

"Hush, child." soothed the motherly woman as she clutched the boy in her arms.

"All I see is Him; everywhere I turn. I am becoming Him!" continued Maxwell, still distraught.

"No child, no. You are Maxwell Asa Hinkley; you are your own person. What happened to your brother was terrible and an accident. You are not bound to his fate."

Burying his head into Amelia's robe, little Maxwell wiped his eyes and embraced the woman, where he continued to breath in an uneasy manner.

Amelia settled in on the floor and ran her hand through the boy's thick hair until he slipped off into sleep.

Across the darkened house, Moses listened to the events occurring between Amelia and his son. The enervated man lay quietly on the large cot that was centered in the blackened room. Beside him remained an open portion of mattress that once served as a cozy cocoon for Sue; and now served as the resting place of young Abigail.

Stroking the coarse, wiry strands of hair that hung from his chin, Moses began to zone off into an entirely different world. His dark pupils, that had become regularity, started to spiral into an even more nebulous and murky color, driving out the last bit of light that filled his soul.

Rising with a grunt, the man approached the bedroom door and opened it very slowly so that not even a tiny creak escaped the opened walkway. Peering around the shadowy, shapeless living room, the man worked his way to the old bedroom of the children, and waited.

Moments later, Amelia snuck out of the room and shut the door gently. "Maxwell is back to sleep, Sir."

Moses did not respond.

"May I be excused to bed now, Sir?" Amelia asked again with a hesitant voice.

"No you may not." was Moses' reply.

A look of confusion crept over Amelia's shadow-ridden face. "I beg your pardon?"

Moses lurched forward and grabbed the woman by her arm and pulled her tight into his chest. Immediately, Amelia turned her head, expecting a blow to the side of her cheek. She could feel the warm, repeated breathe on her lips as Moses stood still, holding her by her arm.

"You have been a great service to this family since Sue's passing." said Moses staring into Amelia's closed eyes.

"I don't understand, Sir?" whimpered Amelia.

"I have lived without a woman's touch for over two years now…it is time you grew to respect me not only as your master, but as your lover."

Amelia's spine tingled as Moses' words pierced her. Desperately she tried to pull away as the hair on the man's face began to poke her soft cheeks.

"You will obey me!" whispered the man.

Amelia pulled again with all of her might, yet the harder she fought the tighter Moses' grip on her bicep became; a sharp, stinging sensation shot through her body as the popping of her shoulder from her socket forced a cry to shoot out of her mouth.

Moses closed his eyes as his execrable lips touched the perspiring face of the captive woman. Without warning, Amelia pushed the man's chest with the force of a bull, knocking him back and breaking his grip. Moses looked down at his chest where a letter opener extruded from his right breast; a ring of blood was built up around the wound.

Amelia backed away toward the door of the home, defenseless, and injured.

"You stabbed me you cussed-fool!"

Tears streaked Amelia's face as she searched for a way to evade the man's impending onslaught.

Moses pulled the object from his chest and gripped it white knuckle-tight. "By God's eye, I swear I will put you in the ground!"

Moses raised the weapon in the air, but stopped as the silhouette of Abigail appeared beside Amelia from the darkness.

"Daddy, what is going on?" she muttered awkwardly, rubbing her eyes.

Moses dropped the letter opener as he glared at his daughter in the dark. Calming his rage, the glaze from his eyes faded back to their normal light. "Leave this house, Amelia...and never come back." he did not look at the woman, nor did she look back when she left. The last figure of hope for the children remaining in the cursed home was gone.

When Maxwell awoke the next morning, his eyes scanned the dull ceiling; it took him a moment to realize that he was not staring at the ornately decorated fixtures of the den, but that he was looking up at the familiar roof of the old bedroom. His face felt tight and dry from the spilt tears that had soaked into his face from the late hours prior; however their presence no longer remained, leaving him to feel cleansed and renewed. Rubbing the sleep from his eyes, the boy looked around and saw that he was in his original bed facing the window. Beside him, Nathan's old bed was unoccupied, and the sheets were tucked under the mattress and pulled to their original position, stopping just shy of the head of the bed where the pillow covered the remaining expanse. In a way, the room seemed peaceful. The frightening aura had faded along with the nightmares that once plagued the boy's mind.

The young child rose from the toasty warm sheets and tossed the hair on his head around as if shaking the sleep from a tight grip. He made his way over to the bureau, and reached a careful hand to the drawer that once belonged to him. He stopped just before his fingers grasped the brown, grainy knob. Tucking his fingers back into his palm, he shifted his arm toward his brother's drawer. He sheepishly looked around as if someone was going to stop him from rooting around in the private dresser, yet no one was around. Slowly, he extended his slender hand once more and closed his fingers around the knob, pulling the drawer open, and releasing a spray of dust that took flight into the morning light that shimmered coarsely through the window. Inside the drawer, Nathan's shirts were folded neatly into small stacks. His pants and nightclothes took place right beside the socks. The boy shoved his hands into the drawer and lifted up a gentle white cotton dress shirt; a shirt Nathan had worn often. Maxwell examined every inch of the cloth before he held it up to his nose. The unique smell that captivated Nathan had faded, and only the musty smell of the wood remained imprisoned in the threads.

The dusty-haired boy tossed the shirt on the bed, followed by a pair of black slacks. He then struggled to unbutton the top of his nightgown, but finally managed to pull the stiff oval through the open hole. He lifted the top of the gown up over his head and tossed it to the ground, feeling the cold air course over his naked body. For a moment he considered retreating back into the warm sanctity of the gown, yet refrained knowing Amelia would be in any moment to bring him to his drawn bath. However something was wrong…there was no Amelia. The boy grabbed the shirt and held it close to his body to shield him from the coldness of the room as he walked over to the window. The golden tub that used to sit out in the yard every morning of bath-day was absent. Maxwell hobbled back over to the bed where he threw the shirt back down beside the pants and picked up his nightgown from its balled up position on the wooden floor. He rotated it end over end, until he found the bottom and pulled the still warm cotton down over his skinny frame, at once feeling cozy and sheltered. Finding what had happened to Amelia became his priority when he exited the room out into the quiet home.

As he made his way into the kitchen, he saw his little sister, Abigail, sitting on the floor playing silently with her cornhusk doll. Maxwell panned the scene, searching for a sign of Amelia or his father. When neither registered, he knelt down beside his younger sibling. "Hey, Abby…" He stated softly.

The little girl smiled brightly at her brother, but said nothing.

Maxwell rubbed her cheek out of kindness and spoke again, "Have you seen Amelia?"

"Amelia is gone." called the hoarse voice of Moses.

"Dad," Maxwell yelped; startled.

"She left ya…" Moses put coldly.

Maxwell stood up, contorting his face as he tried to guess where his belligerent father was taking the conversation. "Why?" he asked.

"She left ya for dead! Just like your damned mother."

"Shut up!" Maxwell screamed at his father, who sipped a strong smelling potion from a tin cup.

"Well, it is true! Amelia left you for dead, just like your momma! Neither of them could handle the stress, Boy."

Maxwell started to seethe, eyeing Moses as he crossed the room over to the window.

"They were weak."

"You are weak! You are the one who needed them all along. Look at you! Ever since Momma died, you have been drinking from that damn cup!" Maxwell spat out in fury.

Moses' knuckles answered fast, striking hard against the child's mouth. "You listen here Maxwell, Amelia forgot her place; as for your mother, she should have kept her place, here, with us, but instead, she died. You, however, know your place, and I swear, like the Sword of Damocles, I will put you back where you belong."

Maxwell massaged the swelling lump on his chin. Abigail reached a hand out and touched the falling tears on her brother's face.

"Abigail, leave us." Moses ordered.

The little girl stood up and gripped her doll with both arms. She waddled two steps toward her room before pausing and saying, "Feel better, Maxy!" Humming, she fled the scene.

"Get up and face me like a man!" Moses grunted.

Maxwell rubbed his eyes and slowly returned to his feet with a face filled with bitterness.

"I do not expect you to know why I do as I do. As a father, it is not my job to be your best friend; however it is my duty to make sure you grow old and wise. Do you understand me?"

Maxwell thought for a moment, and then nodded.

"…You are a Hinkley, and that is a noble name. Your Great Grandfather helped start this Nation, and you will help to reset its course." Moses paused and walked over to an oak chest that sat beside the kitchen wall. He opened it and pulled out a tattered, leather tri-corner hat. "This belonged to him. He wore it

123

during the Battle of Bunker Hill, where over three-thousand British troops marched on the fragile plains of freedom."

Maxwell took the hat from his father's hands and stroked its edges thoughtfully.

"He used this, too…" Moses pulled a musket from the large chest and held it out toward the boy.

Maxwell hesitated at the sight of the gun. The snap of the shot that killed Nathan rang through his ears. "Is that the gun that killed-?"

"Do not say his name!" Moses hollered, cutting him off. "That is the past now." He said before taking another sip from the cup.

Maxwell grabbed the rifle, and held it away from his body. He eyed the trigger with indifferent eyes.

"I want you to honor your family once more in this conflict, and fight for the cause; fight for the South. It is the noble thing to do." Moses looked to the ground and rubbed his beard. "Leave by the end of the week." he said.

Maxwell watched waiting for the man to give him an embrace; not that he would have accepted it, but the gesture would shoot down all feelings of false love that began to take flight in his heart. "Goodbye." he muttered rubbing his chest.

As thoughts of dwindling affection began to rise in the pit of Maxwell's soul, he turned to face his old room once more. As he began to step toward the safe-haven, he stopped remembering Abigail's kindness in the heat of the situation. The boy halted and listened for her innocent voice, which filled the emptiness of the hallway in the home. Changing course, Max walked outside on to the wooden porch, and stepped off into the green grass. He walked out to the edge of the flowing fields to where patches of daises separated the wild nature of the alfalfa, and the tame, shyness of the grass. He knelt down at the flowery edge, his knee absorbing the teary dampness that lay across the surface of the expanse. He grasped the flimsy stem of a small, yellow daisy and plucked it from its home in the purgatory of nature. He walked briskly back to the home and toward Abigail's bedroom.

The young girl sat playing with her green, ragged cornhusk doll on the wooden floor of the white room. She sat helpless, humming a familiar tune; one their Aunt used to sing them.

Maxwell listened for a moment, and then repeated the words softly aloud so he did not startle the playing child.

> *"One little Rabbit caught in a daze,*
> *Followed by a hunter as the rabbit grazed,*
> *Sitting in silence, Mother Rabbit tried to fight,*
> *Help me Mother Rabbit, called the little one in fright…"*

Abigail looked up as Maxwell finished the last stanza of the song to see him leaning on the doorframe, his hands behind his back.

"Yes?" Abigail asked in a playful, innocent tone.

"Nothin' just watching," Maxwell admitted.

The little girl went back to playing with her doll, and humming the familiar tune once more.

Clearing his throat, Maxwell spoke up, "May I come in?"

Abigail shrugged, tossing her doll to the side. She cleared a small spot beside the doll for her older brother to sit.

Maxwell crossed over and sat down, legs crossed, hiding the object in the palm of his hand.

"Want some tea?" Abigail asked.

Maxwell took a sniff of the drink to find an empty cup. "No thank you, it is too strong for my liking!" he giggled in a playful tone.

"But Ms. Popped made it!" she sulked pointing at her doll.

"Oh, alright I suppose." Maxwell said caving in.

He took a sip of the pretend beverage and gave a thumb up in the direction of the doll. From the corner of his eye he could see his baby sister grinning from ear to ear.

"Hey, Abby, I got you something." he said, holding out his hand.

The little girl's eyes opened wide with wonder. She wrapped her small fingers around that of his, and opened them like a present to reveal the golden daisy lying in his palm.

"Mine?!" she asked in disbelief.

"Yup, just for you!" Maxwell said marveling at the girl's simplicity and fascination.

"Thank you, Maxy!" she cried out, leaping in the air to embrace her brother's neck.

The boy paused for a moment, savoring the touch of his sister; something he would soon be without. Raising his arms, he returned the hug before she tore off down the hallway holding the daisy high above her head.

ೞ

It seemed like an eternity since Mary and Father Jed had spent the entirety of their day together with their children like they had back on the farm in Virginia. The brisk afternoon breeze that flowed between the surrounding trees of the Pennsylvanian home was enough to drown out the would-have-been incredibly painful silence that seemed to linger consistently around Logan and Jed's new home.

Jedediah was in his rocking chair on the newly built porch where he did not sway an inch forward or backward. Instead, he sat fixed in an upright position with his feet planted firmly on the wooden deck. He retained a hard stare upon the book in his hand. He became oblivious to the outside world as he devoted his time to filling his mind with the enthralling words of *A Tale of Two Cities.*

Mary walked out of the home, shutting the door quietly behind her. She studied her husband, hoping to catch him at a stopping point in his book, "Jedediah?"

The man held one finger in the air as he mouthed the final words of the chapter, and then shut his book after carefully marking the page.

"Might I have a word?" Mary asked allowing her eyes to wander off over the landscape.

"I suppose," Jedediah answered, slowly rising from his seat.

Mary walked back in to the home with Father Jed right behind her. Once she reached the kitchen, the aging woman stopped in mid-pace and covered her mouth as her eyes scanned a tiny piece of parchment in her hand.

"What are you holding?" Jedediah asked, repositioning the glasses on his nose.

Mary crumpled the paper and clutched it to her breast. "It is a letter-"

"From whom," Jedediah coaxed becoming increasingly curious as to the situation.

Mary filled her lungs with a long, drawn out breath, attempting to settle her rushing emotions. "I sent for a postman last week."

"What for?" asked the man.

"I needed him to deliver a letter to-" Mary halted her sentence.

"Do not think about lying to me, Mary!" Jedediah warned.

"I sent him along with a letter addressed to Sue!" Mary cracked.

Jedediah removed the glasses from his face and rubbed his eyes. In a fiery and quick action he slammed his fist upon the kitchen counter. "Why, Mary? I specifically expressed to all that I did not want any connections to them what-so-ever!"

"I needed to hear from her, Jedediah! Her son died, her husband is cruel; for heaven's sake Jedediah, what she was going through was worse than anything we have experienced so far." Mary massaged her eyes trying to rid herself of the vile tears that dripped down her cheek.

Jedediah put his spectacles back in their prior position, resting upon the bridge of his nose. His face twisted into thought, "Why did you say *was*?"

Mary turned fully around to face her husband. "The letter I hold in my hand is the same letter I sent. When the postman returned it, he said there is no one living at that house by the name of Sue."

Jedediah's eyes shot around his wife's fragile face.

"She is dead, Jedediah."

The man ran a hand through his coarse hair and shook his head in refusal. "No."

Mary continued to weep, watching Jedediah cross to the kitchen table and flop down in shock.

127

"No, no this cannot be," he tossed his glasses from his face, where they made their new home at the center of the mahogany table, "Moses would have sent a letter informing us, he would've sent something, he-"

"He has shut us out of his life too, Jedediah. Just as you have done with him," murmured the aging woman.

After a moment's revelation, Jedediah positioned his glasses once more on his face, and turned to Mary. "Please tell me you are not pinning this on me!" he roared.

"I do not know who to pin this on, Jedediah. Moses had his ways and so did you."

"I did what I had to for my children, Mary!"

"No, Jedediah, you did what you had to for you."

Jedediah coughed furiously in his hand.

"-Food is ready." Mary said without emotion.

In the sweeping fields in the back of the house, Logan busily dug tiny holes in which Jed followed close behind and planted delicate, miniscule seeds that Father Jed hoped would blossom into life.

Logan had started to succumb to exhaustion and threw his small shovel into the dirt after digging one final hole. Wiping the sweat from his forehead, the boy sat back on his heels and let the late afternoon breeze flow across his perspiring face, bringing with it a crisp, yet refreshing smell of the changing season.

"You would think it is getting close to autumn," the boy announced.

"What makes you say that?" Jed asked trying to fill every remaining hole with the tiny seeds.

"The air; it is cool; chilly."

Jed stuffed the last few seeds in the final hole beside Logan and tossed the bag to the side. "Maybe a storm's a comin'?"

Logan shrugged his shoulders as he examined the horizon.

"Do you think it is weird that Ma and Pa still won't mention Nathan?" Jed asked.

Logan shifted his weight back onto his knees as he began to feel uncomfortable about the sudden shift in topic. "Please, Jed, don't."

"Logy, I didn't mean…"

"…Jed, not now!" Logan snapped, wiping his mouth and walking away toward the house. "And do not call me *Logy*."

Both boys reached the water pump just outside the home at the same time. Logan lifted the rusting handle, releasing a murky spray of water that spat out in all directions. Jed waited while Logan rinsed his hands off. Growing impatient, he spoke up again.

"Do you think that Abigail even knew what happened that day?"

Logan slammed his hand down atop the pump shutting off the stream. There was silence. Only the sound of falling droplets of water from the faucet filled the open air.

"Do not make me shut you up, Jed. Let it be; what happened is over."

"I am just curious!" Jed fired back.

"Forget it, Jed! He is dead!"

Both boys averted their gazes as the words hit home.

"…Children, supper." Mary's solemn voice called out into the surrounding valley.

"Coming, Mother!" Logan yelled out.

Logan gripped his brother's collar and pulled him in closer until their noses about touched. "You listen to me, Roo. Not a word about Nathan or any of them anymore you hear me, especially around Mother and Father."

Jed sneered as he pulled away from his older brother's grasp.

Both children trotted off slowly toward the house; Jed remained a few feet behind Logan, kicking the ground with irritation.

When the children entered the home, the dinner table was already set. Father Jed sat emotionless at the head of the table facing Logan, who stood alone in the doorway.

"Dinner is ready." Mary whispered.

Jed pushed passed Logan in a rush to take his seat at the table. Examining the food, his face dropped from eagerness to despair with the realization that the meal would be chicken once more.

"This is the third night in a row!" Jed cried out.

"Shut it, dummy!" Logan lashed out.

Mary stood behind her chair as she watched Father Jed begin to cut his food. The glimmer in her eyes faded as Logan and Jed continued to bicker, and her gaze wandered back and forth between her lonely husband and the two boys.

Jedediah continued to downsize the chicken on his plate, attempting to ignore the eyes that fell upon him. "What is it?" he asked without looking up.

"Are we not saying grace?" Mary asked defensively.

Jedediah took a bite of chicken in his mouth and chewed it slowly. Suddenly, he slammed his fork down on the table, capturing the attention of the entire room. "What should we pray for Mary? We moved from our home, our lives have been torn apart!"

"We should still pray!" Mary fired back.

"For what, that dead boy and his mother," Jedediah roared.

The sentence shot a feeling of numbness through Logan, forcing his jaw to fall open as he watched his father redden with anger.

Mary shook her head in pity, "Jedediah Hinkley, how dare you."

"Mary, what am I supposed to say? Maybe this will make my brother realize the extremes of his actions and beliefs."

"How dare you make Nathan and Sue a martyr for your rage against Moses!"

"I believe I made it perfectly clear that this kind of discussion would not be tolerated in this house!"

Logan and Jed sat helplessly watching their parents fight over the topic forbidden. Logan cleared his throat and the room fell silent as the adults realized the children were still present.

"Aunty Sue passed?" asked Jed in a confused tone.

"There will be no more talk about the family; the people we left behind; who left us behind." Jedediah ordered.

Mary crossed over to the sink and scanned the world outside. Silently she began to weep, allowing the sink to catch her tears.

Jed's attention shifted to his mother. He stood up from his chair and started to walk to her, but Father Jed's thunderous voice halted his movement, "Sit!"

Jed hesitated.

"I said sit!"

"No!" Logan shouted in his brother's defense. "He doesn't have to! None of us have to!"

"Mind your tongue, Boy!" Jedediah ordered.

"Enough!" shouted Mary as a knock came at the door.

Silence…

A second knock echoed.

Father Jed stood up and walked toward the door. His aged hand grasped the brass knob and twisted it, letting the dying light of day flood the home; before him, stood a uniformed officer of the Union army.

Jedediah glanced back at Mary and his children, whose faces held a certain flicker of inquisition.

"May I help you?" Jedediah questioned, leaving a tinge of perception to fill the air.

The uniformed officer cleared his throat and a second man in a similar uniform, however less decorated, stepped on to the porch and handed the first man a piece of parchment.

"Sorry to disrupt your evening, Sir," the finely decorated soldier spoke. His voice held a raspy tone.

"Not at all, officer," Jedediah responded, shutting the door to the home behind him as he stepped foot onto the porch with the two men.

Logan jumped up from the table as the door clicked closed behind his father.

"Logan, sit." Mary asked patiently as she moved to the window nearest the door.

Logan disobeyed and continued on toward the door, opening it with a reticent shaking of the handle.

The uniformed officer glanced at the opening door to see Logan's blue eyes peering out, followed by the boy's body. "Are you Logan Hinkley?" he asked.

"Y-yes, Sir," Logan stuttered.

Father Jed turned around, "Logan, back inside."

"Actually, Sir, this letter is for him." The officer handed the letter to the boy who accepted it hesitantly from the gloved hand of the soldier.

"It is an official order to accompany Colonel Nehemiah Tavert of the 11th Pennsylvania infantry to the town of Perryville tomorrow morning for a medical examination. Should you pass the physical, you are to report to Camp Hamilton for training."

The raspy voice of the officer echoed through the confines of Logan's mind as he tried to piece together the information that had just compounded every waking thought to a feeling of sickness.

"What do you mean? There must be a mistake," Father Jed asked.

"No, Sir, he is to be conscripted by order of our president, Abraham Lincoln." replied the officer in a steadied voice.

"Well, he is not of age. He has just turned seventeen." Jedediah ruled assuredly.

The officer shook his head, "Unfortunately, he has fallen too close to the legal cutoff date for those to be conscripted; he is being ordered to battle."

"I do not see how this is tolerable." Jedediah muttered.

"We need troops, Mr. Hinkley. I hope you can understand," the officer turned his attention to Logan who held the letter in his shaking hands, "Colonel Tavert will be back here tomorrow at first light. Do not make him wait."

Both soldiers marched off of the porch; the clacking of their boots and spurs on the wood ceased once they hit the dusted grass.

Jedediah ran his hand down the length of his face. He pushed passed Logan, back in to the home. The blue-eyed boy studied the letter that called him to a war he truly knew nothing about.

"Logan!" his mother called from inside. The sound of her voice forced him to jump, dropping the letter on the wooden floorboards of the porch.

Once inside the home, Logan stepped awkwardly toward the table. He looked up trying to focus on the faces staring at him: Father Jed sitting once more at the table, Jed watching beside the window, and his mother doing the same.

"What does this mean?" Logan asked trying to control his wavering tone of voice.

Jedediah sighed with twisted resonance. "You are to fight in the war, Son."

Logan's incoherent eyes fell squarely on his father, who rubbed his temples. "What?" he asked, still in shock.

Silence and sullenness gripped the room like a hand around one's throat.

Father Jed stood up and paced a circle around the kitchen. "You will fight."

Logan's lips quivered as he spoke, "For how much you hate this war I figured you would be the one to take a stand!"

"Logan, it is not that easy!" Jedediah answered back sharply.

"Yes it is! You, you tell them no!" Logan watched his father circle like a buzzard about to strike its prey.

The boy began weep as he felt the cold stab of alienation penetrate the deepest remnants of his sanctity.

"I can do nothing, Son."

"How am I supposed to fight? I hardly even know what this war is about, because you, Father, you kept *me*, you kept all of *us* in the dark!"

"Do not raise your voice at me, Logan!" Father Jed cried out, moving in on his son.

"I'll be alone; I'll have to kill, like William, I'll die just like Nathan!"

One swift stroke of Jedediah's hand silenced his weeping child.

Logan fell to the floor as his mother and brother watched in horror. He pressed his hand to his stinging face and glared at his father with eyes swollen from tears.

"You have to grow up *now*; you have to be brave, no matter how frightening things may seem, you must be brave!" Jedediah thundered, panting with anger at his son's innocence.

The boy picked himself up and brushed off his pants. Without looking around at the faces that still watched, he scuttled off toward his room.

Mary turned to face Jedediah, who stood breathing hard, trying to recollect the events that had just transpired. With an absence of words, little Jed ran out of the room, following in Logan's trail.

Sitting before the mirror in his bedroom, Logan watched his reflection mimic every breath he took. A red mark creased his cheek where Father Jed's hand made contact; a quiet bump upon the door brought acknowledgement that Jed had entered the room.

Logan's gaze shifted to his younger brother who stood small in the doorway. The blue-eyed boy rose from the bed and approached the dresser that held his clothes in purgatory. He began to unpack the articles, laying them out flat on his bed. Jed stepped further into the room, and stood behind his brother, eyeing every movement with a sullen disposition. Logan's hands stopped folding the shirt before him, and he turned around to face Jed. The boy's face was tear- streaked. Lunging forward, little Jed hugged

Logan, wrapping his arms tight around his brother's torso, gripping both hands behind the boy's back.

"I love you, Logan." Jed soothed, yet his words fumbled over waves of tears.

Logan said nothing, but his return hug meant all the same.

Clearing his vision, Jed pulled away and looked to Logan's eyes. "I want to go with you."

Logan shook his head, "Mother and Father will need your help around here, Jed."

Jed backed away toward the door, "No, Logan. I do not want to stay here anymore. Father has changed; I don't love him anymore."

"Don't you ever say that, Jed," Logan snapped.

"Logan, I am gonna fight, too!"

Logan sat down upon the bed. "You don't understand, Roo-"

"Yes I do. I want to do this with you. Someday I am going to die, and I do not want to die regretting the day you walked out of this house alone to fight. I am going to be right next to you through all of this," said the boy.

Logan smiled briefly, but the expression faded quickly.

"You can think all you want, but nothing will change. I am going with." Jed finished as he exited the room.

Logan remained seated on the edge of his bed, alone.

In the dining room, Jed gathered the dishes of the unfinished meal and tossed them down in the sink of the kitchen. He began to scrub at them vigorously by the time Logan came stumbling out of the bedroom.

Without any words, Logan walked over to the table and sat down quietly, studying the black sky through the shut window.

"You know sooner or later you are going to have to accept that I'm not a little boy anymore. I'm old enough to be able to fend for myself." Jed said, continuing to fiddle with the porcelain plates.

·

Logan turned his attention from the window and onto Jed. "I never said you weren't old enough, Jed, but what kind of brother would I be if I let you come along with me? I have no idea what life is like beyond this stretch of land. Hampton was the closest thing I knew, that *we* knew, of a life absent of farm work…and that is gone now."

Jed ignored the comment and began stacking the dishes atop one another beside the sink.

Logan glanced around at the darkened, empty room. "Ma and Pa go to bed?"

Jed shook his head, "Yeah."

"Does he hate me, Jed?" Logan asked veering off into thought.

"Does who hate you, Logan?"

The blue-eyed boy paused for a moment, and then shook away the feelings. "No one, I'm just rambling."

Jed finished stacking the plates and stood at the sink with his arms acting as supports for his weight against the counter. Out of the corner of his eye, he saw his brother walk over to the door of the porch and open it. Upon the wooden boards of the deck, remained the papers delivered by the Union officer.

Logan bent down and grasped the furled edges of the parchment. When he re-entered the home, he silently looked over the documents that held his fate.

"You're lucky ya know?" muttered Jed as soon as Logan sat down.

Late to respond, Logan asked, "How so?"

"You have your chance to run from here, to experience adventure. Me, it seems like maybe the world is plotting against me."

"Plotting against you?" Logan snickered at his brother's naivety, "Jed, how is the world plotting against you? You haven't been called to war!"

"No, but I haven't exactly been offered any other options that could lead to a life far from here."

Both boys sat in silence for a moment, until Jed spoke up, "I miss home, Logan. I miss Nathan, and Max, Aunty Sue. I miss running from Amelia when she used to bathe us. I miss feeling

136

like a kid; I miss feeling the security, like nothing could ever harm us when we were in that yard."

"Well it is gone," said Logan plainly.

Jed walked away from the sink and crossed over to the table, sitting opposite Logan; the seat Father Jed usually occupied.

"Can I read it?" Jed asked reaching his wet hand out toward the papers.

Logan nodded and turned the sheet over to his brother.

Jed studied the document for a while; he then set it face down on the table. "Are you scared?"

Logan nodded in admittance.

"Don't be, I'll be right there with you." Jed foretold.

Logan giggled, "Great, now I'm even more frightened."

"Easy!" Jed sneered.

"You sure you want to come with me?" Logan asked studying his brother.

"Absolutely, we have hardly ever done anything without each other, and the one time we did, you killed Moseley's dog."

"Killing a dog is a lot different than going to war, Roo."

"Even more reason for me to go with you."

Logan licked his lips in thought. "Alright, fine." He let his eyes fall upon the boy sitting before him whose face was solid and held the determination and vigor of a stone. "Promise me one thing though, Jed."

"Anything." the younger boy replied squaring up to Logan.

"No matter what happens, no matter where we go, we both come back home alive."

"I promise you."

Logan nodded, and then walked away from the table back to the bedroom where he climbed in his bed and laid awake until the rising sun brought a new day.

The sound of hooves upon the dirt path in front of the home brought Jed and Logan out of the security of the wooden walls. Both boys carried a small bindle, nothing more.

Squinting in the morning light, Logan scanned the wagon just beyond the porch where a lone Union soldier struggled to dismount the carriage.

"Last chance to stay home, Jed." said Logan.

"Nope, we are both coming back." the boy replied staring at the man walking toward them.

"Logan Hinkley?" the man asked, stopping a few feet from the porch stairs.

The man was rather tall and had an even build about him. His eyes were brown and his long beard the color of amber. Attached to his blue uniform were a few medals that dazzled in the morning sunlight. On his belt, the golden hilt of a saber shined bright, compared to the dull, black holster that held a revolver on the opposite hip.

"Yes, Sir," Logan stuttered.

"I'm Colonel Nehemiah Tavert. Who is this?" he asked looking at Jed.

"This here is my brother, Jed. He is coming, too."

Colonel Tavert rubbed his beard when he looked the boy up and down. "What is your age?"

Jed studied the colonel before responding, "I've heard of kids twice as young as me signing up. I can fight."

The colonel smirked, but let the smile dwindle until there was nothing. "I'm sure you can."

Logan stepped off the porch just as Tavert walked back toward the wagon. "Can he come?'

Colonel Tavert mounted the carriage and squinted back toward Jed and Logan. "Yes; if he clears his assessment. He will be a drummer."

Jed brushed past Logan toward the carriage, but stopped when he realized Logan was not following. The older boy stood staring at his feet until a brisk breeze turned his attention to the small porch.

"Father and Mother are still asleep, Logan." Jed cooed.

Logan's face remained sullen while scanning the wooden home.

Jed spoke up after a moment of silence, "Let's just go."

The blue-eyed boy walked away without a word and climbed into the carriage with his brother. With a snap of the reigns the wagon surged forward, off to a new world enveloped in war.

"There is still a chance we can return home…maybe the war is almost over." Jed tried to reassure Logan.

Neither of them spoke again until the outlines of buildings were seen sticking up from the relatively flat hillside that was the make-up of rural Pennsylvania.

The carriage that contained the two young boys and Colonel Tavert rolled up to the rundown town of Perryville. Reluctantly, Logan leaned out of the rickety, black carriage and stepped foot onto the narrow dirt road that ran through the center of the very small town. Perryville had a total of three stores, all selling the same goods: bread, various crops, and a few articles of generic clothing that were almost always guaranteed to be too large for any person to wear comfortably. Across from the row of shops rested an old wooden structure; above the entrance hung a rotting sign that read, *Dr. Aarons, Physician*, in bold white print.

Logan became clairvoyant to the fact that his life, and the life of his brother were about to change dramatically, and it all started in the crummy town of Perryville.

"Get to stepping boys, we have a quota to fill." edged Colonel Tavert pushing the boys forward to the shack. The Colonel walked into the decaying structure to call for Dr. Aarons, leaving the two boys outside on the front porch of the office.

"Logan, what if we don't pass this test?" questioned the anxious Jed.

"I'm more worried what will happen if we do. If we are both healthy, it will be straight to the front lines with us."

"Well either way, I'm sticking with you, Logan." Jed stated.

Logan's heart warmed at the comment. It made him feel secure that his brother was going to be the one constant in his life as everything else changed rapidly.

Peeking in to the office, Logan saw that Colonel Tavert was still waiting for the doctor to show himself. In a hurried fashion, the boy reached into his pocket and withdrew a small rag that he cupped carefully in his hand.

"What the heck is that?" asked Jed drawing back in surprise.

"Hush up, Jed, and listen..." Logan said as he unraveled the balled up rag. The blue-eyed boy held his cupped hand out to his brother presenting a tiny collection of blueberries, which lay nestled in his palm, carefully caressed by the surrounding cloth.

"I'm not hungry, Logan..." Jed announced at the sight.

"No Jed, take a few and crush 'em up real nice so that they make a paste, then smear it on your arms and face..."

Jed watched in mass confusion as his brother pressed the bluish paste onto his skin. "Uh, Logan, I don't get it..."

"Hurry Jed, just do it before Tavert comes back to get us!"

Jed obeyed and dipped his fingers into the blue muck and slapped it onto his forearm. The berries felt cold and slimy on his warm, dry skin. The smell from the paste was refreshing and it made both boys' stomachs churn as the odor brought thoughts of their mother's pie that was prepared every summer as the seasons turned.

Logan looked Jed up and down to make sure he was completely covered. "Okay good. Now, when they ask us what is wrong, we say that we ate somethin' bad and we feel sick. Be sure to cough a lot, too!"

The Union colonel, decked out in his medals, walked out into the sun from the building and motioned for the boys to follow him. Before he walked back inside, the officer spun around on his heels and eyed the boys with a harsh look of bewilderment. Suspiciously, he pushed the brothers inside where Dr. Aarons was waiting behind a solid, cherry-wood counter.

"Boys, I am Dr. Aarons, please wait in the next room while I fetch my tools."

Logan and Jed followed orders and walked the paces into the neighboring room, which was barren and completely absent of any color, holding only one chair, and a small table. The room was dark and damp, and the smell brought on past memories for Logan,

140

who matched the odor to the old red barn that stood beside their house back in Virginia.

Moments later, the doctor entered the room with a bag of instruments. The man was tall for his age, standing about five and a half feet. His hair was almost completely white with the exception of two gray patches on his sideburns.

"My heavens, what is wrong with the color of your skin?!" he asked, laying eyes on the blue-boys.

"We feel very ill, Sir." Logan said whilst coughing.

"…Might I note that they were perfectly fine on the way over here, doctor?" Colonel Tavert stepped in.

The elderly physician ignored the colonel and studied Logan's arm with a large magnifying glass, which he pulled from his leather bag. "It seems as though you have the symptoms of Diphtheria…blue skin, cough, warm to the touch, possibly on account of a fever…" the doctor mumbled to himself.

"Doc, please…" the Colonel demanded growing tired of the wait.

"…But the smell…" the white-haired man paused.

Jed shot a gaze up at Logan, who lowered his head in defeat. Doctor Aarons ran his finger across the top of Logan's arm and sniffed it carefully. "Huh…" he sighed. Slowly, the man stuck his tongue out and licked the blue muck off of his fingertips. "Blueberry…"

"I told you they were fine, doctor!" the colonel shouted.

"Nice try, boys!" laughed Dr. Aarons. "Now, remove your shirts, and strip down to your drawers.

Logan and Jed both shot befuddled looks at each other.

"Pardon me, Sir?" Logan stuttered.

"I have to run a full body exam to see if you are fit for the rigors of Military combat, Son; now both of you strip."

Jed gulped as his face reddened. Dropping his gaze to the floor, he slowly unbuttoned his white shirt, mimicking Logan. A feeling of dehumanization flushed through to two of them; they felt helpless and embarrassed as a complete stranger physically assessed them against their will.

As their attire fell to the floor, settling at their feet, both boys stood nervously, their gazes averted away from the doctor who moved in close, pressing the cold head of a stethoscope to each of their chests.

"Breathe," he ordered.

Their pride fleeting, both Logan and Jed obeyed, inhaling one after the other.

As the doctor continued his assessment, testing the boys' reflexes, Colonel Tavert unraveled the conscription documents for both children that awaited the signature from Dr. Aarons. He watched as the two young children stood shivering half-naked in the dark, chilly room, their innocent eyes wide with the look of fear as they took in the strange experience.

The physician stood up and removed his glasses from the bridge of his nose. "Well, they are both perfectly healthy. You have the papers?"

The colonel handed over the documents to the man who dipped a long pen into a nearby inkwell. Speedily, he scribbled his signature onto the parchment, and returned them to the Union officer.

"Good luck, boys." spoke the doctor in a glum tone. Saluting the colonel, he then wheeled around and exited the room, leaving the group in peace.

"Go on, get dressed. Here are your papers…" Colonel Tavert reached his hand out to Logan, who cautiously took the documents.

"You trust us with these?" Logan asked puzzled by the colonel's action.

Hesitating, the officer nodded slowly and bit his lower lip, then walked toward the door, where he stopped briefly, "Report to Camp Hamilton by 0700 tomorrow…that's seven a.m." He then left the room, a look of pity upon his face, where he left the boys with their thoughts.

When the two young boys arrived at camp with only their knapsacks slung over their shoulders, they immediately felt lost; displaced; all around them men a good two years older than them stood in line as they awaited orders. Logan was somewhat more relaxed then Jed, due to the fact that he was seventeen, whilst Jed was only fourteen. However, there was still a tingling of apprehension in his gut as the reality of where he was settled in.

The sky above them showed no remorse as a light rain started to pick up into a heavy drizzle. The clouds were a faint gray, and the horizon yielded a blackened atmosphere; flocks of birds that once nested in the trees surrounding the barbed fence of the camp took flight, and turned their tails to the wind fleeing the brewing storm. Logan desperately wished he was those birds, flying away from the call of war, just like the birds from nature's fiery offensive.

Logan looked down at Jed whose green eyes were wide with consternation. The camp was no place for children, but then again neither was war. A myriad of blue uniforms walked around the camp, their human occupants buzzing around on constant alert. White tents whose linen linings were bleached like a dove's tail were scattered all over the camp's dirt grounds. Small tables made of pine wood were set up at random points over the camp, a long line of normal clothed people stretching behind them, their formations twisting like a snake. Each table held two men, one seated with an ink pen marking the papers that foretold the future soldier's information, and one standing beside the stamp-man issuing a pair of boots. Logan and Jed watched as one person not much older than either of them walked through the line. The process was like a well oiled machine; after the stamping and boot hand-out, the soldier moved down a long line of blue-clad men, all of whom issued the recruit either clothing or a weapon. Logan took a deep breath and looked to his brother.

"Jed, you know you do not have to go through with this. You weren't drafted. I was." In a way, Logan meant what he said, however despite saying it; he hoped his brother would stay. Taking the step into a new world without him would have been incredibly hard, and desertion probably would have been Logan's means of escaping.

Jed shook his head in defiance, on his face remained the same expression of trepidation. "I am staying, Logan, I'm not leaving you."

Logan sucked on his lower lip as he mustered the courage to take the steps from a free American boy to a Union soldier,

143

defending the freedom that he once enjoyed.

"Let's do this, Jed…"

Both boys walked up into the long twisting line that stretched the length of the camp. Once their papers were stamped, they would become nothing more than another name on the list of soldiers from every state in the crumbling Union; a thought that did not seem very heroic or romanticized like it was in the books that both boys read, which depicted brave knights clad in silver armor fighting off the ferocious dragons that threatened the sanctity of the fictional kingdoms in which they served.

As hard as Jed tried, he could not relate the present situation to that of the stories; he would rather face ten-thousand dragons, than have to face one-thousand bayonets.

"Next!" a stern voice seated at the pine table called out; the voice was as unemotional as anything Logan had ever heard.

The frightened teen saw that the space in front of him that had once held a foreign body was empty, leaving a good five feet between him and the officer behind the desk.

"Name?" snapped the officer as Logan approached the bench, Jed stood right beside him. Both boys looked at each other with open mouths, not sure why the officer was being so blunt.

"Uh, I'm Logan…Hinkley, and this is-" Logan started to speak, but was interrupted by the uniformed man.

"…One at a time!"

Jed swallowed hard, starting to regret his decision on coming.

"Your papers." demanded the man.

Logan held out his shaking hand, which clenched the white draft form that was soggy from the rain falling from above; they were the tears of God, who watched the innocence of his children fade with every passing minute. In the back of Logan's mind he could hear his father's voice saying *be brave, no matter how frightening things may seem…be brave.* The words spurred confidence in the boy. He threw his shoulders behind him and erected his back.

"We're from Hampton, Sir, initially…we moved," announced the courage-stricken teen. Yet, whatever his face showed, his heart strings were torn as he thought about the day they fled Virginia. It was a day that would forever numb his mind,

144

and a day that would forever plague his childhood.

"I see that. How tall are you?" questioned the uniformed officer as he examined the paper.

"I'm just about five-foot-five, Sir."

"Weight?" asked the officer.

"One-hundred and fifteen, Sir." swallowed Logan.

The officer signed off on Logan's sheet, the fresh ink bled off of the drenched parchment.

"Move along." ordered the soldier, the second officer handed the boy a pair of boots.

"What if they don't fit, Sir?" asked Logan in a curious, child-like tone.

"Then you go barefoot," replied the man coldly.

Logan looked back as he slowly walked down the line toward the rest of the soldiers handing out equipment. He felt insecure about leaving Jed behind, even if it was only by a few steps.

With his new equipment in hand, Logan walked to his assigned barracks. Jed was not far behind; however he was slow to move due to the drowning weight of his large snare drum. Peering over the camp, Logan grew increasingly amazed at the number of men that were contained within the defensive walls; rats in a cage.

"Look at them all, Jed." Logan whispered upon his brother's arrival by his side.

"Think any of them are nice?" Jed asked hopeful.

Logan snickered at the remark. "We are in the military now, Jed. Somethin' tells me that *nice* ain't on the agenda."

"At least we will have company and won't be shut out." Jed murmured.

Even with all the recruits that surrounded them, hundreds of men from all over the Star- Spangled Banner, Jed and Logan felt more alone and forgotten than ever, whether they admitted it or not.

"Where are you sleeping?" Jed asked.

"Here. My bunk is inside, you?"

"I'm across camp with the other drummer boys."

The two stood without speaking for a moment.

"I'll see ya around then I guess…" Jed sighed.

Logan nodded and watched as his brother disappeared in the crowd of soldiers that jogged by.

"Hey, you are new?" cried a disembodied voice.

Logan scanned the area and found a man with a crooked smile staring at him. "Yeah," Logan replied.

The man approached the boy and walked a circle around him. "The name is Killian; Killian Diggs O' Sullivan."

"Nice name." Logan said.

"You getting smart with me are ya, little one?" Killian snapped.

"No, I'm just saying."

"Your accent…you are southern?" sneered Killian.

"Yeah, I was born in Virginia."

Killian clapped his hands and tried to draw a crowd, "Virginia-boy, look ore' here lads, a Reb in our camp!"

Logan reddened as a feeling of raw anger flushed through him.

A few nearby soldiers laughed and joined in on the mockery.

"You are Irish?" Logan asked, going on the offensive.

Killian's laughing subsided some, and he turned once more to face the boy. "Aye, what have you?"

"You are from New York?" continued Logan.

"Aye." the creases in Killian's cheeks faded as his tone became more serious.

"Tell me, how does it feel to be a slave to the native-born out there? Feel good?"

Killian grabbed Logan by the throat. "I swear, lad, I'll strangle-"

"You will release him or face serious reprimands!"

Killian turned to find a horse whip an inch from his nose; holding the whip was Colonel Tavert. "Release him!"

Killian's grip diminished, leaving Logan to rub his throat while gasping for air.

"Leave!" thundered Tavert.

Killian scampered off glaring at Tavert and Logan; he raised a thick finger, "Watch yourself, Virginia."

"Are you okay?" asked Colonel Tavert.

"I'm fine." Logan coughed.

"Hurry along to your barracks. Tomorrow will be a rough day."

Logan obeyed, leaving Tavert to stand his ground.

෨෧

Maxwell made his way down the old dirt road that once bore the trails of his family as they departed. He could not help but think how differently the surrounding area looked. Trees that once towered the flowing landscape were no longer present, and in their place, patches of thick green grass cut segments in the alfalfa, giving the area more of an open feel.

As the small boy trekked onward, kicking rocks that lie in his path, he thought about the glory in fighting for a cause his father, and so many others, believed so strongly in. Deep down, he knew little of why men were fighting; however, he knew enough to know that they were willing to die for the cause. That very thought did not sit well with him. He was not sure if he was willing to give up his life for a war he knew little of, yet the glory in fighting and dying in battle seemed like it would bring everlasting fame, and thus please his father; something he longed to do even after their disagreements.

Peering out over the fields, Max searched for some sign of the Confederate camp. He had been told that it was no less than two miles from his home, and sure enough, he could see plumes of smoke reaching high into the sky from the fires of the soldiers. Enthralled by the sight, the boy skipped his way down the path and darted through the fields, laughing as he pictured Jed running beside him. For a moment, he opened his mouth to call to his

147

cousin, but stopped himself remembering that those days were gone. Max halted to find his bearings and let his mind catch back up with reality. Only the chirping of crickets was heard over the distant call of men shouting. Readjusting his path, the boy moved on.

Maxwell arrived at a gate guarded by a few soldiers. Both seemed to be lean, and evenly built. Both had on minimal gear, only the necessary canteen, rifle, and munitions were secured to their torso. As the boy approached, both men perked up and crossed their rifles, halting the dusty-haired boy's path.

"You lost, littlen?" asked one soldier with buckteeth.

"No."

"Then what brings you here?" wondered the other soldier. This one was more appealing to the eye.

"I'm here to fight. I got my own gear, and I can fend for myself." Maxwell answered, standing tall between the two men.

The two soldiers examined the boy.

"He seems good to me." the bucktoothed one spat out.

"In ya go, Boy."

The gate opened, and Maxwell hobbled inside the perimeter fencing. The Confederate camp was a small place. Scattered inside the confines of a wobbly horse fence, three fire pits were encircled by men of all ages and sizes. All were talking to each other about some nonsense event that contained no relevance to the war.

"Looks like we have a newcomer!" shouted a finely dressed man smoking a porcelain pipe.

Maxwell nodded, and tipped his hat. "My name is Maxwell Hinkley. I'm from the farm a few miles from here."

The man lit his pipe. "And what brings you to the warfront, Maxwell?"

"I wanna fight."

The gaggle of men smiled at the youth's determination.

"Well you have come to the right place, Maxwell. Make yourself at home. Everyone is friendly."

Maxwell shuffled his way through the camp, searching for an empty spot beside the fiery warmth. No one acknowledged his presence after the man with the pipe dismissed him to the camp crowd; he felt unwelcome. Dragging his equipment, the boy scooted off to the far corner of the campground and made himself a cozy nook with his blankets. He stared at the sky, which darkened by the minute, listening to the men who sat a few yards away argue about an ensuing card game.

As the thoughts of his brother, Nathan, became ever more haunting, Maxwell started to dream. He dreamt of himself and his role model sitting in the grassy fields talking about anything and everything that came to mind. The two would share stories of their adventures with their cousins, and recollect on times when they would play tricks on their mother. Ever since Nathan had passed, things were just not the same. The boy's father did not listen like Nathan had, nor did he tuck Maxwell in at night with love and comforting words, telling him stories. The brown-haired child felt alone...he felt like a castaway.

Peering around the camp, Maxwell noticed that most of the soldiers were sleeping, and the ones who were not, were drinking. Carefully, he uncovered himself and slipped on his boots. He danced his way around the flames that swelled in the fire pits so he did not cast a shadow over the dimly lit camp. Once out of the light, the boy ran over to the small gate that guarded the entrance; with no sign of the guards in sight, he slipped through its wooden restraints out into the surrounding night.

About an hour later, the child had made his way to his destination. Before him was his home; the windows were black and the doors shut. The wooden structure seemed to hide in the back of the scenery. The air smelt of smoke from the house's chimney; a malodorous stench left to sway in the nightly breeze. The boy took in a deep breath as he walked onto the wet grass that covered the slopes surrounding the home. Above the quiescent countryside, the moon was absent. The silver beams that normally radiated a shimmering wonder over the dormant land ceased to be. Timidly, he approached the two lonely headstones of his mother and brother that seemed dwarfed by the vast, open fields around them. The image of the small child standing before a veil of death seemed dreamlike, and unreal.

Sharply, Maxwell took in a shaky breath as he tried to push the images of the fateful day out of his mind. With a groan, the adolescent boy sat down on his rear, the wet grass seeped through his cotton pants. There, he rested; letting the words he longed to say for years to his brother, but never had the chance to, fill his mind.

"Hi, Nate…" he said clearing his throat. "It has been rough without you…"

The child grew quiet as if anticipating a reply. In his mind he could see his brother sitting before him, the deceased child's golden face and smile peering right into his soul; however the reality was much less glamorous.

"Tell Mother I said hi…" Plucking a blade of grass anxiously, Maxwell spoke again, "…Nathan, am I a bad brother? When you died, I did not cry, I did not shed a tear. Instead, I helped shower dirt on your body." Small tears began to streak the boy's face, which was hidden by the mask of night. "If I could relive that day, just get that one day back, I would spend it all with you. I would never leave your side, and I would stand right there with you when you faced Logan…and who knows, maybe that bullet would hit me." Rubbing his nose with his sleeve, Maxwell reached a hand out and rubbed the gritty headstone that marked Nathan's body. The touch of the stone was cold and rough, the sensation sent shivers down the boy's arm. Calming down, the child continued, "Nathan, should I fight? Is it worth it? There are nights when I consider walking out into the field of battle and letting the hot lead hit me so that I can be with you and Mother, again. Life is not the same anymore…it feels like death." Staring at the gray rock before him, Maxwell gave his ultimatum, "Just give me a sign…"

Maxwell drew his hand back. In that moment, an oil lamp's faint glow filled the porch of the house.

"Papa, someone is in the field!" shouted the shrill voice of Abigail.

Maxwell spun around on his feet and waited. He saw the tall, scruffy outline of his father walk from the doorway of the house, and onto the porch. Maxwell thought for a moment, wondering if he should announce his presence, but chose otherwise. He turned to the gravestone and grasped the photograph of his family, taken the day William left; its corner was buried in the dirt. As quietly as he had slipped onto the property, the child disappeared into the dead of night.

႟

"Good morning, recruits! Today you will learn how to shoot, drill, and behave as a soldier in the United States Army," yelled a large infantry captain dressed in a dark blue uniform.

Sprawled out in an awkward line, the recruits, including Logan and Jed, sleepily stood at attention dressed in their battle fatigues.

"First thing is first, realize that you are no longer the civilians you once were. Realize that you do not have the freedoms you once enjoyed. You are now the property of the United States Government; an investment. Should you be injured in combat, you will receive reparations, and be granted two months leave…" the captain paced in front of the pitiful bunch, his gloved hands gripped the hilt of his saber that dangled gracefully from his leather belt.

The morning air that filled the camp was laced with dust, making the visibility very poor. Above the arid scene, the sky was bright and clear; not a cloud present, nor a bird fluttering. The rows of fresh soldiers, who had been in attendance during the processing phase, were now scattered throughout the camp, filling every corner visible. Most spent the time either jogging the perimeter of the fence line, or learning how to properly drill with their weapons.

"…Now the fun part," laughed the captain, who had yet to introduce himself, "The rules and regulations that you will abide by, not only in this camp, but in your theater of operation. Rule number one: you will keep yourself presentable at all times. Failure to remain clean-shaven, or your uniform properly pressed, will result in punishment. Here, that means that you will receive three days trench-duty, where you will dig until I decide that you can quit for the day…"

Jed smirked at the clean shaven part, for he had never even touched a razor, nor did he have reason to; Logan had not even grown his first few facial hairs, much less, enough to deem shaving necessary.

"Rule number two…" the captain continued, "You will address me, and every officer in this camp by either their rank, or as sir. Is that clear?"

The camp roared with mixed answers, some resulting with sir, the others with captain.

"Leave it at *sir,* for now. Rule number three and I stress this rule the most…" the captain stopped pacing and stood directly in front of the group of recruits. He looked down the line at each man, staring right into his soul. "Should anyone decide that they want a break, and leave this regiment before their time of service is up, you will be tried in a federal court of law. Should you think that the punishment is worth the risk of desertion, and you still try to escape, I may skip the whole trial part, and have you hanged in front of the camp; do I make myself clear?"

An eerie silence fell upon the crowd, as each face grew white with fear. Jed looked up at Logan, who stood perfectly still…motionless, however, the boy's hand was shaking sporadically with disquietude.

"Good." the captain concluded. "Grab your rifles, and fall in."

In a mad dash, the recruits ran back toward the barracks where their rifles stood like tepees; six rifles to a stack, each with the bayonet fixed, serving as a focal point for one another, helping to support the weight of each rifle.

"Logan, he wasn't serious, was he?" Jed asked swallowing hard.

Logan ignored his brother and fell in line, leaving the child back by the white wall of the barracks, his snare drum resting on the ground before him.

"Jerk," mumbled Jed under his breath.

After drill, Jed did not see Logan again until that night; they sat around a large wooden table filled with plates of food. Nothing like Amelia used to cook. The meat was dry, the vegetables practically raw, and the bread was so stale that when one touched its hard surface it flaked into a million pieces.

Conversations were so rare during the meal that speaking to one another seemed toxic. However, despite his hunger, Jed attempted to contact Logan.

"Hey…" he whispered.

"Hey, Jed," Logan replied with a mouthful of peas.

"How was drill?" asked the green-eyed boy.

Logan shrugged and shoved another spoonful of the pale green vegetables in to his mouth.

"Check this out!" Jed exhumed. He stood from the bench and pulled a drumstick out of his belt loop. Biting his lower lip, he concentrated on the stick, balancing it between his middle and forefinger. Rotating his hand in a swirling motion, the stick spun like a windmill, perfectly, for three rotations. "Neat, huh?" asked the boy through a huge smile.

Logan nodded in silence. Tossing the stick on the floor, Jed sat back down and ran his hands through his hair. "You are always so moody-"

Jed's sentence was cut short when a blast of yellow light filled the room. Chunks of cinderblocks hurled through the air like dust in a sandstorm. Trapped under the remnants of burning wood from the rafters, Jed cried out in terror. All around him, the men who sat at his table were no longer present, including Logan. Whistles began to scream in the night air, giving a voice to the stars that shined down through the open hole in the building.

"Pull them out gently!" shouted one of the rescuers to his crew of men in uniform; the stripes of a lieutenant's rank sewn on the sleeve of jacket shot through the wreckage and grasped Jed's collar. "Are you hurt, Boy?" questioned the man tensely as he examined Jed's dust-covered body.

"No, I'm fine! What happened?" he cried.

"Something horribly wrong," the man said; his face was grave.

One by one, the men dug out the soldiers from Jed's table. Once examined, they rested on the ground outside of the rubble.

Colonel Tavert stood watching as the final men were pulled out of the building.

"Sir!" the lieutenant shouted as he approached the colonel. "We have recovered them all, except one."

"Who," Tavert snapped.

"His name was Carl Topp. He was a private under your command."

Tavert did not reply. He looked to the ground when he ordered three more men to help with the cleanup of the destruction.

"What happened?" Jed lashed out in fear.

"A drill went wrong!" Tavert roared. "We called for an artillery strike to hit outside of camp. We wanted to see how everyone would respond to a surprise attack. In the field, the enemy doesn't sleep. They are always thinking of ways to kill you when you are least prepared. We over shot our mark...and hit camp."

No one spoke. All eyes drifted to the crushed body of Carl Topp, as the men pulled him from the wreckage.

"You are all dismissed. If you feel strange or sick, report to the field doctor." Tavert waved his hand and each soldier, including Jed and Logan, walked to their respected barracks, leaving Carl Topp and the destroyed mess hall to sleep forever in the dark of night.

Unable to succumb to exhaustion while tucked down in the thin sheets of his cot, Logan began to reflect. He tried to remember a moment in his life after William left that was not filled with the slightest tinge of depression.

Listening to the snoring and coughing of sleeping men all around him, the boy snaked his hand out from underneath the seclusion of the blanket, and felt around the end table just beside

154

him. He grasped the crumpled edges of a letter; one addressed to him from William, and drew it close to his face after striking a match to illuminate the secrets written.

With wet eyes, Logan scanned the page, allowing each word to take on William's slight accent.

Dear Logan,

In my absence, please take care of the home. The crops will need tending shortly I would imagine, and the younger boys will need to learn the quickest way to harvest 'em. I trust you remember, and have grown wise enough to instruct them. Pa will need comforting from time to time. I feel my departing has left him a sore spot.

As for me, life has not changed much. While writing this, I am lying just outside of Vicksburg, Mississippi. I have not seen action yet, for every time my ship is called to battle we arrive too late, just missing the engagement by a few moments. I consider myself lucky. The smell of death is one nobody can forget. You are blessed to never have to endure such a sense. Please give my love to little Jed, and Mother as well. Give Nathan and Maxwell a hug for me, and most of all, let Pa know I am doing well. I will write often, and I wish to hear back in return.

Loving unconditionally,

William

Logan read the note once more before crumpling into a ball and tossing it across the small, musty room where it hit the wall with a silent impact. He sat up from his prior position and ran his hands through his hair, breathing in a stuttered fashion as he tried to contain his tears.

"Must have been a bad note." called a stranger's voice from the darkness.

"No." Logan objected scanning the blackness for a sign of the illusive perceiver.

"Then why crumple it? And why the tears?" the voice asked.

Logan wiped his eyes and took a few deep breaths as he regained a sense of self-possession. "I'm not crying. You wouldn't understand."

No reply came forth. In the bed across from him, a figure sat up. "Then what is the problem?"

Logan looked down and picked at his finger. "I miss him."

"That is very vague, kid."

"My brother; my older one," answered the blue-eyed boy.

"Is he on vacation or something?"

"No, he's in the west fighting."

The figure stood up and crossed to a window beside Logan's bed and opened it, allowing the night breeze to prance around the room freely. "Many families are fighting each other, don't feel so bad."

Logan studied the black outline of the man before speaking. "We fight for the same side."

"Good." the mysterious stranger fired right back.

Logan kicked his feet out of the covers, and let them hang over the side of the bed as he shifted his body to take in some of the breeze rolling through the window. "Why are you talking to me?" he asked.

"Call me lonely," answered the man with a callus tone.

Logan carefully undid the top three buttons on his shirt and removed it, tossing it to the floor. Sweat shimmered on his skin, illuminated by the moonlight. "What is your story?"

"I haven't one," said the man.

"What is your name?" Logan asked.

The stranger did not reply for a moment or two, nor did he look upon Logan. His gaze remained fixed on the desolate camp outside. Growing impatient, Logan swung around on his bed and laid back down, watching the ceiling above.

"Are you scared to fight, kid?" the stranger asked breaking the subject flow.

Logan played with his fingers once more, thinking. "Yes." he finally replied.

"Don't be," the strange man said.

"That is what my father said." Logan admitted with strains of irritancy.

"War hasn't changed; for thousands of years the principles have remained the same: to slaughter. The only thing that has changed is Man's talent in discovering ways in which to kill…if you dig deep enough, you'll find that the reasons we are here today, are the same as battles fought hundreds, thousands of years prior."

"So what does that mean?" Logan asked.

"It means you aren't walking in to anything new. Simply put, people will try to kill you; all you have to do is kill them first." concluded the stranger walking back to his cot. "The name is Mitchell; I usually prefer to keep that to myself.

The blue-eyed boy watched the outline of Mitchell as he sank down in the sheets of his bed. The window beside Logan remained open, letting the moaning wind carve its way through the room. The sleeping men around the boy shifted in their sleep, attempting to take refuge from nature's breath.

"Nathan!" Logan awoke screaming.

The white walls of the barracks were the only objects in the room that stared at the boy. Dripping with sweat, Logan tried to steady his racing heart. He glanced down and rubbed his wrist, which ached from the nightmarish grip of Nathan's dead hand.

The other men of the company tossed in their sleep, and it was not until the drums sounded the morning call that they sat up and rubbed the weariness from their eyes. Logan kicked the wool covers off of his body and slipped out of bed, planting his feet firmly on the floor. He leaned forward and rested his elbows on his knees, letting his hands caress his sweaty hair.

157

"Mornin' boys!" one of the soldiers shouted while dancing up and down the row of cots, wearing nothing but his drawers. "Who's a ready to do some marchin'?"

"That's today?" asked another soldier whose eyes were set really close to his nose.

"Darn right; ten miles to the maneuvering field, and ten back!"

The close-eyed soldier shook his head with a cocky smirk, "You are far too excited my friend. I will surely make the march, but I don't think you will."

Logan watched as the soldiers started to dress themselves in their blue uniforms.

The half-naked man fired back, "We'll see about that Cameron.

A man sitting beside Cameron spoke up. "Why are we headed to the maneuvering field?"

"I heard them officers speakin' about field drills with the artillery units."

"Haven't we had enough artillery drills? For cryin' out loud, we've already lost a man." Cameron intervened.

"Sounds like you is scared, Cameron." the half-naked man giggled.

"I'm not scared."

"What time is the drill?" asked the soldier beside Cameron.

"Not for an hour or so. Jarret Dempsey over in the Guard unit is givin' haircuts to anyone who wants one fo' free."

Logan tugged on his bangs, pondering the idea. "I'll take one."

"Take one what?" Jed asked as he entered the barracks, his drum dangling from his neck.

"Nothing, Jed, just a haircut." answered Logan

Jed approached Logan and tossed his drum down, however he continued to grip his drumsticks. "I'll get one, too."

Logan stood up from the bed and started to dress himself in his uniform. "Why?" he asked. "Your hair is already short."

"So, I could use a trimming. If Mother were here I'm sure she'd agree."

Logan shook his head as Jed revealed a cheeky grin. "Where were you?"

Jed clicked his drumsticks together. "Mornin' call."

"You hear about the maneuver drill after the march?" Logan asked.

Jed's face lit up. "No! I'm excited!"

"How come, it is dangerous, and you'll be up in the front banging on your drum."

"That is why I'm excited, my first command!"

Logan laughed, "Not quite, Jed."

Once dressed, both boys followed the man, who was previously half-naked, over to where Jarret Dempsey and half a dozen other men sat around outside, their hair cut flat and neat.

"Got some more for ya, Jarret."

Jarret looked up from clipping a final clump of hair from a fellow soldier's head, "Great, sit on down, Son."

Logan walked over to the wooden stool in front of Jarret and sat down.

"How would you like it cut?" Jarret asked, immediately receiving a round of laughs from the other men.

"I'm assuming there is only one choice?" Logan asked nervously feeling the attention of the group on him.

"Just hold still, kid. It won't take long."

Logan sat in silence as locks of his dark blond hair fell to the ground. The slicing of the scissors around his ears forced him wince as the cold steel touched his skin.

Snip after snip, sections of the boy's lengthy hair fell to the ground where it met the long clippings of the grass.

"And that should do it!" Jarret said running his hand through Logan's scalp, removing the leftover follicles.

Jed handed his brother a mirror. Gazing at his reflection, Logan thought he looked even more like William. The top of his head was cut perfectly even, and left slightly longer than the hair along the sides and back.

"What do you think?" Jarret asked in excitement.

"I like it. I feel…lighter." Logan replied.

The group laughed, and Jed replaced Logan on the stool.

Clean cut, and dressed sharp in their clean blue uniforms, the boys and men of the company grabbed their gear and lined up in front of the old barracks. Jed stood just in front of the line of soldiers, his drum suspended around his neck by a strap. Colonel Tavert watched the men from the comfort of a gaming table, while the captain gave the order to start the march.

The company rolled out of the gates of camp, down the dirt roads headed to the open fields, following in rhythm to the snap of the snare drum.

After a few hundred feet, the captain rode his horse up alongside Jed, and ordered him to fall in to formation with the others.

"Yes, Sir," Jed nodded, tucking his drumsticks into his waistband. The boy took off down the line of men who continued marching forward past him. While searching for Logan amongst the crowd of monotonous blue, Jed lost his footing and slipped down off of the raised road and into a ditch on the side. A few of the passing soldiers chuckled and shook their heads.

Determined to bring redemption before being marked a klutz, Jed stood up and attempted to conquer the rise to the road, however, upon digging his foot in the dirt to climb, a stinging pain severed his muscle control, causing him to collapse back down in the ditch, moaning in agony. The boy rolled his pant leg up to examine his ankle. A purple swollen knot had formed around the top of his bony foot. Desperate for help, the boy looked around at the marching column, pleading to be lifted from the ditch.

The final few men at the tail end of the column noticed the boy, and slid down to help.

"My ankle, it hurts!" Jed whined.

"You probably sprained it," one of the soldiers said while pulling Jed out.

"What should I do?" Jed asked as the soldiers hurried off to catch up with the marching soldiers.

"Better hurry to catch up!"

When the dust cloud settled, Jed was left alone on the desolate trail, in the footprints of his so called brothers-in-arms.

Despite the pain in his throbbing foot, he tied the laces on his boot as tight as possible, almost cutting off the circulation in his aching extremity. After a moment of rest, the pain subsided a little. Forgetting the intensity of his injury, he took a step carelessly, and immediately a surge of throbbing pain shot through his left leg, causing him to lash out with a tearful sob. Hoping for some help, the child looked around, yet no one had heard his cry. In aberration, Jed took another step, afraid of what his consequence would be if he waited any longer as the group trotted along up ahead, turning into small dots on the horizon. In a careful, yet hurried motion, Jed touched the ground with his toes and waited for the pain to reawaken in his foot. When the numbing sensation was felt again, he realized he would have to fight through the agony.

By the time the injured boy reached his brother in the line of men, he could no longer feel his foot. Limping without intention, another uncomfortable feeling began to arise as the weight of his gear was becoming unsettling and increasingly annoying.

Panting as droplets of sweat fell from his brow, Jed asked, "Why do we have to carry so much gear?"

Marching along the side of the column, a slim boy who appeared slightly older than Logan answered the lingering question. "When you walk amongst giants, you best be prepared to get squashed."

Jed squinted in confusion, trying to decipher the words. "What does giants have to do with carrying gear?"

Logan shook his head at his brother's lack of knowledge. "He means when you are going to war, you better be ready for anything."

"I get it!" Jed shouted as his face lit up.

The older boy turned around and continued to march backwards as he held out a hand toward Logan. The boy's face was smeared with freckles and his eyes reflected a hazy brown color, ignited by his reddish locks underneath a dark blue Kepi-hat. "The name's Henry. Henry Woodson."

"I'm Logan Hinkley, and this here is my brother, Jed…unfortunately." Logan said laughing at his brother's expense.

"Nice to meet you two, you from around here?" asked Henry.

Jed shook his head in a negative response, but corrected himself when he realized that his days in Virginia were that of the past. "Yes, we are."

"I'm from New York. I moved here when the war broke out." Henry said, trying to keep a low whisper so the officers did not hear him speak.

"What made you move?" Logan asked.

"I wanted to escape the city. My friends and family stayed behind, but something inside me forced me to leave. I am thankful I did. It is pretty country here."

Jed glanced around, marveling at the landscape. The way the clouds melted into the rolling hillside ignited a vibrant juxtaposition that forced the blades of grass atop the earth to stand out strong and clear amongst the pink sky.

"You fellas hear about the orders?" Henry asked, switching the subject.

"What orders?" Logan questioned.

Henry chuckled, "I guess you haven't then. After the march we are heading straight northwest to a small town called Craysville. You ever hear of it?"

Both Logan and Jed shook their heads.

"It's nothing special; dirty little place. We are to check the town for any Rebel spies. Craysville is notorious for its Southern sympathy. Caleb Burnett from 4th Calvary says he overheard command saying they expect an attack on Northern soil by the Army of Northern Virginia. Remnants of Lee's III Corps are thought to be heading this way. Word has it if they are to stop anywhere to rest, it'd be Craysville."

"So, we are guaranteed action?" asked Logan nervously.

Henry shook his head, "Not necessarily. Intelligence could be wrong, but I wouldn't doubt any word of it."

"So, you don't know?" Jed asked reiterating.

"I mean don't believe it or disbelieve it. Just go with the flow."

Just as Henry finished speaking, the column of soldiers stopped.

"Break into line formation! Drummers sound the call!" shouted the captain from atop his steed. In a wild, yet controlled break of formation, the troops conjoined into a long line, two men deep. Jed made his way to the front of the line, sounding the battle call on his drum. When he stopped, the stretch of blue reached from the hills a solid two hundred yards to the right, and another fifty yards to the left where it ceased, the last man in line hidden under a thicket of trees. Each soldier held his rifle taught against his right soldier; the butt-plates of their rifles dug into their hands, causing them to shift the dead weight to relieve the growing soreness.

"Where is the artillery?" Logan asked quietly to Henry, who still stood by his side.

"Forward, march!" cried the captain. The rattle of the war drums continued and the men stepped forward in unison; left foot, followed by right. Just then, the deafening thump of cannon fire cracked through the tapping of the drums; a loud hiss followed as the shell hurled through the air, and impacted face first in the dirt thirty yards in front of the column.

Pushing through the falling debris, Henry smiled ear-to-ear, "You got your answer, Hinkley!"

The soldiers marched onward through the fields, under cover of the rumbling cannons that rained down searing hot lead on the invisible enemy. That night, the boys-in-blue would march two days northwest from the fields, leaving the serenity and calm of the camp, and out into the theater of war; their destination, Craysville.

Chapter V: Enemies in the night
ೞ

Maxwell seemed to be the first to rise in the sleeping Confederate camp. His muscles were tight and a fierce burning sensation began to fizzle in the backs of his legs. Despite the soreness, the boy stood up tall from his blanket that laid upon the uneven ground, and peered out at the sunrise; a gentle luminescence peeked its way through the shades of the trees above the grassy plains that surrounded the vast expanse all the way to the mountains that reached for the sky on the horizon.

"Look at the colors…" Maxwell whispered to himself with an open jaw.

Luscious shades of crimson and sapphire trickled through the leaves of the trees and settled upon the boy's body, making him glow in the still darkened camp.

"It is a marvel isn't it?" a voice called behind the boy.

Maxwell spun around to witness a man sitting upon a stump, tying his boots.

"I did not even hear you wake." Maxwell replied with a startled tone.

"Oh, I've been up for some time now, just didn't feel like moving." the man said.

Maxwell turned his attention back out onto the horizon, bearing witness once more to the start of a new day. "Do you think the whole country can see this?"

The man rubbed the stubble on his chin for a moment, as he repeated the question in his head. "I'm sure it appears different."

Maxwell yawned, and then looked at the man again, "Like our views?"

"Yes, everyone views the sunrise differently."

"No…I mean slavery." Maxwell muttered, almost regretting speaking.

The man reacted differently than the boy thought. He stood up and chuckled briefly and crossed over to a still smoldering fire. "I guess you have a point there, youngling," The man motioned for Max to approach the fire as he set a pan over the flame, "I assume most civilians, or even those who fight, don't see the world through our eyes. We see slavery as not only our right, but also our survival. We will have nothing without their labor. There are more reasons for rebellion, but slavery is a key part in the cause."

The man paused. Maxwell crossed his legs and sat down in the dirt next to the orange flame.

"It is like the rising sun; most people look at it and think the start of a new day. We look at it and think: is it the last we will see?"

Maxwell watched the fire dance in the morning breeze. "Well, then why don't we explain that to people?" he asked innocently.

The man removed two eggs from a tin box and cracked them on the corner of the pan, spilling the yolk, "No one wants to listen."

"Why? Don't they want to understand?" Max asked accepting a small piece of bread from the man.

"Once the public gets an idea in their minds of what is right, only action and bloodshed will change their minds." The man rose from the fire and walked over to his sleeping bag. "Want some spirits with your eggs?"

"I don't drink, Sir." Maxwell giggled.

"…Neither did I!" the man said returning to the fire. "So what is your name, kid?"

Maxwell shifted around, trying to return feeling to his rear that had grown numb from sitting still. "I don't have one." he answered.

The man took a sip of his drink and nodded his head. "Well, I am sure you do, but I respect your privacy."

Maxwell's ears went numb to the man's reply, for his hands had found the tattered corners of the tri-corner hat. He removed the family photograph he had taken from his brother's headstone and ran his thumb over the face. "Have you ever been forced to make a choice?" he asked without realizing he cut off the man in the middle of a sentence.

The man studied Maxwell, and the two objects clutched in his hands with wonder as the boy spoke again.

"I feel like I'm on a train I cannot control. Everything happening to me seems out of my hands, even the choices I make."

The man nodded slowly, giving the appearance he understood, even though he was completely at a loss. "Here have a swig of this!" he said holding out the cup of liquor.

"I'm not in control of my future." Maxwell said coldly as he eyed the man.

The fighter tossed what remained of the liquid into the fire, causing the flame to jump. "…Kid, who really is in control? Hell, if we could choose what happened to us, I'd be home sucking away on my pipe watching my little girls play in the fields; a care-free life."

"Nothing feels right, yet, I feel like I cannot give up." Maxwell admitted. Frustrated, he stood up and pulled the hat down on his dusty-brown hair.

The man watched Maxwell leave to pack up his blanket, and then turned his attention on the black eggs. "Ah! They're burnt to a crisp!"

Maxwell giggled helplessly at the man's tirade.

"Finally, I made you laugh! Children, no matter how old, should not have to be here, kid, but seeing as how you are, you might as well have some laughs…you have to make your own little heaven in the hell you've been thrust in to."

"Thanks…" Maxwell smiled as he tucked the photograph into his chest pocket.

"Let's get this wagon rolling, men!" yelled an officer as the camp started to bustle with activity. "We head toward Pennsylvania!"

The awakening crowd jeered with an immense roar, "To arms!"

One by one, the tattered soles of Confederate boots struck the muddy ground surrounding the stables at the outskirts of the town of Craysville. The company of troops jogged with a quickened pace, their hearts racing. Maxwell followed behind two men in long overcoats; their words muffled as they spoke in a foreign tongue. As the wind blew the cape-like fabric behind their backs, an array of knives on their belts caught the reflecting glow of the town's fires, which illuminated the night sky.

As the band of soldiers poured into the sleeping town, a man dressed in white took up a position upon the top of an empty wagon. He pulled out his pistol and fired one shot in the air, "Take the town!" he cried.

Maxwell paused and watched in confusion as the men he traveled with ran like mice through a maze, breaking into the houses and dragging woman into the streets by their flaxen hair. Few tried to fight back to his surprise. Men in dull dress came pouring out of bars, laughing and making mockery of the situation. The entire town seemed the cross of a riot and party. Maxwell jogged up to the man in white.

"Sir, where should we set up camp?!" he asked in mass confusion.

The man smiled revealing yellow teeth, "Pick a room and a broad, Boy!"

Maxwell winced, backing away from the man who continued to fire off rounds into the night air. As the dusty-haired boy scanned the lust scene, he could feel the grime and grit of sweat and dirt as it ran from his perspiring pores, and into the fibers of his clothing. He had not bathed in at least a month and in an uncomforting sense, felt connected to the men around him, for they shared the same filth.

Watching in shock at the sinful scenes unfolding before his eyes, he wandered down the center of Craysville, dragging his rifle behind him by the sling. Out of the corner of his eye, he saw a woman his mother's age watching him. Around her, men performed barbarous acts of looting and thieving, laughing cynically in the process.

"Boy!" the woman called, her dark hair blew in the chilly wind.

Maxwell halted and turned his focus upon her.

"Come to me!" she hollered in a tone that did not set well with the youth.

Maxwell shook his head in refusal; however his legs would not carry him away from the approaching woman. As she moved in closer, the familiar smell of whiskey escaped her blackened mouth, and for a moment, Maxwell felt like calling his father's name.

"You fight?" asked the wretch.

Little Maxwell pulled his rifle to his chest and nodded, swallowing hard.

"Well, my little Yankee Doodle, want to have a good night?"

Max's face twisted in revulsion and he pulled away, attempting to resume his march away from the madness. The woman's bruised arm reached out and her black fingernails scraped the back of his neck as she tugged on the collar of his shirt. "Let me tuck you in, little boy!" she cried out, laughing hysterically.

Maxwell lunged forward with all his might, releasing her grip from his shirt. The woman had already moved on, targeting another man. *Where is General Heth?!* Maxwell thought hoping the commander would be his savior in the dark town.

With no sign of the man's familiar face, the boy worked his way back to the stables where he found a small shower used for cleansing horses. Anxiously, he began to remove his gear, but hesitated for a moment when he heard the breaking of glass amongst the shouts in the town. As the chaos was followed by laughter, the boy removed his clothing and sheltered himself inside the box-like shower stall. He pulled the chain hanging down from above, releasing a cooling spray of water that cascaded down his face; the water trickled off of his chin and into the grass at his feet. The water removed weeks of sweat and caked on dirt, just like the daylight would wash away the sins of the soldiers.

Maxwell awoke to the silent call of a morning dove, which sat nestled atop a jutting corner of a roof. As he yawned away the sleep from a small nook in a barn, his safe haven from the outside world, he watched the bird's calm breathing. Suddenly, the animal's head jerked toward the western horizon. Max's eyes remained trained upon the creature as its breathing quickened. In one graceful swoop of its wings, the dove took flight into the pink light of the sky, flying off as the world was awakening.

Moments later, a gray rider and his Bronco sped through the center square of Craysville. The rider and his horse spun in a circle three times before the man pulled a pistol from his saddle and fired two shots into the air. Maxwell stood up sorely, and rubbed his aching neck. The man dismounted from his horse and removed a scarf covering his mouth. Another man exited from one of the houses in a full uniform. General Heth. Maxwell watched eagerly as the man finally made an appearance; his presence was illusive during the chaos of the night prior.

The rider whispered something to the General, and then remounted his steed and took off in the opposite direction. As he passed the barn where Maxwell stood, their eyes met. For a moment there seemed a flicker of sorrow in the rider's eyes, yet only a flicker. Maxwell sprinted toward the town where men had already started to gather.

"Listen up! Douse all the fires, gather all your weapons and belongings, and be ready to move in ten minutes! Our scouts have spotted Yankee divisions heading our way in full strength." Heth ordered.

Hell broke loose left and right, as the town exploded with movement and noise. Maxwell ran back to the barn where he had slept and stamped out what remained of a dying fire. He grabbed his musket, patted his old hat down tight upon his head, then rushed off toward the rest of the evacuating troops, however in his rush, the photograph of his family feel from his pocket and onto the dying ashes of the fire, which thirsted for air.

CRASO

The light of day faded from the surrounding landscape, bringing forth the creatures of Craysville. From the low-lying hills, Jed and Logan watched as the fires of torches, and oils from the lamps burned into the night, giving the town a ghostly silhouette.

"So this is Craysville?" Jed asked seeming unimpressed.

"Looks like it." Logan replied.

"Silence," Colonel Tavert's voice thundered. "Men, we search the town and if we should locate any Rebel troops, we take them into custody. Do not meddle with the civilians, unless they give you cause. Be alert, and watch each other's backs."

Jed and Logan nodded to each other, accepting the order.

Tavert continued, "We will split into squads and search every house." The Colonel turned to face another officer standing at the ready beside him. "Bravinsky, take half the strength and enter the town, we will move through after you take the initial sweep, that way we have reserves should something arise."

Bravinsky nodded and blew a high-pitched whistle. Half of the division scuttled forward, responding like dogs to the noise, moving toward the town. Jed and Logan watched as they all disappeared into the night.

"What squad are we in?" Jed asked anxiously.

"No one's said, but I see Killian already pairing up. Let's find Henry." Logan said scanning the faces of the blue soldiers. "There!"

Henry moved into view with one other man; he was tall with blond hair that fell to his shoulders.

"Henry!" Logan called in a forced whisper.

Henry perked up when he saw Logan's hand waving in the air. He pushed his way through the crowd until he reached Jed and Logan, the other man followed close behind.

"So we need a squad, want to roll with us?" Logan asked motioning to himself and Jed.

"Definitely; by the way, this is Ronan." Henry said pointing to the blond man. "Ronan, these are the Hinkley brothers, Jed and Logan."

"It is nice to meet you." Ronan voiced in a German accent.

Henry tapped Logan's rifle, "You might want to fix your bayonet; this town is a rough one."

Without hesitating, Logan pulled his bayonet out and ran his hand over the sharp edges of the triangle blade; the metal glistened in the moonlight.

Sharp cracks of gunfire echoed from the town, causing every head to turn toward the ghostly outline of Craysville.

"Well, they are in. There looks to be some resistance, but only drunk civilians." Tavert proclaimed quietly, but loud enough for Logan to hear. "Let's move in."

In one massive surge, the rest of the 11th Pennsylvania took their steps toward the cursed town.

The waist-high grain that flowed through the fields became entangled in the soldier's gear as they marched ever closer to the artificial light of the town. Ghostly shouts of drunken men and women filled the air, followed by the loud crack of a gunshot here and there.

"Are you alright, Hinkley?" Henry asked.

Logan wheeled around to see the trooper's eyes staring at him, surrounded by the dark blue panorama. For a moment, Logan had forgotten he was in a pack. "I'm-"

"Virginia-boy will be okay, it is the crotch on his uniform that will need replacing!" shouted Killian at a level he tried to suppress unsuccessfully.

Logan shook his head and turned back forward to see that the tall grass was dying, shifting to the pebbles and dirt that lined the town's streets.

"Logan, let Ronan take point," Henry addressed shifting his rifle into a ready position, "Move into triangle-formation; you take the left flank, I'll cover the right. Jed, you stick right in the middle."

The line broke and the boys moved to their respective positions as they started their march through the foreign town. The main square was crawling with people; the homeless clung to soldiers, begging for rations and clothing; the drunk argued and egged the columns of Union troops, while the wenches looked for prey.

"How ya holding up, Jed?" Logan asked, unsure himself.

The boy did not respond, only the click of his drumsticks signified that he was still alive in the rear.

Ronan pointed to a man wearing a bright red shirt with a blue painted face at the far end of the square. "That man is armed, and he is heading this way. Be ready!" he shouted with a hint of excitement outlining his German accent.

172

Logan cocked the hammer on his rifle and shouldered it in a readied fashion. The reflection of orange streetlights on his polished bayonet caught his eye, drawing his attention away from the man.

"Logan, hold formation!" Henry cried out.

The blue-eyed boy glanced up, breaking his trance. He was about twenty feet from the group, openly exposed with the man in the red jacket squaring off directly in front of him, pistol drawn.

"Stand down!" wailed Henry pointing the glistening blade of his bayonet at the man's distant face.

The civilian's intoxicated mind did not render the order.

"Stand down!" Henry repeated, with Ronan chiming in.

The red-shirted man raised his weapon and fixed his aim on Logan's chest, and squeezed the trigger; an empty click. The man cocked the revolver once more; an empty click. As he raised the gun for the third time, the backs of his knees gave out and the crushing blow of a side-palm met his throat. As the man collapsed, Henry stood in the wake breathing heavily; staring at Logan's befuddled face, "Fight, don't think!" he shouted.

The group fanned out into a defensive formation as more Union troops poured in to the setting.

"Hinkley, scout that barn!" shouted Ronan motioning with his hand, his boot acted as a restraint against the assailant's chest.

Logan nodded with riddance and jogged across the dusty street toward the offset reclusive nature of the barn. When he approached, he raised his rifle scanning the bleak structure for any signs of life. "Is anyone there?" he called out, trying to control his wavering tone. When no reply came, the boy's attention turned toward a small pile of extinguished embers near the far corner of the barn. Carefully, Logan stepped toward it, looking around the area one last time. He knelt down beside the ash and ran his fingers through the cinders. His tips brushed a hardened edge of something unnatural. Curious, he gripped the point of the object and lifted it up from the ashen debris. The light that reflected off of its face revealed a family gathered around a house; a house with red shutters.

The shock of seeing the familiar faces in the photograph sent a cold chill, like needles, down his spine.

"Is that us?" called Jed's voice from behind.

Logan rose and turned his attention upon the boy who stood child-like against the backdrop of the besieged town. "Yeah, Roo; It is us."

Jed shook his head trying to piece together the answer he may have already known, "But how?"

"Maxwell."

Chapter VI: Gettysburg
CออD

Maxwell had not closed his eyes to dream in two days. Ever since the notion to push north was proposed, the armies were marching day in and day out in all conditions, rain or shine. Sleep tugged on his sleeve like a mosquito buzzing about in the hot air-- always there, yet no matter how hard you try to ignore it, it ends up getting the best of you. Glancing around, Maxwell noticed a sudden liveliness in the men; there seemed something growing on the horizon, something that warmed everyone's blood and shot adrenaline through their veins. Maxwell rubbed his weary eyes and desperately tried to find more energy, and a hint as to what was causing the sudden shift in moral.

"Load up, men!" General Heth's melodic voice called out over the sound of clanking gear. "The sun is just arising and the early bird catches the worm!"

Maxwell quickened his step, moving up through the ranks of men to where another boy who appeared to be his age, stood.

"What is goin' on?" he asked curiously.

The strange boy looked at Maxwell, his left eye bore a long scar that stopped just shy of his cheekbone. "We've reached Gettysburg. I suppose we're moving in."

Maxwell's heart suddenly began to race as the thought of taking the town hung over his head. They were in Federal territory, and around every corner, and in every hole they could easily happen upon the slithering tail of the Union army, or worse, the venom spewing fangs.

As the column of gray-backs weaseled their way toward the outskirts of the town, soldiers started dropping excess equipment along the side of the road. Maxwell figured it was a good way to lighten the load, however when he examined his person, he could not think of anything he could go without. His canteen was necessary for water, which unfortunately was running scarce, his knapsack carried his blanket and food, and the cap-box, which carried the ammunition for his rifle, was a must-need. He glanced at the boy whom he had just met and noticed that he had even less equipment. The child's feet were bare and bruised from endless marching without the comfort and protection of boots. Maxwell could not imagine the pain that the boy must have felt from the jagged rocks and uneasy terrain they encountered while on march.

"What happened to your shoes?" he asked without realizing his blunt tone.

The boy took a moment to realize that Max was talking to him. His solemn, dirtied face perked up before he spoke. "I lost 'em at Chancellorsville…"

Maxwell had heard of that battle. It had taken place just a month before he joined the rebellion, and was the battle that consequently killed the great "Stonewall" Jackson. When Maxwell's father heard the news about the famed officer's death, he about threw a funeral right there on the front lawn of the house with red shutters.

"You have been without boots that long?" Maxwell asked amazed at the boy's tenacity and resilience.

"Yeah, I have tried to find another pair, but every dead body I come across the shoes have been long gone. My luck I guess…"

Feeling sympathy for the kid, Maxwell changed the subject trying to pass the time until they reached the city limits. "So, are you from Virginia?" he asked.

The scarred kid shook his head. "No, I'm from Mississippi originally. Somehow I found my way into this mess." The boy rubbed his chin trying to strike up a conversation. "I find it somewhat ironic…"

"What's ironic?" asked Maxwell.

"That we are out here fighting for a better country, yet it seems like no matter how hard we try, we are always going to have to bear the scars of our past."

"I meant what does ironic mean…" Maxwell clarified.

"Oh! It means the opposite of what you'd expect. Some kinda fancy word I suppose. Like I was saying, we are doing what our forefathers once did, you know, the whole fighting for a new country thing. Yet, even if we win, we will still be the same as before, only different in name…on top of that, we will have to live with the fact that we severed friendships and bonds because we put a cause before ourselves, and in the end, cutting our loved ones out of our lives will be like taking a knife to our own throats and leaving a mark. That mark will always serve as a reminder that unlike or forefathers, we were unable to forget our families and friends because we will be alone, and the question of 'what if' will always plague our minds: what if there was some other way besides war? It's ironic."

Maxwell tried to wrap his head around the whole concept. The boy may have been right. Maybe leaving the Union was a bad idea. Maybe they should have tried further reasoning, after all, in the end you can rebuild a country, but you cannot rebuild family that has passed on or forgotten you, even if you have not forgotten them.

"I don't know though, I'm just thirteen, and a soldier, and that right there is about the lowest of the low." the scarred boy joked.

"My name is Maxwell, I'm from Virginia." the shy boy introduced himself.

"Howdy, Maxwell from Virginia!" the other child said shaking his new friend's hand. "My name is Nathaniel."

When Maxwell heard the name, he felt a sting inside him. It had been two years since anyone had uttered that name to him.

"Are you alright?" asked Nathaniel noting the expression of raw nerves on Maxwell's face.

"I'm fine-" Max was finally able to spit out. Fiddling with the hammer on his rifle, he remembered the days when his older brother was alive. The days when he played with his cousins care free in the fields that engulfed his home, and the brutality of innocence cut short was unfathomable, and abysmal.

"Have you lost family?" Maxwell asked the boy, hoping to find common ground.

"I lost my sister; a brigade of Union troops set fire to my home when they marched through our town back in Mississippi. She wasn't able to make it out."

Maxwell frowned realizing that his situation was absent from this boy's history.

The view of Gettysburg's structures had started to come into view through the morning fog that hung high in the air. An eerie aura presented itself, as the town seemed vacant; from what they could tell, wagons were left in the streets and shops unattended. The column of soldiers, including Maxwell, started to jog at a faster pace so they could reach the safety of the town's buildings and not be left out in the open, susceptible to any Union artillery that may have been watching over the village from the ridges that encompassed the pocket-like valley.

Maxwell could feel his heart start to race as the fear of not knowing what possibly lay in front of him became overwhelming. Nathan, the boy with the scar, readjusted the grip on his rifle in anticipation for a fight.

"Push forward, men! Ninety yards to go until the fences!" shouted Heth over the roar of footsteps on harsh ground. Maxwell pulled the hammer back on his musket and ran a quick check of his gear. In his head he could hear the thundering concussion of twelve-pounder cannons; he envisioned the ranks of men before him being tossed up in the sky like helpless crops caught in a storm.

"Fifty paces!"

The musty smell of manure became abundant as the soldiers pressed on through the fields littered with freshly planted crops.

"Thirty paces!"

Stinging beads of sweat fell from Maxwell's hair and into his eyes, forcing him to run blind.

"Twenty…"

This is it, he thought. The moment was upon them. Fate was in control of their lives.

"Ten paces…"

Then there was nothing. The column of gray-clad Confederate soldiers stopped at the edge of two rotten fences that signified the start of the town's boundaries. No one was about, yet no less than one hundred yards away every shop in the town was open. A few horses trotted through the streets, their saddles packed with gear, however their masters remained invisible.

"Where is everybody?" whispered a toothless man beside Maxwell.

"Company hold…" General Heth shouted, dismounting from his white equestrian.

Maxwell breathed in quick succession as emotions churned inside of him.

"Hey…" spoke a bearded man in his late forties. "What is that?" he asked pointing to a piece of cloth slung over the side of an abandoned wagon just beyond the fence line.

"Do not break column, Sir!" shouted on officer to the man who continued to make his way slowly to the wagon.

The man set his rifle down on the ground and tipped his hat up on the back of his balding head. "Looks to be a flag…" The man's bony hands gripped the fabric and lifted it up to reveal an abundance of white stars and red stripes.

"A Federal flag," Maxwell whispered tensely to himself.

In that very second, a shot rang out that forced the entire brigade to duck in cover of the illusive shooter; the man holding the flag dropped forward against the wooden boards of the cart, and fell dead on the ground beside his rifle.

"Over there!" came a voice from the crowd.

Maxwell shifted his eyes toward the town where a line of blue uniforms stood facing them, bayonets fixed.

෧෨

The 11th Pennsylvania infantry marched toward the mountains in the distance, leaving behind them the filth of Craysville. In orderly fashion, their column stretched a good hundred yards back, making their movement relate to that of a caterpillar's.

Logan and Jed marched beside each other; each occasionally glancing around at the view of the landscape surrounding them. Logan pressed his hand to his chest, feeling the rough edges of the photograph in his pocket.

Catching sight of the motion, Jed asked, "Do you think he is still alive?"

Logan nodded almost immediately as he adjusted the cap on his head. "I know he is."

"How?" asked the younger boy while he tapped the skin of his drum.

Logan removed his Kepi-hat entirely and rubbed his dirty hand through his buzzed hair. "I just have this feeling. He's Maxy after all; he always was able to get away from Amelia back in the day remember?" Logan waited for a reply from Jed. When none came, he turned and smirked at his brother, nudging the boy's arm with his shoulder.

"I guess you are right." Jed said apathetically. "He was always a little sneak."

The green-eyed boy began to incessantly tap the top of his drum with his forefinger. "But, Logan…"

"Yeah?" he replied.

"What if we find him? What if we find him, and he has changed; if he tries to kill us?"

"We are family; no matter what, we are family."

Jed's face showed reassurance, but his fingers continued to dance atop the white skin of the drum.

"Colonel Tavert!" shouted a foreign voice in the distance.

The company halted as Tavert turned his horse and trotted toward a scout riding away from the sun.

"Colonel, there's action a few miles from here." gasped the rider trying to keep a handle on his impatient steed.

"What field?" Tavert questioned sternly.

"No field, Sir; town…Gettysburg."

"East of us?" asked Tavert scanning the horizon around him as sounds of cannons began to erupt in the distance.

"Absolutely." replied the rider directing his attention toward the source of the thunderous sound.

Tavert stroked his gloved hand down his beard, "How many strong?"

"I counted two divisions of gray-backs with more pouring in. As I was leaving they were deploying their long guns, which by the sound of it, are already engaging."

"How many divisions do we have in the town?"

"Not many, we had two cavalry divisions that met the Rebs as they were entering the town limits." The rider pulled out a map from his saddle pouch and held it up for Tavert to examine.

"Here is their position. We have the two divisions stationed here, and here, with more units bringing up reinforcements from this end here." he said pointing to lined positions on the map.

"Is it imperative I bring my men into this engagement?" Tavert asked with mixed tones rising from the depths of his vocal chords.

"Word has it that General Lee has learned of the skirmish and is headed toward the town as we speak." the rider scanned the long line of blue soldiers. "If your men are ready for combat, I would suggest moving in to reinforce. This could be the battle we need to turn the tide."

Tavert peaked over his shoulder at the troops standing patiently at attention. "I will lose a lot of good men."

"It is war, colonel." grieved the rider.

Tavert paused for a moment debating his answer, finally he replied, "Tell whoever holds Gettysburg that the 11th Penn are moving in."

"Excellent, Sir!" grinned the rider briefly, before sinking into an emotionless state. He turned his horse around and started back toward the direction of Gettysburg.

Colonel Tavert removed his hat and stroked the brim of it. Captain Gold trotted up beside Tavert and studied the horizon as the sound of distant guns echoed like the voices of the Gods. "To Gettysburg?" he asked.

Tavert set the hat gently back upon his balding scalp, "To Gettysburg."

⊰⊱

"Form the line!" screamed a Confederate captain, decorated with rusty, old medals; he tried to direct the men over the sound of the erupting gunfire.

Maxwell's instincts took control as he stepped forward in sync with the other men around him. The captain walked down the line of soldiers, his sword drawn. As he approached Maxwell, he tapped the top of the old tri-corner hat. "Aim high!" he said while smiling at the boy.

Fifty yards away, the line of blue Union troops broke up into two firing squads as the buildings of Gettysburg behind them began to crumble as Confederate shells pounded the structures.

The captain stepped backward, raising his sword high into the air. He began to speak, his voice long and drawn out, unlike the quick succession of gunshots by the Union troops. "Today, we die, but our cause lives on!" The captain turned to face the wall of Federals, and shouted the firing orders, "Load!"

Maxwell pulled a lead ball from the leather pouch on his waist. He pressed it to the barrel of his musket, and rammed it down. He then filled the pan with powder and cocked the hammer backwards, taking aim at the row of soldiers before him. The smell of gunpowder filled his nostrils, and the images of death grasped his retinas, yet his instincts held control. He licked the tip of his finger, tasting the tart, bitter metallic taste of lead on his tongue. He slid his hand down the length of the stock in a divine manner until his finger touched the slick, cold metal of the trigger. His eyes, a radiant fusion of green and brown, glowed with an animalistic fever as he searched for a single body in the line of perfect targets no less than fifty yards before him.

"Fire!" shouted the captain.

In a wild flash of smoke and fire, the world around the boy became a blinding maze. The pain in his ears subsided, and the ringing finally became audible. When a gust of wind blew in, removing the smoke, the captain turned around and shouted an order to reload. Maxwell glanced down to remove another lead ball when he realized he had not fired his weapon. He raised the rifle to his cheek and once again sighted the enemy down the muzzle. As he touched his finger to the trigger, a warm spray fell across his face and trickled into his mouth, forcing him to gag as the taste of copper filled his taste buds. The boy dropped his rifle and looked at his hands to find the spatter of blood all over his arms and upon his chest. The boy began to spit up profusely as the red blood gave color to his saliva. He scrubbed his face with his sleeve, removing splotches of the red liquid. When he averted his eyes forward, he saw the lifeless, mangled corpse of the captain lying in a deathly-seductive pose upon the lush, green grass.

"Charge their lines!" screamed a man taking the lead with three others, forming the spearhead of the Rebel wall. Maxwell surged forward with the bodies of men charging the two small Union skirmish lines.

As the Rebels neared within twenty feet of the kneeling Federal troops, a wall of smoke and ash from burning gunpowder transpired before them, dropping a large number of the Confederates that ran before Maxwell. "Hold the Lines!" cried a Union officer; the last words that were audible before the Rebels smashed into the Union line of men.

High-pitched cries for help and the squealing of impaled men pounded upon Maxwell's eardrums as he raised his arms to take aim at a soldier a few feet from him. It was then that he realized he had never picked his rifle back up after he had dropped it. In desperation, the boy tackled the man, knocking him onto his back. The man punched with what force he could muster from under Maxwell's body, hitting the boy above the eye, impairing his vision slightly. Maxwell slammed his head forward as hard as he could, crushing the man's jaw and simultaneously releasing a stream of blood from the man's nose. The man swung again, catching the side of Maxwell's head, throwing him in the air and onto the ground. Unable to coordinate any motion to move, Maxwell laid exposed on the ground as the screams and horrors of man strangling man unfolded around him. He watched as his assailant sat up and snapped his jaw back into place, letting out a sharp cry of pain that resembled the sounds of an injured wolf. The man spit globs of blood from his mouth and turned toward Maxwell with fiery eyes. Max started to kick his legs intermittently, trying to stand or even crawl away, yet his head throbbed with every move he made, forcing tears out of his eyes. The soldier leaned over on to his elbows and crawled to the boy, his face painted in shades of scarlet from the dripping blood. Maxwell's voice cracked as he tried to form words to plead for

183

life, but fear and nausea held his tongue prisoner. The soldier smiled sadistically as he rolled Maxwell over and mounted him, pinning the boy's arms under his knees. The soldier leaned in close to Maxwell. The smell of his bloodied wounds snaked its way up the boy's nostrils. The man pressed his lips to Max's ear and whispered, "Poor, little boy."

The pain from his breaking arms under the man's crushing weight faded as a surge of adrenaline pumped through the boy's small frame. Maxwell threw his head sideways and sank his teeth into the man's neck, releasing a tepid spray of blood that coated the inside of his mouth. In a shriek of desperation and pain, the soldier thrashed violently, however in doing so, he assisted in the removal of the skin over his jugular, and the stream of blood flowed from his wound and turned to mist in the ash filled air. Maxwell stood up and sprinted with the strength he had remaining, back to the location of his lost rifle, just as the dirt and earth around him flew up as Union artillery opened fire on the battleground with the arrival of Federal reinforcements.

CRED

Jed's demeanor sank when his eyes peaked over the billowing tops of wheat on a rise in terrain that governed over the acres of fields, and the town of Gettysburg below. Hundreds of bodies already littered the ground, and the air was filled with the gray fog of war. Even from his position on the hill, a solid two miles from the battleground, he could make out the unmistakable color of death as it splashed its dull saturation across the lifeless bodies. The boy looked to Logan who squirmed, a look of anticipation running rampant across his face.

"Logan…we have to go down there?" he asked fighting the feeling of dizziness.

"Jed," Logan replied. "I see why Father kept this away from us."

Jed's mind raced back to all the times he tried to steal the morning paper that carried news of the action; the innocent, emotionless black text held discretion compared to the actual carnage he was witnessing first hand.

Colonel Tavert dismounted his horse and removed a pair of binoculars from his belt. As he peered through them, the muscles in his jaw began to relax forcing his mouth to hang open in disbelief. "Dear, God." he muttered under his breath.

Captain Gold also dismounted from his stallion and walked up beside the colonel, "Your orders, Sir?"

"Well isn't it obvious? We fight." Tavert turned to face his men with eyes that glazed over. "Gentlemen…"

Jed looked back to Logan and whispered to his brother in a hushed tone. "Logan, I-"

Tavert continued, "It is no secret what we are about to walk in to…"

"Logan, I want to tell you I'm sorry for bothering you and being an annoyance when we were younger." Jed paused, waiting for a reply, letting his eyes drift aimlessly over the death that surely awaited them all.

Tavert pulled his sword letting the tip of the blade skim the top of the grain. "We will fight, and we will do our duty. No matter how you arrived in my division, you are here now…"

Logan looked down at Jed, and for a brief second, let his mind slip away from his current surroundings, and back to the house with red shutters where his little brother knelt by his bedside. "Don't be Jed, we are brothers."

"We are brothers," Tavert concluded. "Fight for each other, and I guarantee you that we can do no wrong."

Jed and Logan brought their attention back toward Tavert.

"Glory awaits us." With the wave of his sword, the men of the 11th Pennsylvania marched toward the killing fields surrounding the small village; their blue uniforms united them, the red of blood in their hearts matched that spilt on the green grass, and the white smoke from the cannons became a blanket to hide the killing from God's sight.

℀℁

As Maxwell slid to a stop, he grabbed up his rifle; his foot dug a hole in the ground; searching for an escape from the artillery shells that continued to pound the ground around him, his eyes darted left and right. Flashes of decapitated and dismembered bodies pierced his soul as he tried to locate a safe-haven among the combat.

The explosion of a nearby shell sent a cloud of dust in all directions, blinding the boy's senses. Desperate to get out of the target zone, he began to crawl back toward the outlying fence around the battlefield. As he crawled, his hands found the missing pieces of limbs that belonged to human bodies. Maxwell stood up, no longer able to handle the gore and grit of the situation. Against his will, he keeled over and threw up on the dirt at his feet.

Voices shouted left and right, giving and receiving orders; the crackle of gunfire settled, and then suddenly picked back up in frenzy as skirmish lines formed once more. Maxwell wiped his mouth clean and tried to regain his composure. A line of Rebel soldiers marched through the fog before him, and continued on in direction of the town. Maxwell pulled his hat down tight on his head and joined their ranks.

"Push through!" one officer yelled down the line.

The men kept on marching as the faint sound of cannon fire opened up behind them. Two seconds later, the buzz of the flying shells soaring overhead linked up with the deafening cry of Mother Earth as the shells pummeled the ground before them.

"Firing lines to the ready," another officer wearing a hat that held a white feather screamed.

The column of soldiers beside Maxwell broke up in to two groups. Maxwell joined the second group as they continued forward.

"First line, fire!" cried the officer.

The first line of Rebels opened fire to give cover for Maxwell and his fellow troops, as they continued marching ahead toward the leveled streets of Gettysburg that lay covered in rubble and debris.

"Secure the town, push forward!" cheered a Rebel soldier; kneeling in the rubble of a bombed out building on the edge of the town, he attempted to nurse a wounded man back to health.

"Reform the line! Adams, move to secure the left flank!" yelled the man in the feathered hat.

Maxwell and a group of six men broke their line and followed the soldier, known as Adams, off in to the remnants of buildings that met the initial destruction by Union and Confederate shells.

Adams' voice cut through the melody of cannon and musket fire, "Move through the buildings, use them as cover!" Maxwell darted through the wreckage of an exterior wall to a flower shop, hopping over the shattered glass cases and support beams. What walls remained, were riddled with cracks from the concussion of the barrage of lead that fell upon the town from both enemy and friendly cannons.

As Maxwell leapt over a splintered armoire, his foot landed in a divot in the wooden floor. Two of the six soldiers passed him by in a rush to find a position to take up as cover.

"Help me, my foot is stuck!" he cried out with a catch in his voice.

One of the soldiers wearing a crisp, white shirt turned back to help. As the man reached out with his hand, his brown eyes opened in shock and he quickly thrust his hand upon Max's sternum, knocking him onto his back; his ankle crunched. Before Maxwell's cry of pain could be voiced, the ceiling of the building collapsed, and all went silent. The sounds of war outside the crippled walls were no longer audible. The sky above Maxwell was as black as iron, yet what light entered held a silver glimmer as it cascaded its mystic beauty through the cracks in the rubble upon him.

Maxwell shoved his hand through the rock and wood that smothered him; light flooded his eyes, giving the scene an angelic glow. Dust fell gracefully from an unknown source, as the only remains around him were the four standing walls of the building. The men who had accompanied him were no longer present; only a sleeve from the white shirt that belonged to the man, who saved the boy's life, was visible peaking from the rubble. Maxwell pushed the rest of the destruction from his body and crawled over the mound of bricks toward a gaping hole in the building's wall nearest the street. Outside, the line of Confederates whose flank Maxwell was sent to protect stood in two lines, one kneeling, the other standing; both with rifles aimed forward, bayonets fixed. Maxwell shifted his gaze to the left in the direction of pointed guns to find three rows of Union soldiers, twenty in each line, marching no less than ten feet from his view point in the path of the Confederate muzzles.

The cannons in the distance seemed to cease as the Union machine stopped their approach and dispersed into their firing lines.

"Company, load arms!" shouted a Union officer. His voice echoed throughout the walls of the town.

"First line, hold your ground!" cried the Confederate officer with the feather in his hat; his voice projected louder than the Federal officer's.

"Second and third lines, fix blades!" screamed the Union man, stepping forward from the mass of soldiers, his sword bloodied and raised high to the sky.

The Union troops in the second and third defensive lines fixed their bayonets in preparation for a charge. Maxwell studied the faces of the men who stood closer to him than Nathan had the day he died on the porch of the house with red shutters. Only the crumbling wall separated Maxwell from the men of war in the streets.

"Jonathan Miller, last chance to surrender and keep your lives!" the Federal officer hollered out to the Confederate lines, where the officer with the white feather and a thick mustache rose from the ranks.

"I am sorry Hector, but our friendship ends in blood!" the mustached man shouted removing his sword from his sheath and waving it in the air. The Confederate troops let out a massive Rebel yell that was answered by a volley of lead from the lips of the Union's rifles.

Maxwell's hands hugged his ears as he tucked down in the rubble. Unwanted tears streamed down his cheeks as the smell of roses from under the rubble filled his nostrils, and the sound of murder slipped through his fingers and into his ears.

After a minute of violent fighting, the fire trickled down to nothing. Maxwell opened his eyes and raised his head, peaking up from the mound of debris to see the Union soldiers scrambling to reform their lines as the Confederate machine surged forward with two more companies backing them. When the silhouettes of the soldiers passed by, they blocked out the light that shined through the building; Maxwell spun around and dug down in the pile of bricks where he gripped the stock of his musket, and the stem of a rose.

Clambering out of the remains of the flower shop, Maxwell stopped beside the hole in the wall, and looked back inside at the arm of the man who saved his life. Buried under the dirt and masonry from the building's roof, the lifeless hand rested with an open palm. Maxwell approached the hand and brushed it free. He knelt down and placed the rose gently in the exposed palm, pausing for a moment to reflect. The dusty-haired boy turned around bearing witness to the Rebel soldiers racing in pursuit of the retreating Union lines.

"Protect me, Nathan," he whispered aloud as he departed the makeshift grave and joined the other soldiers fighting toward the hills and ridges surrounding the town.

CREO

Colonel Tavert led his men through the fields to the outskirts of Gettysburg. The sea of uniformed soldiers took up positions of cover against the brick and stonewalls of the buildings a few hundred yards from the center of the town, where the fighting was locked in.

Jed and Logan were the last to trot up to the buildings.

"Keep behind me, Jed. That drum won't do you any good to shoot back." Logan whispered to the boy while simultaneously trying to listen in on Tavert's conversation with another officer from the 13th Indiana regiment.

"What is the state of the battle?" Tavert questioned with a voice full of composure.

The other officer removed his cap to reveal long golden hair that shimmered with beads of sweat. "Most of the fighting has been to the front of the town. All regiments are in retreat, pulling back toward Cemetery Hill behind us."

Tavert interrupted, "Any word on who is in command for the Confederacy?"

"General Lee arrived roughly two hours ago. He ordered A.P. Hill to attack General Meredith and the Iron Brigade."

"They couldn't hold off the attack?" questioned Tavert.

"No, they retreated through the seminary, and are now linking up with the other regiments and remains of Buford's Calvary divisions. Every unit is in full retreat toward our position through the center of town."

Tavert removed his hat, revealing small streaks of gray hair that neither Logan, nor Jed had noticed before. "Who is in command of our forces?"

"Well, that's been the enigma of the day. About fifteen minutes ago Winfield Hancock took control from Doubleday."

"Who ordered that?"

"General Meade."

"Meade knows about this?" Tavert asked surprised.

"Everyone knows about this colonel. I have a feeling by the time this battle is over, we will be living history."

Tavert paused to watch the structure of a building crumble in the distance as cannon balls concussed the center of the town. "What are my orders?"

"Stand this ground until the rest of the regiments retreat past us, and then join in the retreat up the hill to take defensive positions."

"We are giving them the town?!" Tavert asked in shock.

"They were able to reinforce before we were; they win round one."

Tavert turned away, his face red and flustered. Logan watched him, trying to guess his doomed words.

"*Abyssus abyssum invocat.*" the colonel muttered with a glum look of despair.

"What does that mean?" Logan asked.

Tavert studied the boy's face before speaking. "Hell calls hell; one misstep leads to another."

The battle in the center of Gettysburg Square raged. Union lines buckled one after the other as each regiment tried to retain ground. A bugle sounded with a short chirp, breaking the crackle of gunfire. Waves of blue uniforms started to withdraw back toward the hills surrounding the town. Logan and the rest of the 11th Pennsylvania readied themselves to defend their retreating comrades as they neared the defensive position.

"Drummers, sound the battle call!" hollered a captain from the wall.

Jed stood up and grasped the drumsticks in his hands, which were soaked with sweat from the combination of heat from the stagnant summer day, and inflicted fear. His eyes scanned the broken town, searching for any sign of life. He heard the shouting of orders, the signal calls of bugles and horns signifying another regiment's retreat. Suddenly, through the dust and fog, blue uniforms broke into the visible horizon, hundreds in an all out rush for the protection of the hill.

Jed looked around at the soldiers in cover from the wall of buildings; all were kneeling with rifles aimed at the enemy. He slid his hand down his pant leg to remove the sweat escaping his pores before his took up a drumstick once more. One by one, the Union drummers started to play their battle cadence as the first wave of retreating soldiers crossed the road out of town and into the mistakenly serene grass.

Logan closed his eyes to block out the sight of bloodstained uniforms as they passed him by.

"Hold ground!" cried Tavert.

Immediately behind the retreating Federals, yet in front of the arterial barrage, columns of Rebels ran screaming with animosity. Jed dropped to the ground, screaming in terror as the snap of lead munitions hitting the sides of the buildings near him became too much to bear. Tavert knelt down behind cover, and attempted to shout the next round of firing orders, yet the cry of battle swallowed his words. Catching sight of movement within the building before him, Logan peaked through the window where three small children laid cuddled up with their mother in the corner of the building, shaking with fear. The oldest child in the family glared at Logan; not with anger, but with blue eyes that held a glimmer of heartbreak and hopelessness.

With the anticipation of the fight growing, Logan ducked around the textured edge of a home to witness hundreds of Confederate troops doing the same. In a brief moment of hysteria and confusion, he stepped out to the middle of the road.

Jed's body became numb; his eyes glued to his brother standing before the hands of death. "Logan run!" he cried, but the screams seemed hollowed.

The blue-eyed boy's radiant gaze watched the columns of enemy soldiers' fire in intermittent bouts, dropping the retreating Federals like flies, yet he remained untouched. The boy's mind stopped asking why and began wondering how he had ended up in the situation so far from home. Dazed and emotionally vexed, Logan fell to his knees; his hands combed the bloodied ground searching for an object. They met the cold steel blade of a knife. As if instinctive, he grasped the handle and raised the blade to his neck.

In a moment of desperation, Jed rose up from his chest and raced through the gunfire to his brother, tackling him down in the rubble of the street. The younger boy wept with misunderstanding as he tried to find words of reason. "Logan, we're going to die!"

As the final words slithered from Jed's tongue, the building Logan previously sought as cover exploded into hundreds of pieces, and the surrounding area was blanketed with chunks of masonry and dust. Beneath the piles of stone and ash, the world faded; the screams and gunfire melted together forming a hypnologic undertone, leaving only little Jed and his brother huddled together in a world awash in blood.

"Tell me we won't die!" Jed ordered clenching his brother's chest.

Logan looked skyward watching as the clouds above blocked the sun from reaching them. He dropped his eyes and scanned the men that surrounded him, who continued to fight off the horde of Confederates. The blue-eyed boy dug his hand in his pocket and felt the frayed corners of the photograph Maxwell once held, before him. "Roo, do you remember the day we stole the paper from Father?"

Little Jed wiped his tears on Logan's shirt, and raised his head from the darkness of the cloth. His eyes were red, and his face tear streaked.

"Nathan was there, and so was Max. Can you believe that we are here now? Living what we read?"

Jed sat up more, continuing to look at his brother; forgetting the outside world.

"You told us to give the papers back, but I didn't listen."

Logan looked to the hills behind the fighting Rebels where artillery smoke transpired, and drifted to the sky. Turning back to Jed, he spoke quickly, "When this next round hits the ground, you run; you run as fast as you can with the other men back to safety."

"What about you-" Jed asked in fear.

The shell struck the ground before the boys and a plume of destruction blocked the vision of the enemy.

"Run, Jed!" Logan screamed, pushing his brother away.

In a flash, the boy took off, following in the footsteps of the other retreating Union troops. Logan rolled over, retrieved his rifle, and ran toward Colonel Tavert, just as the wall of dust from the shot settled.

Settling in amongst the rest of the troops still holding a defensive line, Logan took up aim with his rifle, only glancing back once to make sure Jed was long gone.

"Hinkley, forget it, you go!" Henry shouted over the growing chaos as he moved to replace Logan's position beside Tavert.

"But-"

"No! Protect Jed; we're going to be rebounding back up the hill anyway!"

"You promise?" Logan asked worriedly.

Henry smirked showing his teeth, "Don't you get all soppy on me, Hinkley!"

Logan took off toward Cemetery Hill. As he made his ascent, he glanced back. The defensive line broke almost immediately, following the Confederate surge. Left and right bodies dropped gaping with holes from bullet wounds, leaving men to cry out, sucking in the open air one last time before death.

Colonel Tavert and Henry were nowhere to be seen, nor was Ronan, the German soldier who seemed attached to Henry's hip. What view of the streets of town Logan could see, lay paved with blood and bodies broken and frail. As the Rebels steamed forward within a few hundred yards, Logan rushed up the hill to where a small picket line, fortified by logs and rocks, rested; Manning the defenses, the Federal soldiers who had escaped the hell occurring in and around the town.

"Men, they will not take this hill!" ordered a Union captain dressed in a simple uniform.

Logan tucked down behind the barricade of logs and listened as the distant gunfire and roaring cries grew, transpiring into an ear splitting barrage of perpetual agony. Bodies of living and dead soldiers fell atop Logan as they attempted to leap over the barricade for subliminal safety, some successful, others not so.

Covering his ears to shield the concussion of war, Logan's piercing eyes became the gateway of interpretation of man killing man. Before him, no less than five feet away, a young Union soldier crawled to a tree that stood unharmed, and untouched away from the action. The soldier's legs were absent from his torso; only the bloodied flesh hung in place. His shirt was torn in zigzag patterns where exposed flesh smiled with a bloodied grin at the world; the after effect of saber strokes. The man crawled until he was just feet from the tree. He reached out a desperate hand toward the jutting roots, and died instantly. Logan watched in horror; in grief; in sadness; in pity. Gripped by the hand of death, he could not move. Left and right, bodies continued to fall over the wall of logs, and the dragons of war spit fire back at the enemy in the form of lead.

A maladroit cry from a bugle sucked in the sounds of death and pushed forth a refurbished and melodic song. One by one, the bodies ceased to fall over the logs, and the Confederates withdrew down the hill.

Logan uncovered his ears, yet his sight remained cast on the dead soldier beside the tree. The jeering of Union troops broke his trance.

As the Confederate's ran away from the Union lines, he felt a wave of relaxation brush over him. He had survived the first hours of combat. Swallowing hard, he looked out over the barricades where he saw a sight all too familiar. The red, burgundy colored blood, like the kind that had escaped from Nathan's fatal wound, lay in puddles across the razor-like grass. Bodies of soldiers of all ages were scattered about in unnatural poses, some taking in their last few breathes before departing to a new life. The air was wrought with the smell of decaying flesh, and a reddish mist hung over the field. Logan felt sick to his stomach as his sky-blue eyes peered out at the scene torn from the pages of the Book of the Dead. Through all of this however, something caught his attention; a butterfly gracefully fluttered carelessly over the mass of bodies, its white wings moved its little body up and down as if it was dancing throughout the contrasting scene.

At the image of the lone butterfly, Logan collapsed backward onto the barricade. His dark blue Kepi-hat slid down his head and fell onto his chest. He began to hit his forehead with his fist repeatedly, expelling tears that slid down his muddy cheeks, leaving little streaks where the watery drops descended to his chin, and dripped onto his tattered uniform. The barbarity of the situation was something that he could not comprehend. These men were all Americans, yet they killed as if they had never known it.

Jed slowly worked his way over to Logan, his large wooden snare drum suspended from his neck. Tossing it to the ground, he sat across from his brother. The small boy was breathing heavily, his face flustered as he tried to make sense of the situation.

"Logan…"

"Ah!" Logan shouted, snapping his head up and gripping his rifle with terrified eyes.

"It's me!" Jed soothed.

Logan's heavy breathing settled into a steady rhythm. Jed looked at his brother's neck where droplets of blood stained his skin.

"You are bleeding," the boy noticed.

Logan lifted a shivering hand cautiously to his neck, where his fingers felt the warm liquid. Gritting his teeth in revulsion, a feeling of nausea settled over him as he quickly wiped the dark blood onto his navy blue jacket. "It's not mine…"

Jed shivered at the remark. Neither one of them said anything more for their fear-stricken faces showed all.

"Company, make camp!" shouted a grizzly voice.

At the order, the troops that held the barricade began to unhitch their bags and gather sticks for fires. Logan stood up leaving Jed at the wooden logs that served as a defensive line, and walked over to where his haversack had fallen.

"Hey, Virginia…" Killian's rustic voice called.

Slowly, Logan glanced behind him. The hardened Irishman stood with three others, all at least twice Logan's age.

"How come you don't fight?" the man asked.

Logan brushed off the comment and continued on his mission to find his belongings.

"I said, why didn't you pull the trigger once, lassie? We're all putting our lives on the line to fight, and you are just sitting around on your arse watchin' us."

Rushing to the battered boy's side, Henry spoke up. "Take it easy on him guys, he is still just a kid!"

Logan pulled his bag angrily over his shoulder; his depressed mood was apparent, unlike the other soldiers who seemed to think nothing of the prior battle.

Henry leaned in close to the blue-eyed boy and whispered sympathetically, "Why didn't you shoot, Logan?"

The group of bloodied soldiers around the boy grew quiet. Jed made his way to the front of the pack and rested on a wooden log, waiting to hear his brother's reply.

Logan licked his lips as he tried to detach himself from his feelings. "Because, I don't know which one is him…"

"Huh?" Henry asked puzzled.

"Because, I don't know which one is him…imagine waking up one morning, and having everything you hold dear be ripped apart in front of your eyes." Logan paused as he desperately tried to keep from feeling the pain that once tugged on his soul.

Around him, the soldiers watched and listened intently as the boy continued.

"…I sat there and watched my cousin, my best friend, die by my side. I can still feel his fingers grip my arm as he tried to hold on to every last ounce of life that he could. His little brother and sister watched in horror as their oldest sibling died in a pool of his own blood…" Logan sniffled and wiped his nose. He looked up shyly at the soldiers who watched him with empathy.

"I'm terrified of watching another one of my family members die again…anyway…the little brother's name is Maxwell, and I haven't seen him in two years. But he is out there somewhere," Logan said motioning with his head to the field, "And that's why I don't shoot…because I don't know which one is him."

The camp said nothing more to criticize the boy. The realization of his past was enough to make them mind their tongues. Henry patted Logan on the shoulder just as Jed walked up beside his brother from the dispersing crowd. The two hobbled off to a remote section of the camp where they could be alone. Henry watched them walk off for a moment longer, then turned around and joined the other soldiers.

The sun that once ruled over the bloody battlefield finally closed its weary eyes. All around the Union camp, soldiers sat around fires, the flames reaching for the night sky, as if trying to escape the cursed place. Logan and Jed were lying beside each other a few feet from the flame pit, a large gap between them. Around them, logs served as benches, but only a few men occupied them, the rest were sprawled out beside their fires that lay just beyond the logs. The ground was damp, and the air was dry. No crickets chirped, nor did birds sing goodnight. The land was filled with thick grass, and trees and bushes of all sorts, yet through all its beauty, there was a sense of eeriness: thousands of men had just fought and died on the very ground that served as a pillow to Jed and Logan. Mother Nature had a front row seat to the destruction of Man.

Jed was lying on his back, his eyes peering off into the stars, his hands cupped on his chest. Logan was turned on his side, facing his little brother. He watched as the boy's body moved up and down with each breath he took, the air escaped his mouth and turned into a smoky glimmer in the night. Neither one would talk about what they saw that...each had eyes that were robbed of innocence; the sparkle that once made them children was gone.

"Roo," cooed Logan, still watching his brother.

Jed breathed in odd time, taking a deep breath, followed by a quick one. His eyes did not move from the stars, but he answered, "Yeah?"

"Are you alright?" Logan asked in a wavering tone that signaled his true emotions.

"I'm scared, Logan."

Logan clenched his teeth together picturing the red, bloody carnage that swept the beautiful, lush green fields, "Yeah, me too, Roo."

Logan scooted himself closer to his brother until they were side by side, and pulled the blanket over the both of them. Jed still focused on the night sky, and soon, so did Logan.

"Do you think that Pa would ever believe what happened here?" wondered Jed.

Logan chewed on the question before giving his answer. "I don't know, Roo...I hope he never asks."

Jed glanced at his brother for a split second, "Why do you wish that?" he questioned.

"Because I never want to hear those screams again; I never want to see what I have seen. Jed, those boys who died today were no different from us. How is this right?" he asked confused about the justice in war.

Jed turned facing his older brother, trying not to think about what Logan just asked.

"Logan, do you remember that song Momma used to sing us?"

198

Logan searched his mind, "The one about the rabbit?"

"Yeah, that's the one." Jed answered.

"I believe so."

Logan cleared his throat and started to whisper the words in a soothing voice. All around him the camp was silent, absent of voices; only the coughing of sick men and the crackling laugh of fire was heard. Jed closed his eyes and rested his head on his brother's chest, as Logan sang the song, looking up at the angels in the stars.

> *"One little Rabbit caught in a daze,*
> *Followed by a hunter as the rabbit grazed,*
> *Sitting in silence, Mother Rabbit tried to fight,*
> *Help me Mother Rabbit, called the little one in fright…"*

Logan glanced down at Jed, whose breathing was finally synchronized; his eyes no longer looked at the world in fear. Logan continued,

> *"Run to the den, hold your head up high,*
> *Do not fret, little one, I'll always be nearby,*
> *Forever my child, close your precious eyes,*
> *Remember your bearings and home you will fly…"*

Logan finished the song and yawned in exhaustion. Jed was finally asleep. The camp seemed to be sleeping as well. The golden silence seemed surreal compared to the day's events. Logan pulled his arms out from behind his head and wrapped them around little Jed; shutting his eyes, his mind drifted into sleep where he could forget, just for a while, the horrors of war.

ଔଛ

Sauntering back exhausted and delirious, Maxwell made his way through the wreckage of farm houses that were previously caught up in the hurricane of war, through the fortified lines, and out to the fields where his unit was assigned to make camp. As he stepped around the bodies of the dead, he collapsed. Drowsy, sickened, tired, and alone, he laid face down in the grass as the eerie silence filled the summer night around him. When he listened more closely, he could just make out the faint cries for a savior in the distance, brought forth from dying victims.

The boy rolled over on to his back and glowered at the constellations above, searching for an answer to the madness surrounding him. "What sort of punishment is this?" he squeaked in a raspy voice.

The crickets humming in the grass were the only response to the question still lingering in the air.

Reaching for his pocket, Maxwell attempted to grasp the photograph of his family, only to find it missing. *Not even a picture remains of them,* he thought. A chilling wind swept through the grass, deafening his ears to the night serenity, and forcing him to shiver. He set his rifle down in the dirt, and removed his hat; Maxwell hugged his arms around his shoulders and hunkered down in the grass, closing his eyes from what light remained from the gleaming moon. As he slipped off to sleep, a lone soldier approached him slowly, and covered him up with a woolen blanket.

CRD

The shouting of a horn broke the silent barrier of Logan's dream. The youth rose from his makeshift bed; nothing more than a listless pile of leaves, and a standard-issue wool blanket he had used to shield himself from the elements. Shedding the sleep from his eyes, it took a moment for the adolescent to realize his surroundings. The taught fibers of the jacket on his chest, different from his usual bagginess of his nightgown, ignited the morose images of the carnage that had swept the fields of Gettysburg the day prior. The sensation threw him back into frame; feeling sick to his stomach, Logan reluctantly slipped his hand from his eyes reveling a colorful painting of death. Beyond the camp, hundreds, if not thousands of lifeless bodies still laid in barbarous fashion, their extremities frosted by night's algid breath. The buzzing of flies around the hands of the dead tickled the ear like a sinister whisper, a whisper that forces one's hair to stand on end.

On the exterior of the macabre depiction, Logan pulled his sleeping brother to his feet just as the second horn sounded. Scurrying like mice, both boys grabbed their gear and started to break down camp. The other soldiers of the 11th Pennsylvania hauled logs and sizable rocks over to the crest of the hill to form some shelter against the impending Confederate attack.

"I need to see Captain Gold, Lieutenant Morris, and Davidson on the right flank now!" shouted Colonel Tavert.

Jed watched as the uniformed officers hurried down the sea of blue, which were occupied building up the wall of earthen debris. In the back of his mind, he could not help but wonder how many of the brave soldiers who stood behind him were about to meet their fate.

"Hey, Hinkleys," came Henry's voice.

Logan and Jed turned around to see the soldier, no older than their brother William, approach them with a handful of bread.

"Here, take some, a few other fellas and I raided the supply wagon just before dawn. This here is worth at least two days rations." Henry pushed a handful of bread into each of the teen's hands.

Jed shoved the entirety of the meal into his mouth only to fall under a coughing fit, spitting it all back up. "It is bone dry!" he hissed.

"Well yeah, scout, it's about three days old! Here, pour some of this on it." Henry reached into his haversack and pulled out a glass jar of molasses.

Logan ripped off a piece of his share and handed it to Jed, who dowsed the stale provision with the syrupy substance. The soldiers scarfed the food like it was their last meal. Ironically, it very well could have been.

Cannon fire began to rumble throughout the surrounding valley just as the brothers chewed their last bite. The screaming projectiles shaved the tops of the trees overhead, causing branches from the canopy to fall to the ground, and onto the encamped soldiers.

"Listen up! Form the line and prepare to defend at all costs!" hollered Colonel Tavert returning from the right end of the line.

As the cannons continued to spit fire, the anxious Union troops formed a barrier along the wall of rocks and logs. Tavert made his way to the front of the Union barricade and hushed all the men before him by holding up his gloved hand. "Gentlemen, today we begin a new fight in the War for Preservation. Today we have a chance to route the infernal enemy, and bring this war back to Richmond where it began…I expect every man to stand his ground, every man to wield his sword, and when the smoke clears, I expect every body of the boys-in-gray to litter this landscape! Do you hear me?!"

In a unanimous hurrah, the Federal troops jeered, tossing their fists in the air. Jed and Logan watched the colonel as he turned to face the windswept plains, unsheathing his golden saber, exposing the bloodied blade. Logan shifted his attention down the line where flags fluttered in the wind, displaying the trinity of faithful colors: the red, white, and blue. From the left of the troop, a voice shouted in a harsh tone, "Here they come!"

༄༅

Maxwell's eyes were red and raw from a night spent weeping, tossing and turning with failed attempts to block out the sounds of the dead and dying. He had already been up; sorting

202

through his rations by the time the formations of other units began to disappear around him on their way to the ridges in the distance. He gathered his gear and hurried to find the men of his troop.

"Maxwell, right?" asked a man who appeared to be taking charge of the small band of soldiers present in a tightly tucked circle.

"Yes." he replied, slinking over to the group.

"Alright, that's all of us-"

"What do you mean?" Maxwell asked in disgruntled confusion.

The man in charge looked around the circle. "This is all of what's left of the unit."

Maxwell rubbed his eyes wearily. "No it isn't, what about the kid with the scar, Nathan, or the man who I met cooking eggs…or Heth?"

"Boy, most everyone is dead or wounded. However our unit has been downsized. All morning it has been a race to capture the hill to the south; Little Round Top. The units have been pulled and blended to make up for losses in the ranks. Heth is still alive, and I'm sure the others are, too."

Maxwell tried to make sense of the situation.

"Listen now," the man in charge began, "We need to push up toward Cemetery Hill in conjunction with the other brigades. Be ready to rush 'em."

The men around Maxwell loaded their arms and secured all loose baggage. They formed a makeshift picket line and marched onward to the ridges, stepping over the dead along the way.

CRUESO

From the woods below, columns of Rebel soldiers charged forward unfazed by the sudden eruption of gunfire from the Federal line. Logan ducked down, hugging tight to the rocks, cowering from the advancing wall of gray. Unable to see, he listened as the crackle of guns was answered by screams of dying victims. Carefully, he removed a rock in front of him to see that the enemy was closing the distance to a matter of meters.

Jed stood just a few feet away, holding a steady rhythm on his drum while the marching of the enemy changed sporadically, following a large explosion from an unseen artillery shell. Through the falling ash of dirt and limbs, a lone man rushed at the green-eyed boy. Jed did not notice the adrenaline-driven man, for his eyes were closed as he desperately tried to shield his mind from the reality around him. Logan tensed as he watched the armed assailant charge his brother. In a flash of wild instinct, the pacifistic-boy raised his rifle and squeezed the trigger, sending a volley of hot lead into the adult's chest cavity, exposing bone and severed flesh.

The shot startled Jed; he stumbled backward in a fit of shell shock, landing on his back. The Confederate soldier continued to stumble, changing course toward Logan, who crouched in hysteria clenching his musket, his bayonet drawn. The man tripped over the wall of rocks, and fell forward onto the boy; his warm fingers caressed the child's lips as he slipped down the youth, leaving a trail of red blood across the blue, wool uniform. The fresh, mint smell of the dying man's aftershave cream flooded Logan's nostrils. The way in which the man fell was nostalgic for Logan; Nathan had collapsed on him in a similar fashion the day he was killed. Trembling, Logan desperately held in the rushing emotions of fear and panic, and slowly rose up, letting the man fall to the ground before him. The boy looked to the sky and ran his trembling hand down his face, smearing the crimson blood across his features. His crystal-blue eyes glazed over into a cold, desolate stare as he lowered his head to the dead body of the unknown man before him. Trance-like, he bent down and pulled his bayonet out of the deceased victim's stomach and reattached it to his smoking gun. From the side, Jed watched his older brother as his innocent nature metamorphosed into one of sinful impurity.

"Help…" a fateful moan arose from beyond the breastworks, through the fading smoke.

Logan shifted his stare out among the Confederate wounded. Jed remained motionless, watching the boy's every move.

"Please…" the same voice repeated through dying lips.

Jed swallowed hard as he fought an inner battle. "Do we help him?" he asked hoping for a reply from his brother.

Through shell-shocked eyes, Logan turned to face Jed. His mouth hung open, attributing to the expression of depleted humanity.

"Logan, answer me!" Jed shouted as the dying man's wishes remained unanswered, leaving a stinging ring in his ear.

A breath of life shot back into the blue-eyed boy as he quickly regained his awareness. Logan looked around quickly before leaping over the log barricade and down the bluff to the lost voice.

Jed followed, his heart pounding as his mind raced. Images of torn bodies and severed limbs filled his thoughts so much so, he could see them with his waking eyes. When the boy looked up to find Logan, all he saw was the white smoke from battle floating over the flowers in the field. In a panic, the child spun around in circles as tears of fright flooded his green eyes. "Logan!" he cried out.

"Jed! Bring your canteen!" Logan's voice echoed over the eerie silence of the landscape.

Jed pulled the metal can from his hip and rushed to the sound of his brother's voice. Through the blinding smoke, he saw the faint outline of his brother crouched over a larger figure.

"Help me," the dying man pleaded.

Jed knelt down beside Logan, trying not to look at the man.

"Jed, it is Mr. Mosley…" Logan said through gritting teeth.

Searching his mind, Jed remembered the man's name. At first it seemed foreign to his ears, but then he recalled the incident with the rabid dog and Logan, back before the family split…back before Nathan was killed. "He owned the dog…"

Logan clenched his jaw and studied Jed's face, then nodded quickly.

Mr. Mosley raised a dying hand and touched Logan's cheek, pulling the boy's gaze back on him. "You...I know you."

Logan breathed in deeply, trying to hold back the rushing emotions of frustration and sorrow, "Yes, Sir."

"You are William's brother?" asked the man through agonizing breathes.

"Yes, Sir."

A brief smile appeared on the man's face, but was pushed away by a surge of pain.

Jed ran his hand down the man's jacket to where a puddle of blood formed in the creases of the man's stomach. The child closed his eyes as he applied pressure to the wound. When he pushed, he felt the tepid liquid flow from the wound, through his fingers, and onto the top of his knuckles. "Logan." he whispered trying to inform the boy of the wound's nature.

"Mr. Mosley, we are going to get you help." Logan promised the man.

"No, Son." he said shaking his head whilst gasping for breath. "My time has arrived." "Help me," the man said trying to reach his dagger that rested sheathed on his belt.

Logan looked to Jed. Both knew what the man wanted, and both felt a moment of resistance.

"Please..." Mosley whimpered.

Logan let out a breath of pity, and reached to the man's leather belt and gripped the handle of the dagger. Slowly, he pulled on the weapon revealing the long, metal blade that glimmered in the sun.

Jed reached his hand over to the knife, and held on to the top of the handle as he helped Logan position it over the man's heart. Logan aided Mr. Mosley in raising his weak hand onto the knife's eccentric handle. As the icy touch of the cold, metal point barely pierced the fabric of the man's shirt, Mr. Mosley closed his eyes and sucked in three large breaths of air. He then opened his brown eyes and looked at the two boys. "What a shame it is that life should be wasted with such violence as war..."

Droplets of tears fell from Jed's eyes as he watched the man he had known throughout the early years of his childhood in his final moments.

With one fluid motion, Mr. Mosley plunged the dagger down through his chest, letting out a quick gasp, then a sigh of relief. Jed reeled backwards onto his rear where he broke down in anguish. Another part of his childhood had been lost at the hands of war.

Logan ran his hand over the man's shimmering brown eyes that no longer looked on the world in suffering. The boy rose to his feet, and pulled Jed to his. "Let's get back to our lines before they consider us missing in action."

Chapter VII: We are Brothers
 C3⁊O

Beaten, tired, and alone, Maxwell laid in a small ditch along the base of a splintered walnut tree. All around him, soldiers from defeated battalions returned from the front lines bearing the scars of war; bloodied reminders of the horrid assaults of the morning.

In the back of his mind, Maxwell stirred a curious thought as to why he remained at the doomed town of Gettysburg. With all the chaos of action, he could easily escape to a remote section of the wilderness, and be presumed dead. He would no longer have to tempt fate, nor would he have to continue to muster every last bit of strength his fragile body contained to live one more day. The boy smiled deliriously at the thought of faking his death. A mix of heat stroke, and severe exhaustion had rattled his mental psyche to the point at which he wanted nothing more than to relax against the tree and forget the world. Despite his thoughts of false bereavement, something kept him on the field, something he could not explain.

"Why am I here?" he asked himself aloud.

Nathaniel, the scar-faced boy, passed in front of Maxwell carrying all his gear, "Did you say something?" he asked.

"Huh?" Maxwell asked, partially acknowledging the little soldier's presence.

"You said: *why am I here.*"

Maxwell painfully shifted his weight onto his left arm, and sat himself up; his back rested on a hollowed out portion of the damaged tree. "I was wondering why I'm still here."

Nathaniel scanned the area for the rest of his unit before dropping his gear beside the beaten boy. "Mind if I sit for a moment?"

Maxwell shook his head; his eyes were blackened from lack of sleep.

"I know why you are still here..." Nathaniel spoke up after a long moment's pause.

Maxwell did not speak; he only listened.

"Pride..."

Rubbing the dirt from his hands, Max sat his body more upright.

Nathaniel ran a hand down his brow, following the path of his scar. "Pride is what keeps you here. Sometimes people have too much of it, and it drives them to do crazy things...those people are the heroes you see, the ones who storm trenches with nothing but a knife and pistol. Do they fear death? Probably not..."

Nathan looked Maxwell in the eye. "You have just enough. Your pride isn't as great as those heroes, but yours has a purpose."

Frustrated and exhausted, Maxwell shrugged Nathaniel's explanation off as he lay back down on the tree's roots.

"I'm not finished," Nathan, continued, "you told me once that your brother was killed. He was taken from you. You didn't get the chance to have him see you grow up and become like him, to become a true family, and have him help you grow and be a kid. Well, I think that is why you have pride. You have a drive to find and protect something, something that was taken from you. I'm not certain I know exactly what it is, but I think you will find it by the time this battle is over…whenever that is."

Maxwell shifted his gaze to a pair of soldiers walking from the direction of distant guns; he followed them visually over to a small cask that held a few gallons of water. One of the soldiers had massive tears down the chest and sleeves of his uniform that were matched by blood, and bullet holes in the trousers. "Hey, Nathan…"

The prophetic kid turned his attention back on Maxwell as he laced his newfound leather brogans on his feet. "Yeah?" he asked.

"You know, people say that war is an opportunity…an opportunity to be something, to become someone." Maxwell paused to piece together his sentence. "They say that it is a stepping stone, a sort of jumping off point where men can become Gods; become immortalized."

Nathan stirred the words around in his head.

"Yet, all I see is grown-ups fightin' and dying; none of them have done anything holy, not one." Maxwell hesitated as he listened to an artillery shell whiz overhead. "I don't know much, but I do know that killing isn't the way to become a saint…"

Nathan squinted through the afternoon sun as blotches of shade passed over his face from the shaking tree caught in the wind. "Maybe not, Max, but opportunities are what you make of them; you can let them pass unnoticed, or grab them and ride them to where they take you." Rising from the sporadic shade of the tree, Nathaniel threw his knapsack over his shoulder and saluted Jed. "Good luck, friend. Maybe someday I'll see you again." With that, Nathaniel scuttled off into a group of troops marching toward the rumbling guns.

CR&O

After repeated assaults to the Union defensive line, the troops began to grow weary. Logan ran ammunition up and down the left side of the Federal strong point, delivering it to the soldiers in need.

"This is all?" a lieutenant with thick sideburns asked upon examining the few crates Logan and two others had hauled in.

"This is all that is left, Sir." Logan sighed above the ricocheting rounds hitting the log barricade.

"It will have to do; thank you, gentlemen."

The men saluted and scurried off toward their section. As they jogged down the line, Logan noticed for the first time the true extent of the carnage, when his eyes peered through a gap in the tree line overlooking the seminary in the distance. Columns of soldiers fired volley after volley toward his position on the hill and the troops occupying Cemetery Ridge. Littering the ground at their feet, the dead and wounded, stretching as far as he could see. Flags fluttered left and right marking the different units and divisions; the men who died still clutching the flags in their hands, led their men to the gates of hell.

"It truly is a sight ain't it, Hinkley?" panted one of the couriers, watching Logan and the action unfolding on the horizon.

Logan studied the battlefield with eyes like a hawk, "I don't understand it. In a way it is beautiful, not the death, but the sheer amount of them. They just keep on comin' for us."

"And one day they will all die." the courier sneered.

"Do you have family out there?" Logan asked.

"Not that I know of here. I did at Bull Run two years ago. Some of the dead that day were my family, but it doesn't matter, as soon as they devoted themselves to the Southern cause, they died in my heart."

The gray outline of soldiers continued on by the time Logan and the other couriers hustled off, back to their position. When they trotted up, the men of their unit were stacking themselves against the log palisade, prepping for another assault. Jed was sitting on his drum with his hands shaking on his knee.

"Jed?" Logan asked worriedly trying to catch his breath.

Jed turned his attention to Logan, and pointed a stiff finger to a bloody body lying on the ground, "Henry."

ℭℬ

"Stand up, Son!"

"What?!" gasped Maxwell.

"You dozed off, the Yank's have held their lines all day, and we intend on breaking them and send 'em runnin' for Washington!" an older man with no teeth grinned.

Maxwell looked up at the sky above him. The once bright and vivid colors of the afternoon were dulled by the appearance of heavy rain clouds. "How long was I asleep?!" he asked in a panic as he tried to gather his equipment in record time.

"Lord knows, Boy, get to stepping!"

Maxwell did his best to follow after the elderly man, who disappeared in the mass gathering of gray uniforms.

All around, men from detachments of the militias, guard units, and regular army stood in a line. Max guessed that there were easily two to three hundred soldiers present.

"Listen up! This will be the final assault by us! General Lee himself has asked that every single one of you give your last valiant effort to push the Federals back from their lines to their capitol. Boys, let's make all of Pennsylvania, and Washington, and every damned state of the Union shake with fright as we bring a wall of gray to their doorstep!"

Every man in the crowd cheered as the mysterious officer moved out from the cover of the woods with the mass of bodies following close behind. Normally, Maxwell would have rejoiced at the words spoken by the officer, yet he had begun to grow tired of supporting a cause he felt was dwindling.

As the Confederate battalions moved from their cover of the trees, the massive cannonade that had been firing for almost two complete hours, ceased. The silence was ear piercing. Maxwell's senses rang as he tried to remember the last time he had heard the quiet nature of his surroundings.

"Form the line!" the officer's voice announced, defeating the moment of serenity.

The clank of tin cups on bayonet sheaths, and musket slings on leather cap boxes filled the remaining void as the troops settled into formation.

Maxwell snuck a glance down the left flank and in an instant, his jaw dropped. As far as he could see, ant-like figures stretched the miles of grassy field. Hundreds of flags fluttered in the gale-like winds that blew the grass flat on its side, revealing piles of bodies that had not lived to see the breath-taking spectacle. The true numbers of how many soldiers were present in the tiny town in Pennsylvania had never been truly apparent to the child, yet upon seeing the row of Confederates alone, Maxwell knew that the forthcoming battle, and the battles prior, were much more than small skirmishes…they were key in deciding the fate of his country.

കൈ

"Stack the line, hold all positions!" screamed the officers of the 11th Pennsylvania, while they rushed down the line checking to be sure all soldiers were present for the defense of the ridge.

Logan's eyes were fixed upon the lifeless body of Henry, the only person beside Jed and Colonel Tavert he considered family. Soldiers rushing past bumped into the confused boy, almost knocking him to the ground. Jed's gaze soon fell off of his brother and on to Henry.

"Did he say anything before he died?" Logan murmured trying to hold back the rushing emotions that were coming to a climax.

Ronan stood up from a stump beside Logan. "He said to not get all soppy when you saw him."

Logan's brief smile combusted into tears as he looked down on the body of his friend, "Thank you for being a friend, Henry."

Jed rose from his drum and strapped it over his neck. He gripped the sleeve of Logan's jacket and pulled him away to the line where both boys gazed out upon the thousands of enemy soldiers marching toward them in a single line, stretching from the Wheatfield to their left, all the way as far as the eye could see to their right.

Wiping away the tears from his eyes, Logan shook off the weight of a passing friend, and let the emotions turn to pure concentration; concentration that would be the deciding factor in his life or death. "There are so many of them, Jed."

The green-eyed boy said nothing. He watched soldier after soldier step from the cover of trees marching toward him in perfect unison. Suddenly, the screaming cries of artillery called out; the cannon shells flew, bringing a letter of death to all who marched in their path. Miles out in the fields, the rounds made contact hitting the earth and sending plumes of debris into the air, covering a section of the line in ash, however, through the ash, more soldiers marched forward, continuing through the onslaught.

Colonel Tavert unsheathed his sword once more, exposing the gleaming blade. "They will keep on coming, men," he warned as the anxious faces of the soldiers around him turned white with fear.

"It has been a pleasure fighting with you, colonel." a bearded man announced tipping his cap.

One by one, the men of the unit saluted their leader who pursed his lips, holding in his feelings. Sighing deeply, Tavert peered out over the golden wheat littered with craters and bodies, where he let his gaze rise to settle upon the trees, and saluted back, "When the trees of the world shake us free, fear not the fall, for we shall land among the leaves of a greener yesterday," turning to face his troops, he continued, "We cannot fail here in these final hours, for we have already seeded this land with our blood, we have given our all, and that my boys, spells victory."

The men focused on the man for a moment longer before turning back to the sight in the fields before them. The cannons continued to fire, and the enemy soldiers continued to fall, only to be replaced in tenfold.

ᏻᏺ

The wall of gray continued their march against the Union line. All around them, shells exploded, sending hordes of searing hot metal through the air to where they found their marks on the exposed flesh of the Rebel troops.

Maxwell continued to march, holding his rifle tight to his shoulder. In his head he desperately tried to block out the agonizing screams of injured men, and the abrupt silence around him after the cannon blasts. As he marched, he hummed to himself hoping to further drown out the horror that surrounded him. Falling chunks of dirt and debris fell onto his head, reminding him of how close the arm of the Union army was to touching him.

The low, thunderous rumble of cannons embellished the crackle of musket fire as it continued to rain heated metal onto the soldiers below. As the fear and desire to look ahead tugged on Maxwell's eyelids, the boy continued onward. Finally, he gave in

and answered to desperation. Flashes of red and black filled his
retinas as remnants of human bodies fell to the ground, then rose
back up again following another shot from the Union guns.
Maxwell looked beside him to where three men marched with
bayonets fixed; a useless weapon against the raw power of the
rifled guns. In a wild flash of yellow, Maxwell was thrown on his
back. When he regained his bearings, he looked to where the men
once stood…there was nothing; they had been completely
vaporized by a direct hit.

The boy hammered the ground with his fists repeatedly;
each time with more ferocity. He began to kick and scream wildly
as the artillery shells continued to fall all around him. "Stop it!" he
screamed through a waterfall of tears that drowned his words. The
noise was so deafening that he could not even hear his own
screams for peace. In a desperate attempt to hide from the reign of
fire, the boy rolled over and began to dig hysterically with his
hands in the dirt. The clay filled his fingernails and dried on his
hands and face, as he hunkered down as close to the ground as
possible. With each breath he took, particles of dirt and soil filled
his throat causing him to choke in a coughing fit.

"Get up!" came a cry, followed by a hand that grasped the
back of Maxwell's shirt, and pulled him up from the ground and
further toward the Federal line.

Looking back, the boy watched as a lone shell pounded the
earth where he laid just seconds prior.

Through the roar of battle, the child looked at his savior
and tried to make out what the man was saying.

"Grab a rifle and fight damn it!"

Maxwell swallowed hard as he tried to overcome the strong
desire to run and hide. He searched the ground around him for a
weapon...any weapon. Picking up a revolver from a dead soldier,
the boy turned his attention back to the Union defenses and
charged head on with the thousands of attacking men.

The unrelenting lashes from the Union artillery continued to pound the ground; the concussion lifted a vaporous plume of dirt and blood into the air, showering chunks of human flesh across the scarred earth. Logan and Jed dodged musket fire that snapped off the logs in front of them in a repeated fashion as the Confederate machine continued to close the gap between the lines.

Running for their lives, the boys sprinted down the defensive line, hurdling over the bodies that littered their path. A stray shot from a Rebel musket ricocheted off a rock beside them with a twang that echoed throughout the enclosed perimeter of the breastworks, and hit an unfortunate private in the forehead. The man dropped to his knees instantly like a doll made of stuffing.

"Don't look at him, Jed!" screamed Logan over the massive reverberation of combat.

Falling on his stomach, Logan took cover behind a shattered fence. Jed stood frozen, his eyes fixated on the surging mob of Rebels that were about to hit the Union wall like a tsunami.

Raising his rifle to his shoulder, Logan took aim at the mass crowd of soldiers before him. The boy pulled the trigger, only to hear the deafening click of an empty weapon.

"Lord, help me!" he cried out as he hurriedly pulled the ramrod from his rifle and loaded in the shot and powder. His hands fumbled the stick as he desperately tried to slip it back into place under the barrel of the musket. His clammy palms slipped down the grip of the wooden stock where his index finger found its place on the smooth, metal trigger that would deliver a round of lead one thousand feet per second into the unfortunate soul who crossed his path.

Without a moment's hesitation, Logan closed his eyes and pressed his finger against the cold trigger, delivering the fatal shot. The rifle recoiled with the force of a hammer driving a nail into rail tie.

"We gotta keep moving!" Logan hollered as he pulled his delirious brother with him down the line, trying to evade the ensuing onslaught.

Jed desperately tried to keep up, however his legs could only take him so far. Dropping to his knees, the child began to vomit, spewing out a pale, yellow liquid that stained his uniform.

Turning back, Logan saw his kid brother kneeling beside a flag bearer. A rushing wave of fear swept through his body as he sprinted toward the boy who continued to dry-heave over the stained grass.

"Jed, run!"

Unaware of the potential danger he was in, Jed brought his gaze forward upon Logan. In a blinding instant, the flag bearer's stomach exploded releasing a crimson spray that splattered upon Jed's face.

The man holding the flag fell to the grass, screaming in high-pitched terror, as another man rushed to raise the colors.

Logan reached Jed just as another bullet struck the second man in the head, rendering him incapable of further life. "Color guards make good targets for sharpshooters!"

The two Hinkley brothers continued on, outrunning death himself, when suddenly a magnificent force shook the earth, dropping the two boys to the ground like a bag of bricks.

A swift shooting pain pulsed through Logan's body causing him to drop his rifle, and let out an ear-piercing scream. Looking to his shoulder, he found a chunk of metal extruding from his socket; its splintered edges coated with blood.

"Pull it out, Jed!" yelled Logan.

Jed lifted a shaking hand to the wound and gripped the sharp edges of the shrapnel. With a swift tug, the metal withdrew itself halfway. Writhing in agony, Logan bit his knuckle with closed eyes, trying to concentrate on something other than the throbbing pain.

Jed pressed one hand on Logan's chest for leverage, while the other grasped the shard of metal once more. With a violent pull, the piece flew out of the boy's shoulder. Jed held it up in the air as he marveled at its size, for a moment forgetting the hell surrounding him.

"Don't show me it, Jed!" pleaded the wounded boy.

Jed stood up and grabbed his brother by the opposite arm. "Get up, we have to find cover!"

Logan stood, but buckled under his weight. "My leg, something is wrong with my leg!"

Looking down, both discovered a piece of Logan's calf missing, revealing the shredded muscle.

Jed's eyes bulged in sheer horror as Logan dragged himself to a makeshift barrier of logs. All around them, only whitewash was visible, and the sounds of battling armies echoed throughout the once quiet village.

Just as Jed was making his way over to the wounded Logan, a soldier clad in gray broke through the veil of fog; a wooden stake, and bayonet in his hands. Stiffened with cowardice, Jed could do nothing. With a slashing motion, the demonic soldier cracked Jed in the face with the stake, sending blood pouring out of his nose. The man then disappeared into the blinding mixture of smoke and gunpowder that filled the air.

Crippled, and blind, both Jed and Logan rested with their backs on the log fence; their only means of blocking out the war that once seemed so far away. Logan placed his arm around his green-eyed brother, and pulled him in tight. Looks of debility and languor dripped over the boy' faces as they began to accept the inevitable fate of two young soldiers caught in a maelstrom of war.

"Logan, I don't want to die." cooed Jed with sorrow, no longer able to cry.

"I don't want to be forgotten…" Logan whispered as he faded in and out of consciousness.

Two Confederate soldiers approached the boys, their muskets fixated upon the chests of the brothers. Jed looked each soldier in the eye, his body trembling. It seemed as if no life was left in the enemy before him; only a rage conjured by war. The soldiers pulled the hammers on their rifles back with a click. Swallowing hard, Jed closed his eyes, not wanting his last image on earth to be of the men who killed him.

Darting from the smoke, a small boy rushed into the sides of the attackers, knocking them into each other. Falling away, one of the soldiers slashed at the assailant with his knife.

Hearing the scuffle, Jed opened his eyes to see Maxwell standing before him, a long gash open across his stomach.

"Jed, take my sleeve and wrap his wound." Logan ordered, still slightly disarranged.

The injured Maxwell fell awkwardly to his knees as the sharp stinging pain started to increase across his exposed abdomen. Jed tore a chunk of fabric from Logan's uniform jacket and wrapped it tight around his cousin's stomach.

"What do we do?!" shouted Jed in disarray. Realizing that both his brother and Maxwell were in dire need of medical attention, the boy started to recede inside, forcing out tears that smeared the blood from his nose down his face.

The crackling of gunfire had started to die down when three Union soldiers approached the group of kids. Jed examined their faces; each just as chiseled and cold as the Rebels he had witnessed moments earlier. A gritty slim, composed of dirt and sweat, was embedded in their skin, and their eyes were blackened and bruised. Jed continued to look upon them, realizing the difference between men like them, and children like him: those men knew nothing other than war; their kinship was comprised of those around them at the given moment…there was nothing left for them to go home to, and their eyes told all.

Two of the soldiers dressed in blue approached Logan, and gently lifted him up from the cracked earth, and called for a stretcher. Jed held his arm around Maxwell's shoulder, and pulled him up to his feet. One of the soldiers turned and pointed his gun at Maxwell, the barrel inches from the boy's face.

"No! He is with me!" cried Jed.

The soldier glanced at his peers with a moment of hesitation, and then carefully dropped the aim of his rifle to the dirt.

"Jed, take care of Max. Bring him home, I'll be fine." stated Logan, wincing in pain as the Union troops lowered him on to a stretcher.

Jed shook his head refusing the order, "What is gonna happen to you?!"

"Give the boy a dose of chloroform, his leg will need amputation," said the soldier who brought the stretcher.

Logan shut his eyes and breathed in deeply trying to calm his nerves. The soldiers lifted the boy and stretcher, and started to walk away from the barricade.

"I don't know where to go, Logan!" Jed screamed in a panic.

"The song, Jed…remember your bearings, and home you will fly."

The frightened Jed watched as Logan disappeared into the mob of blue men all around him. "Take care, brother," he whispered to himself.

ଓଡ଼୦

Maxwell awoke under the shade of a cypress tree. He could hear the faint whistling of the wind through the canopy causing the branches to dance under the high noon sun. The dusty-haired boy sat up; he let out a high-pitched scream as the excruciating pain from his wound surged through his abdomen.

In a flash, Jed stood up from the brush, a canteen in his hand. "Lie down!" he shouted rushing to his cousin's side.

"It hurts, Jed!" Maxwell moaned, trying to remove the bloodied bandages encasing his stomach.

Jed helped to ease Max onto his back and finished pulling off the makeshift bandage, stained red with blood, to reveal a dark gash filled with a yellow puss.

"I could be wrong, but I'd say that's a nasty infection." Jed said frowning at the cut. "I'm gonna try to clean it. This could hurt…" he warned.

Maxwell swallowed hard and clenched what lush grass he could in his palms. Jed removed a torn flag from his haversack and placed it over the nozzle of his canteen. Gracefully, he tipped the object end over end, sloshing the liquid into the flag, then poured some more onto the wound. The moment the fresh water touched the wound, Max tensed up, but let out a sigh of relief as the heated flesh cooled.

"This could hurt," he foretold once more, bringing the balled up flag close to the boy's stomach; gently, Jed began to apply pressure, then scrubbed at the infection, clearing away some of the puss.

"-Easy!" wailed Maxwell gritting his teeth.

"Hang on, almost done," Jed consoled.

Jed set the flag down and inspected the cut. It had begun to open again in the middle, reveling pink flesh, followed by crimson seepage. "I'm gonna wrap it again."

Max nodded in approval and sat up as best he could. Taking the old shirtsleeve in his hands once more, Jed tied the bloodied fabric around his cousin's torso and helped to prop him up on the gritty tree trunk.

"We need a clean bandage. It's only a matter of time until that wound gets worse."

Maxwell attempted to button his shirt back up with one hand while he leaned his weight against the other. "Why did we stop?" he questioned wincing in discomfort.

Jed worked his way over to his scattered gear a few feet away. "You collapsed about twenty minutes ago..."

"Was I unconscious?" asked the dusty-haired boy.

Jed nodded his head.

"I don't even remember walking." Maxwell admitted rubbing his forehead.

The two sat in silence for a moment, listening to nothing more than the buzz of cicadas in the distance.

Maxwell finally broke the silence, "How long have we been away?"

"You mean from the battle?" Jed asked.

"Yes."

"A little more than a day; nightfall will make it two," answered the green-eyed boy. "I wonder how Logan is..."

Maxwell leaned his head back against the rotting bark of the cypress tree and closed his eyes. "He will be fine."

"I hope so," whispered Jed.

"You are taking me home?" Maxwell asked, as he started to squirm around, switching support arms.

Jed watched him for a moment, "Yeah; to your home."

"It was your home once, too; remember?"

Jed shook his head frowning at the memories. "I never forgot."

Both boys locked eyes for a moment until Maxwell looked away over the grassy fields. "Jed…"

Jed Jr. perked up waiting for Max's question.

"Ya gotta take me back…"

"Back where?" he asked.

Max continued, "Back to Gettysburg."

Jed squinted in confusion, "What? No way, you need-"

"You don't understand! I have to go back, I have to! You can't take me home, not like this!"

"Maxy, you will die unless we get you home where you can get that cut treated!" Jed protested.

"Then let me die here! I can't go back and face my father like this. He'll say a true soldier would have died on the field, and not come home crying with a small cut."

Jed quieted down and watched as Max's eyes began to drip. "He was happy I left to fight. He was proud. The one thing in his life he had control over was going away to fight for a cause that could fix the world. I was noble, and he was proud!"

Jed watched in discomfort and pity. "Max, you fought; you put your life at risk. That's enough to offer. Death is too much."

"No it's not! I should have died. Those soldiers were going to shoot me after I saved you and Logan. They could have made me a hero, but you stopped them!"

"A hero in whose eyes, Max? Moses'?" Jed asked raising his voice.

Maxwell rubbed his knuckles over his eyes, removing his tears.

"What kind of man wishes for his son's death? Wasn't Nathan enough?"

"Don't speak of him-"

"No Max, he was my brother as much as he was yours! Death doesn't make you a hero! Saving me and Logan does; if you are too warped to see that, then I'm sorry!" Jed said panting with emotion. "What about your views. Did you even want to fight? Or was that Uncle Moses' bidding, too?"

"My opinion doesn't matter." Maxwell whispered.

"Yes it does-"

"It doesn't matter! I still fought. Even if I chose not to, I couldn't go back home. You should've just let me die…" Max sobbed.

Jed scanned the surrounding bluffs and looked to the east where the giant mountains stood in the distance like watchful eyes. "What has happened to us all, Max?"

The boy ignored him, and continued to fight between his stinging wound and aching arms.

"We used to be so close…" Jed said softly, bringing his attention back upon his cousin.

"Things change. Whether it is bad or good, things change." Maxwell said bluntly.

Jed stood up and walked over to the boy; he brushed the injured boy's bangs off of his forehead and pressed the back of his hand to Max's skin. "Max, you're burning up with fever."

"I feel like hell," he muttered.

"Have some more of my water, and let's get moving. You're getting worse by the hour."

CR&O

The invigorating smell of oranges filled Logan's nose. His blackened state faded when he came around. Moaning in pain, the boy opened his eyes; his vision was blurred, but he could hear the chatter of men and women around him. He was just able to make sense the outlines of three figures standing around his left leg.

"Sit up gently, Boy." one of the figures announced, helping to ease the teen up into a regular sitting position.

Logan's body ached. The last thing he remembered was watching Jed walk off with Maxwell toward the fields beyond Gettysburg. "Where am I?" he asked with a scratchy throat.

"A field hospital a few miles from the ridge." replied a woman. Her clothes had started to become visible as the effects of the chloroform dispersed from the boy's system.

Logan ran a hand across his chest to find thick padding over his shoulder, wrapping around his torso and back once more.

"You were banged up bad." the woman spoke, handing Logan a cup full of water.

Logan sipped the water, gagging at the taste. "Who are you, Ma'am?"

The lady's face was comprised of deep cavernous wrinkles, but her complexion was fair and her eyes soft and gentle. "You may call me, Miss Fridley. You are in my home."

Logan peered around the small cottage. He was not the only soldier in the home. Bodies of the dead and dying rested along the walls, seeking attention or burial. The luckiest soldiers held the comfort of lying in a bed or couch nearby.

"Do you remember arriving in my home?" Miss Fridley asked.

"No, Ma'am," Logan frowned.

Miss Fridley's expression dampened into that of depression. "Child, can you stand for me?"

Logan glanced at her in puzzlement, yet not for long. He set the cup of water down and removed the covers to spin off of the table he rested on. It was then that he saw what remained of his left leg. Where his underwear stopped, his right leg continued, but on the left half of his body, a bandaged nub was all that remained.

"I am sorry, Son. It was the only way to save your life." Miss Fridley whispered in heartfelt torment.

Logan stared at the remnants of his leg in bewilderment. "It was only my calf that got hurt," he moaned in disbelief of the entire situation.

"We could not risk infection."

Logan nodded and slowly sunk back down on the table, shivering in the cool air that flowed through the home.

"We can remove the bandage on your shoulder now if you would like?"

The blue-eyed boy rubbed his chest, feeling the difference in texture between the bandage and his warm skin. "Can I go home?" he murmured.

Miss Fridley walked around the front of the table to where Logan's gaze drifted. She knelt down beside him and ran her hand through his hair. "I will make you a deal. If you promise me you will not let this injury cripple you for life, then I shall agree to let you go."

The words settled into Logan's mind and he nodded solemnly.

"Promise me?"

"I promise."

"Very good; let us get you dressed and we can arrange for a carriage to take you back toward your home."

ೞ

It was early morning by the time Maxwell and Jed had started down the long dirt road to the house with red shutters. The morning haze that seemed to be ever apparent years ago was absent from the scene letting the heat of the sun, shine with all intensity upon the boys.

Maxwell clung desperately to his green-eyed cousin, his clothes tattered and torn. The boy's hat, which had seen three generations of war, was tipped back on his shaggy head, brimming with sweat.

Jed glanced at Maxwell, and saw the expression of exhaustion rampant through his pale, hollow face.

"We're almost home, Maxy. Hang in there." he tried to soothe.

Toughing out the last hundred yards, Jed had finally reached the old white porch. He stopped shy of its stairs and looked to the spot where Nathan had laid in his final minutes. Lifting his boot, Jed placed his foot on the spot and shivered as thoughts of the scarring day exploded in his mind. Opening his eyes, he quickly took another step with determination, and let the images fade to nothing.

The youth approached the porch swing that danced slightly in the breeze, and set his injured cousin down on it. Removing his Union jacket, Jed placed it over the rags that sealed Max's wound. "You are home now," he muttered looking around at the place where his childhood once thrived, and died.

Jed turned and started down the steps of the porch back toward the dirt road once more. He felt like an ant when started to realize how the events around him had shaped his life and how little he was able to change them alone. Entranced with thought, he walked on until the menacing click of the hammer on a gun shattered his daze.

Turning around, Jed's green eyes settled upon the door of the house where Moses stood, revolver in hand; his aim was fixed directly on the boy's chest. Jed stood perfectly still. Tired of war, and sick of fighting, he relaxed, letting his true emotions flood his face. The barren expression of loneliness and depression fell like a curtain over the boy's features.

Moses watched the adolescent's every move with his own look of despondency.

"He needs water. I did the best I could to stop the infection." Jed said, breaking the silence.

Moses did not move; he cast a bleak gaze upon his nephew. "You walked all this way with him?" he questioned.

"…Three days…" Jed admitted.

Moses rancorously lowered the aim of his weapon to the floor of the porch. "Why would you do that?" he asked. Pointing to Maxwell he added, "He is the enemy."

Jed shifted his stare upon Maxwell, who had not moved since he had been set down. Turning his shoulders square to his uncle, Jed stood tall. "I did it because I do not see him as the enemy, or even my cousin…I see him as my brother." Letting the answer sink in, Jed lowered his gaze back to the ground, and then started off down the dirt road once more; the sun continued to rise above his head.

Chapter VIII: Home again
ೞ⃝ೞ

The pansophical Virginian breeze that had once swept the fruitful plains, carrying with it the emotions of sweet euphoric bliss, detestable anguish, and content alleviation, finally turned northward bearing the loathsome affliction of a youth who had been cleansed in a baptism of fire. Despite the atrocities witnessed in the years prior, the airy gust was renewed in spirit by the hopes of a normal life…hopes, which flooded forth from young Jed's soul.

Upon leaving his old home in Virginia, the boy felt a sense of closure. Being able to look upon the house with red shutters through eyes that no longer winked at terror or fright was relieving. He could finally move on from the nightmares of the day when Nathan died.

The return trip home to Pennsylvania was quicker than the boy had expected. Hitchhiking his way via passing wagons helped to speed his pace. No longer willing to fight or hold another weapon, Jed turned tail from the direction of Gettysburg and fled home to where his mother and father would surely be waiting.

Jedediah sat in the bedroom of the dainty home, puffing on his pipe. Around him, a pluming cloud of grayish smoke filled the humid air, forcing Mary to cough whenever she passed from the room. A sense of revelation arose in Jedediah, and in that moment, he took the pipe from his mouth and tossed it to the ground without remorse.

Believing that the aged man had dropped his wooden utensil, Mary rushed over to her husband's side and reached a frail hand over the object. The veins in her wrist extruded through her wrinkled skin, showing her growing age.

"No, Mary." Jedediah roared.

The woman glanced up at her husband in disbelief.

"It is time I quit. I have become a hypocrite, always telling Moses to rid himself of the dirty habit, and here I am puffing away on my own poison."

Glowing with giddiness, Mary stood up leaving the pipe on the floor. Her heart swelled as she repeated the man's words in her head. It had been almost a year since Jedediah had called his brother by his name.

"I'm proud of you, Jedediah." Mary said, studying her beloved with heartfelt eyes.

228

"I do not do it for your attraction, my dear." Jedediah admitted.

"And that is why I envy you...you have taken strides to fix the wrongs in your life."

Jedediah shied away, shaking his head in defiance. "There are too many wrongs to right I am afraid."

"No, Jedediah!" Mary approached her husband with a soothing voice, resembling that of a Morning Dove's call.

"Mary, this family would still be together were it not for my actions."

Mary settled down on the bed beside her husband. Trying to show empathy, she ran her fingertips down the crease of his back in a repeated swaying motion.

"Mary, do things really happen for a reason? Or is that just something we tell ourselves as an excuse for missed opportunities?"

Mary thought for a moment. When she could not pinpoint where her husband was going with the conversation, she answered, "In what sense?"

"Nathan...Moses...Sue...the whole family. Did Nathan die for a reason? Did we split apart because it was God's will? Or did I fail to seize an opportunity, an opportunity to fix things with my brother?"

"Jedediah, no one could have guessed that Nathan's death would be a result of this separation. Everything this family has gone through has made us stronger. Maybe the opportunity was not to fix things with Moses, but to fix things between us."

"...Us?" Jedediah asked puzzled.

"Before, when we lived in Virginia, we rarely talked to each other. Sure, we would have conversations over dinner with the kids, but we never spent any time with just the two of us...we were growing apart."

"And now?" he asked.

"And now, all we have is each other."

Jedediah brushed his eye with his hand, removing a tear of rejoice. "Mary, you mean the world to me."

The two embraced for what seemed like the first time in a lifetime. No longer were their words strained, nor their worlds separated. Each were sound and in perfect harmony.

Suddenly, Mary perked up. "Did you hear that?"

"It sounded like…"

Both parents left the bedroom and ran outside onto the creaking porch where they peeked through squinted eyes at the figure walking down the hill toward the cottage.

"Mary! That cannot be!" Jedediah groaned in disbelief.

"It is Jed!"

From the sloping banks of the green hill came Jed, his hat in his hands, and his boots caked with mud.

"Oh, dear God do my eyes deceive me?!" Mary cried out with joy.

Jed stopped at the bottom of the hill and looked around at the beautiful scenery. Nowhere in sight was his brother.

"Jed!" cried a faint voice.

Spinning on his heels, the boy held his hand to his brow, blocking out the sun; atop the crest of the grassy slope stood Logan, his blue uniform swaying in the breeze.

"Logan!" called Jed running to his brother's side. Logan leaned his weight on Jed's shoulder as the two slowly made their way to their parents.

Mary and Jedediah watched as their sons descended the hill toward them. Inside, a strong urge to cry out and run to the children filled them, yet the same urge crippled them; the family had not spoken since the night before Logan and Jed left for boot camp.

The two boys finally reached the front yard of the small home. Jedediah was the first to step off of the old porch. Slowly, he worked his way over to Logan, and stopped just shy of him.

Logan looked his father in his weeping eyes, and in an instant forgave everything that was said before he left. He no longer felt anger toward the man, only compassion and the longing to be held by him.

Jedediah scanned his son up and down. The boy seemed cold and fragile. The aged man's gaze settled on Logan's missing leg, and at the sight, Jedediah lost control. Tears of regret and

230

sorrow poured down his face. Through quivering lips, Jedediah muttered prayers of forgiveness. Lifting a shaking arm from his side, the guilty man cocked his elbow and rested his weak fingers upon his eyebrow, saluting his child of seventeen years.

Logan stood frozen with emotion. He watched his father salute him, and it was at that moment that he dropped his crutches to the ground and fell forward onto the sad man, and let everything out.

Through bouts of falling tears, Logan cried out mournful sobs, as he held tight onto the chest of his father's shirt. The two of them collapsed onto the grassy ground, and embraced each other, not caring about the surrounding world.

"Never again; Daddy, never again," Logan bawled.

"You won't have to, Son. I promise!" replied Father Jed wiping away the falling tears from Logan's cheek.

Mary wept, watching the scene from the shelter of the porch. Looking at Jed who stood alone, she mustered the courage to run to the child, and embraced him.

"I missed you so much, Jed!" she cried.

"Mom, promise me you will always love me!" Jed wailed as salty tears began to fill his grieving eyes.

"Of course my child, of course!" she said as she squeezed her son with all of her love.

Chapter IX: Songs to the Nation
ॐ

Months had passed, and the seasons began to change. The greenery of summer was replaced with the fiery fluorescence of autumn, bringing in a new feeling of tranquility amidst the harsh backdrop of the months prior. The sweeping valleys and steep rises of the Pennsylvanian hills were no longer covered in tall, razor-like grass, but were filled with the straw-like wheat: a flowing sea of grain.

The sun, a gem in the darkening sky, had started to dip below the tallest of trees in the land, giving off a glow resembling that of amber. The golden rays penetrated the teal glass of the Hinkley home that rested at the bottom of a hill, awash in a sea of shed leaves.

Jed's eyes opened as a single beam of light brushed his cheek, illuminating even the darkest crevices of his relaxed face. Rising from the pocket of his mattress, he looked around the quiet room. Before him, white sheets covered his legs, and a small tray with cooled soup rested on the beige nightstand beside his bed. Across the room was Logan, who still lied in a somber state. Jed reached over to the beige table and picked up his pocket watch. Opening the golden clasp, the lid flipped open to reveal two large hands that signaled to numbers inscribed with intricate detail.

"It's afternoon already?" Jed asked aloud in disbelief.

Since returning home from duty, he had become severely sleep-deprived, always awakening in the night with terrors of the grizzly scenes of war. As the months proceeded however, he had slowly regained his ability to dream peacefully.

"Hey, Logan." he called softly.

The sleeping boy did not move in his bed. Fit on alerting his brother of the time of day, Jed hobbled out of bed and worked his way over to Logan's bedside.

Sitting down gently at the edge of the bed frame, the green-eyed boy poked his brother's side carefully. For a moment, he twitched fearing the infamous backhand that Logan flung when bothered whilst sleeping, however no such hand came.

"Logan." Jed whispered again.

The sleeping boy's eyes opened briefly, then squinted shut at the sun penetrating through the window.

"What time is it, Jed?" Logan asked with a scratchy voice after a moment of recuperation from grogginess.

"It's getting late. We best get ready if you still wanted to go," replied Jed.

Logan slowly turned over in the bed, and lifted the covers with a heavy hand. The boy swung his leg over the edge of the bed, and brought his body around so that he was in a seated position.

Jed glanced down and shivered upon seeing the nub where the boy's left leg once existed. Logan ran his hand down his right thigh, and mimicked with his left hand on the opposite leg, however, he drew the hand back once it reached the point of where his knee should have been. The boy looked up at Jed with eyes full of sorrow and loss.

For the first time in his life, Jed could not understand what Logan was feeling. Normally, the two were like twins, sensing every emotion the other felt; this time, Jed could not fathom the obvious hurt that the blue-eyed boy suffered.

"My crutches, Jed." said Logan motioning toward the two wooden supports against the wall.

Responding to the request for help, the adolescent sprang up and retrieved the rough textured blocks for his crippled sibling.

"Thanks." Logan said appreciatively as he struggled to shift his weight onto the artificial legs.

Jed walked over to the bureau that sat against the front wall of the room, just as it had in the house with the red shutters. He opened it with ease and withdrew a pair of brown slacks, and a white shirt with three buttons at the collar. Throwing off his nightgown, he held open the pants and started to slip his leg in, but stopped suddenly as he noticed Logan watching from the corner of his eye.

A look of redolence was abundant on Logan's pitiful face as he watched Jed dress with ease. Swallowing hard, Jed pulled his pants up to his waist and buttoned them.

"I'm sorry," he said.

Logan shook his head sheepishly as he pushed away the apology. "Don't be, Jed." After a moment of silence, the blond haired boy asked kindly, "Will you call Mother?"

Jed breathed in calmly and nodded with acceptance. Opening his mouth, the boy yelled for his mother, who entered the room moments later to aid Logan with getting dressed.

Aside from the serenity of a life absent of war, the scars of a youth who had aged through a baptism of fire remained.

The afternoon heat was replaced with a cooling breeze that rushed through the woods where Jed and Logan trekked toward the hallowed ground of Gettysburg. All around the boys, trees were dropping their leaves as if growing tired of the weight they held, leaving bare branches that remained naked in the open air. The only thing separating the travelers from the wild nature of the bush was a thin, dusty trail that worked its way up the crest of the hill where it stopped atop a wide clearing overlooking the once decrepit and maniacal landscape that seemed completely transformed into a field of beauty.

"Only a few more steps!" shouted Jed as both boys continued up the path.

Finally reaching the top of the hill, Jed looked back at Logan, who struggled to overcome the last incline to the top. Without thinking twice, the green-eyed child reached his hand out and gripped his brother's shoulder, and helped to pull him up.

"It's beautiful…" Logan murmured, his eyes sparkling in the diming daylight as he overlooked the scene.

Upon the flatlands below, a small stage rested in a crowd of hundreds of people and photographers that stretched from the outskirts of the small town, to the farmland to the east.

Both boys settled in, finding a seat on the lush grass that flooded the hilltop overlooking the sight. The late afternoon dew seeped through their pants, causing them to shift around to find a dry spot. Below, a tall man wearing a black suit and top hat walked to the front of the tiny stage, and began to speak; his words echoed throughout the valley as every person and animal present seemed to listen with interest.

"Is that Lincoln?" Jed asked.

Logan nodded as he stared at the man who was no larger than an ant from where he sat. Despite the distance separating them, the boy could still hear the man's powerful words.

"…But in a larger sense we cannot dedicate, we cannot consecrate, we cannot hallow this ground. The brave men, living and dead, who struggled here, have consecrated it far above our poor power to add or detract. The world will little note, nor remember what we say here, but can never forget what they did here…"

Shifting with uneasiness, Jed broke Logan's concentration on the words, "Hey, Logan?"

"Yeah, Jed?" the blue-eyed boy responded.

"What is gonna happen to us? Will things ever be the same?"

Logan looked down at the ground, and then turned his attention out to the setting sun. A relaxing thought flushed through the boy's mind as he smiled slightly, and drew his arm up and around Jed's neck. "I do not know, Jed…but what I do know is that as long as we are together, we will always have a chance at making things right again."

Jed breathed in deeply feeling reassured, and moved his gaze from Logan back out over the battlefield that still held his youthfulness prisoner. It was at that moment that Jed realized that he would forever have a bond with the men who fought there: those who stood beside him were his brothers…and that was a bond sealed in blood.

Withdrawing from their thoughts, both boys closed their eyes and listened to Lincoln's words as the last rays from the sun settled on the fragile world.

"…It is rather for us to be here dedicated to the great task remaining before us-that from these honored we take increased devotion to that cause for which they here gave the last full measure of devotion-that we here highly resolve that these dead shall not have died in vain; that this nation shall have a new birth of freedom; and that this government of the people, by the people, for the people, shall not perish from the Earth."

THE END

❧SEEDS OF SYMBOLISM❧
-A background on the underlying theme-

     I would like to start off by mentioning one of my favorite quotes by Anthony Brandt, a quote that I feel sums up this entire novel: "Other things may change us, but we start and end with family." That very message rings true throughout the entirety of *War of Brothers*. From the delightful and sweet upbringing of a family in a world their own, to the heart wrenching sorrow that ultimately tears them apart, yet mends their wounds making them stronger in the end, that very quote is *War of Brothers*. Our journey into the underlying theme of the book starts off in the title itself: *War of Brothers*. At first glance, the reader may believe the deceitfully obvious: the book is only about a war between two brothers. However, this is not entirely so. The title is a representation of the external battle between Jedediah Hinkley, father to the main children, and his brother Moses Hinkley, as well as the Civil War itself: a nation versus itself, brother versus brother. Delving deeper, the title expresses another sense of torn bondage in the relations between Maxwell and the family. Early on in the story, the quiet child seems mute, never expressing much emotion. My intention for this was manifested by the idea that when the family breaks and we visit the boy two years later, he is (in a sense) a new character. The strained relationship between him and his father takes on the titled meaning if viewed in terms of bondage rather than kinship.

Moving past the title, the opening dream sequence involving a blue-eyed boy on the destroyed ship of which William served, is a premonition for lack of better terms. Progressing through the novel, William makes a connection between the blue-eyed boy of his nightmares, and his blue-eyed brother, Logan. While William is unable to pinpoint the relation of the two boys, the meaning is the foreshadowing of innocence lost. Fast forward to Gettysburg during the harrowing assaults of day one where we find Logan and Jed on the outskirts of the town, preparing to give cover to the retreating Union troops as they flee the Confederate onslaught. During the temporary stalemate between the two armies, Logan moves forward and grasps a knife, and holds it to his throat, just like the boy in William's dream. That moment is the defining point in which Logan has completely changed; he is no longer the child-like youth he once was, for having witnessed the carnage and bloodshed that he was thrown into he has changed.

While on the topic of the character Logan, the boy was developed to symbolize one-half of a link. Jed Jr., Logan's brother, is the other half. Together, both adolescents stand for the brotherhood men had, and continue to have during war. Soldiers tend develop a bond that is thicker than family, strengthened by the events they witness, and the catastrophe they commit, so what better way to show that bond than by making the two family? After the battle of Gettysburg, Logan's leg is amputated due to extreme and potentially life-threatening wounds. The remnants of his missing leg are meant to symbolize the healing of the nation after the war, where the scars of the incident are forever visible and felt.

The character of Maxwell is a rather complex character, despite his lack of dialogue early on. The boy was written to represent the youth of the war, both fighting and enduring. Like a child, Maxwell is very bright and looks at the world with indifferent eyes. He is able to see and understand all points of view, even after living with his strong-willed father. Out of all the characters, Maxwell was one I really enjoyed writing. His ability to find beauty in the ravished world makes him a truly unique individual, one that took on a special personality as I continued.

Nathan Hinkley, the martyr of the family, is one of the most crucial characters in the book. While his appearance is miniscule when compared to his siblings, he leaves a lasting impression even after death. Writing the death of Nathan was something I planned from the beginning conception of this piece. I knew I needed a character to fall victim, since the role needed to symbolize the loss of life due to ignorant actions. The very first drafts of the novel (at the time, screenplay), the character that ended up becoming Nathan was named Ben. The boy was the exact same age as Logan (fifteen years at the start of the book), and was more of a straight shooting character. As I continued my planning, I began to feel the need to change the personality to that of a prank-playing teen; someone who loves life and being young. Once I made the decision to continue with the change, and adapted the name Ben to Nathan, I started to write the death scene immediately. Truth be told, I almost decided not to kill him off after I fell in love with the character's easy-going personality, however, his death would make people feel the shock of the separation more. Nathan was a great character, one that I truly hated to kill off, but in the end, it had to be done.

The final scene, the Gettysburg Address, is one of my favorites. Logan and Jed listen to Lincoln give his speech while overlooking the battlefield they fought and almost died on, through changed eyes. The field that once contained the dead and dying had transformed to a beautiful compilation of greenery and life. In the final moments of the scene, Jed makes the connection between himself and the soldiers who fought...they were brothers, just like

Logan. The reason I chose to put the boys on the hill, rather than have them in the crowd was to make them seem alienated. Those in the crowd (a majority were reporters, and civilians) did not know the true extent of the horror caused and dealt, unlike the two main characters. Putting the two on the hill also made for a pretty dynamic ending, one which I feel leaves the readers, and characters alike, in relative peace.

By far this book has been one of my most personal, and an absolute thrill to research and write. Each character not only takes on an element of the war or people alive during the period, they share a part of me. From Father Jed to littlest Maxwell, the characters, nay family, in this book are as real to me than those who I meet and speak to everyday. Departing from the Hinkley family is something I knew would come, and hoped would come, but in hindsight I realize that I, myself, have formed a bond to the family spawned within these pages...letting them go is like a war...a war fought by blood, a war of brothers.